PENGU

TO A (

Born in Salinas, California, in 1902, John Steinbeck grew up in a fertile agricultural valley about twenty-five miles from the Pacific Coast—and both valley and coast would serve as settings for some of his best fiction. In 1919 he went to Stanford University, where he intermittently enrolled in literature and writing courses until he left in 1925 without taking a degree. During the next five years he supported himself as a laborer and journalist in New York City and then as a caretaker for a Lake Tahoe estate, all the time working on his first novel, *Cup of Gold* (1929). After marriage and a move to Pacific Grove, he published two California fictions, *The Pastures of Heaven* (1932) and *To a God Unknown* (1933), and worked on short stories collected in *The Long Valley* (1938). Popular success and financial security came only with *Tortilla Flat* (1935), stories about Monterey's paisanos. A ceaseless experimenter throughout his career, Steinbeck changed courses regularly. Three powerful novels of the late 1930s focused on the California laboring class: *In Dubious Battle* (1936), *Of Mice and Men* (1937), and the book considered by many his finest, *The Grapes of Wrath* (1939). Early in the 1940s, Steinbeck became a filmmaker with *The Forgotten Village* (1941) and a serious student of marine biology with *Sea of Cortez* (1941). He devoted his services to the war, writing *Bombs Away* (1942) and the controversial play-novelette *The Moon Is Down* (1942). *Cannery Row* (1945), *The Wayward Bus* (1947), *The Pearl* (1947), *A Russian Journal* (1948), another experimental drama, *Burning Bright* (1950), and *The Log from the* Sea of Cortez (1951) preceded publication of the monumental *East of Eden* (1952), an ambitious saga of the Salinas Valley and his own family's history. The last decades of his life were spent in New York City and Sag Harbor with his third wife, with whom he traveled widely. Later books include *Sweet Thursday* (1954), *The Short Reign of Pippin IV: A Fabrication* (1957), *Once There Was a War* (1958), *The Winter of Our Discontent* (1961), *Travels with Charley in Search of America* (1962), *America and Americans* (1966), and the posthumously published *Journal of a Novel: The* East of Eden *Letters* (1969), *Viva Zapata!* (1975), *The Acts of King Arthur and His Noble Knights* (1976), and *Working Days: The Journals of* The Grapes of Wrath (1989). He died in 1968, having won a Nobel Prize in 1962.

Robert DeMott is Professor of English at Ohio University, where he teaches American literature and has received both graduate and undergraduate teaching awards. His books include *Steinbeck's Reading* (1984) and the forthcoming *Steinbeck's Typewriter: Essays on Creative Dimensions of His Art.* He edited Steinbeck's *Working Days: The Journals of* The Grapes of Wrath (1989), and co-edited Steinbeck's *Novels and Stories, 1932–1937*, for the Library of America (1994).

TO A GOD UNKNOWN

JOHN STEINBECK

WITH AN INTRODUCTION
AND NOTES BY
ROBERT DEMOTT

PENGUIN BOOKS

PENGUIN BOOKS
Published by the Penguin Group
Penguin Group (USA) Inc., 375 Hudson Street, New York, New York 10014, U.S.A.
Penguin Group (Canada), 90 Eglinton Avenue East, Suite 700, Toronto, Ontario,
Canada M4P 2Y3 (a division of Pearson Penguin Canada Inc.)
Penguin Books Ltd, 80 Strand, London WC2R 0RL, England
Penguin Ireland, 25 St Stephen's Green, Dublin 2, Ireland (a division of Penguin Books Ltd)
Penguin Group (Australia), 250 Camberwell Road, Camberwell, Victoria 3124,
Australia (a division of Pearson Australia Group Pty Ltd)
Penguin Books India Pvt Ltd, 11 Community Centre, Panchsheel Park,
New Delhi – 110 017, India
Penguin Group (NZ), 67 Apollo Drive, Rosedale, North Shore 0632, New Zealand
(a division of Pearson New Zealand Ltd)
Penguin Books (South Africa) (Pty) Ltd, 24 Sturdee Avenue, Rosebank,
Johannesburg 2196, South Africa

Penguin Books Ltd, Registered Offices: 80 Strand, London WC2R 0RL, England

First published in the United States of America by Robert O. Ballou Inc. 1933
Published by Covici, Friede, Inc. 1935
Published by The Viking Press Inc. 1938
Published in Penguin Books 1976
This edition with an introduction and notes by Robert DeMott
published in Penguin Books 1995

Grateful acknowledgment is made for permission to reprint an excerpt from
"Roan Stallion" from *The Selected Poetry of Robinson Jeffers*.
Copyright © 1925 and renewed 1953 by Robinson Jeffers.
Reprinted by permission of Random House, Inc.

LIBRARY OF CONGRESS CATALOGING IN PUBLICATION DATA
Steinbeck, John, 1902–1968.
To a God unknown / by John Steinbeck; with an introd.
by Robert DeMott.
p. cm.
ISBN 978-0-14-018751-9
I. Title.
PS3537.T3234T6   1995
813'.52—dc20   95-6761

Printed in the United States of America
Set in Stempel Garamond

CONTENTS

INTRODUCTION

"Primus ego in patriam mecum . . . deducam Musas"; "for I shall be the first, if I live, to bring the Muse into my country. . . ." This was not a boast, but a hope, at once bold and devoutly humble, that he might bring the Muse . . . to his own little "country." . . .

—Jim Burden on Virgil's *Georgics*, in
Willa Cather, *My Antonia* (1918)

This story has grown since I started it. From a novel about people, it has become a novel about the world. . . . The new eye is being opened here in the west—the new seeing.

—John Steinbeck in a 1932 journal

I

In the margin of an older sister's copy of Robert Louis Stevenson's *Prince Otto*, a very young John Steinbeck marked in pencil his intention to be a writer. It was startling because, as Steinbeck later claimed in an early draft of *To a God Unknown*, "Artists and poets were not much thought of in western America." But at that time, when the definition of *writer* seemed less ambiguous and contested (but no less fraught with dilemma) than it has become in our post-structuralist age, Steinbeck's desire would become a self-fulfilling prophecy, which he addressed with such undeflected intensity for the rest of his life that he often considered himself "monomaniacal": "When there is no writing, I feel like an uninhabited body," he remarked in 1931. He belonged to a turn-of-the-century generation of white male novelists for whom the act of writing would be considered an essential, even exalted, pursuit. (William Faulkner and Ernest Hemingway were his contemporaries; born within four years of each other, all three eventually won the Nobel Prize for Literature.) For Steinbeck, as with many modernist-era writers, literary creativity took precedence over nearly all other life endeavors. He reached maturity in a period when becoming an author was a self-willed act with a romantic, rebellious aura to it; consequently, two of his first three books—*Cup of Gold* (1929) and *To a God Unknown* (1933)

—feature larger-than-life heroes. More than that, however, throughout Steinbeck's life, writing was all things to him—a purely enjoyable activity, a sustaining addiction, a way of establishing and maintaining personal and economic identity, and perhaps most of all, a habit of being, a necessary condition of existence: "As long as [I] can eat and write more books, that's all I require," he stated in November 1933.

Though occasionally he played the role of Artist with capital *A*, Steinbeck was more often than not extremely humble and self-deprecating. He learned early to distrust and even eschew the glamorous, celebrity side of authorship (with its emphasis on publicity and fame), and instead focused his energy on its private workaday side. If living so deeply in his fiction made him less than fully comfortable in the social, domestic, and emotional spheres of real life, it also provided therapeutic, compensatory benefits for a man who was intensely shy and inward-looking. Novels "regulate our lives and give us a responsibility," he claimed in 1930. Five years later, having tasted his first critical and commercial success with his fourth novel, *Tortilla Flat*, he confessed to the *San Francisco Chronicle*'s book critic Joseph Henry Jackson, "The work has been the means of making me feel that I am living richly, diversely, and, in a few cases and for a few moments, even heroically. All of these things are not me, for I am none of these things. But sometimes in my own mind at least I can create something which is larger and richer than I am." More than two decades later, Steinbeck was still espousing the priority of the life in art; he counseled Denis Murphy, a young novelist and family friend, that "work is your only weapon" against life's tragedies.

John Ernst Steinbeck was born into a respected middle-class household in Salinas, California, on February 27, 1902. He was the third of four children of John Ernst Steinbeck (1862–1935), a quiet, emotionally distant man who was, until 1911, manager of the Sperry Flour Mill, then became a private tradesman with his own feed and grain store (which failed), a bookkeeper at the Spreckels Sugar Refinery, and, in 1926, elected treasurer of Monterey County. Steinbeck's mother, Olive Hamilton Steinbeck (1867–1934), was an energetic, formidable, and socially active former schoolteacher, who encouraged Steinbeck's intellectual habits and fostered his sense of privilege at being the only son among the four children. His bookish side, however, was colored by a sensitivity—passed down from the Hamiltons—toward ghostly apparitions and paranormal reality; throughout Steinbeck's work, beginning with *Cup of Gold*, detachment exists side by side with an attraction for archetypes, visionary experiences, and mythic patterns. The great live oak under which Joseph Wayne, the protagonist of *To a God Unknown*, builds his house has its counterpart in a "brother" pine tree the young Steinbeck planted next to the family's Monterey Bay summer cottage on Eleventh Avenue in Pacific Grove: "If the tree should die, I am pretty sure I should be ill," he claimed in 1930.

Steinbeck's parents were proper, civic-minded citizens in Salinas, a predominantly conservative agricultural community toward which Steinbeck exhibited antipathy for most of his adult life. Writing was his ticket out of town, though once gone he remained in close contact with his family. (Like Joseph Wayne, Steinbeck always chafed between the desire to be "at home" and the need to be independent and court adventure; metaphorically speaking, writing fulfilled both urges.) His father hoped Steinbeck would do something suitably practical with his life, such as be an engineer or lawyer, but accepted his son's "ruthless" decision to become a writer. Beginning sporadically in 1929, he allowed John—and after August 1930, and continuing for most of the next five years, John and his wife, Carol—to occupy rent-free the family's three-room Pacific Grove cottage, and also provided a twenty-five-dollar monthly living allowance so that his son could concentrate solely on writing daily. From that time on, Steinbeck never held an outside job; working in words became his profession and vocation.

Steinbeck's mother, never quite satisfied with her son's radical decision, hoped that, if he became a novelist at all, he would be like the successful Booth Tarkington. Well into his twenties, Steinbeck was still influenced by the flabby sensibility and wordy excesses of Donn Byrne and James Branch Cabell. Fortunately, however, besides devouring the Bible and Sir Thomas Malory's *Morte d'Arthur*, Steinbeck also read widely in translations of ancient classics (notably by Aeschylus, Herodotus, Homer, and Virgil) and modern American and world literature, philosophy, history, science, anthropology, and mythology. His acquaintance, begun in 1930, with Edward F. Ricketts—a philosophical marine biologist at whose Pacific Biological Laboratory, on Ocean View Avenue in Monterey, Steinbeck spent countless hours of discussion and debate—would, by the early 1930s, curb the mawkishness in his writing and enlarge his view of fictional taste and artistic propriety. In 1932, urged by a friend to read Oswald Spengler's *The Decline of the West*, Steinbeck perused the first chapter, then returned the book, claiming he could not read it because it would "kill" his art. Despite frequent lapses of self-confidence, on his way to becoming a full-fledged novelist Steinbeck relied upon little more than enormous dedication and commitment, unflagging endurance and independence, strong convictions, sincere intentions, an honest desire to improve, and a blistering capacity for self-criticism. To these aspects of his talent, he was fortunate to add the support of his family and the generosity and goodwill of several trustworthy friends.

After graduating from Salinas High School in June 1919, Steinbeck entered Stanford University and attended classes for a total of six semesters through June 1925, without earning a degree. His nominal major was English. In eleven of his fourteen English Department courses (which included Journalism), Steinbeck's grades ranged from D to B+; his only three A's were in courses where more than the usual amount of imagination was called for—Versification, Feature Article Writing, and especially Short Story Writing, which he took twice (the first time earning a B). More importantly, Edith Ronald Mirrielees, Steinbeck's creative-writing professor in English 136, instilled in him an extraordinary—and lifelong—awareness that there was no "magic formula," no "secret ingredient," for writing "effective" fiction except experience, the desire to communicate, reverence for precise language, a terse, lean style, and plenty of discipline and humility. Some of these elements were in lesser supply than others in Steinbeck's brash juvenile period, when he managed only two stories in Stanford's literary magazine in 1924, and another, "The Gifts of Iban," by "John Stern," in *The Smoker's Companion* in 1927. Throughout the twenties, in a succession of odd jobs in California and New York as surveyor, day laborer, carpenter's helper, bench chemist, ship's steward, journalist, and fish hatchery attendant, Steinbeck built a reservoir of practical experience (which he would draw upon for the rest of his life), and continued writing stories and submitting them for publication, but without success.

In 1927–1928, seeking solitude to devote himself seriously to writing, he wintered at Lake Tahoe as an estate caretaker, and began reworking "The Lady in Infra-Red," a story he had written at Stanford. The result was his first novel, *Cup of Gold*, a historical work set in Wales and Panama, about the seventeenth-century pirate Henry Morgan. It was published in August 1929 by the New York firm Robert M. McBride (which also optioned his next book). Steinbeck considered *Cup of Gold* "an immature experiment" necessary to purge a beginning novelist's enthusiasms and to sweep "all the Cabellyo-Byrneish preciousness out for good." As Steinbeck was soon to discover, however, *Cup of Gold*'s publication guaranteed nothing as far as mastery of his art was concerned. "It is an awful lot of work to write a novel," he reported to A. Grove Day, a Stanford classmate, in late 1929.

From 1929 through 1934, when Steinbeck was struggling to establish confidence and credibility, and trying to perfect a tighter style, he wrote constantly, but with mixed success; more often than not he wrote only for himself, but at other times he labored with an eye on the marketplace, such as it was in the early stages of the Depression. Besides *Cup of Gold*, he published two other books of fiction—a linked collection of stories, *Pastures of Heaven* (1932), and *To a God Unknown*—and he published several stories that would later become part of his classic tale of childhood, *The Red Pony*, and others—"The Chrysanthemums" among them—that would make up *The Long Valley* in 1938. Under the stress of his parents' illnesses in 1933 and 1934, he wrote a large portion of *Tortilla Flat*. He also wrote other longer fictions during that five-year stretch, including "Dissonant Symphony," which he destroyed, and "Murder at Full Moon," a shameless commercial satire of pulp-detective novels, written under a pseudonym, Peter Pym (named for a character in Edgar Allan Poe's *Narrative of Arthur Gordon Pym*), which was never published. During this apprenticeship period, alternately dejected and elated by his progress, and sometimes living hand-to-mouth, Steinbeck tried out different methods, forms, and styles, but never wavered from his purpose: "Fine artistic things seem always to be done in the face of difficulties, and the rocky soil, which seems to give the finest flower, is contempt. Don't fool yourself," he informed fellow novelist George Albee in 1931, "appreciation doesn't make artists. It ruins them. A man's best work is done when he is fighting to make himself heard, not when swooning audiences wait for his paragraphs." (Until *Tortilla Flat* succeeded commercially in 1935,

Steinbeck earned less than a thousand dollars from publications.) With *The Pastures of Heaven* and *To a God Unknown* he was on his way toward establishing a new fictional voice in California. Like Virgil, whose *Georgics* Steinbeck admired, he too hoped, against great personal and cultural odds, to be the first of his generation to bring the Muse into "my country."

In the wake of such politicized, socially conscious novels as *In Dubious Battle* (1936), *Of Mice and Men* (1937), and *The Grapes of Wrath* (1939), John Steinbeck has come to be regarded as one of America's foremost documentary stylists; but the truth is that, in a career spanning nearly forty years, during which he wrote thirty books of fiction, drama, and nonfiction, he was never fully comfortable with or in control of a strictly realistic mode. Like Pilon, a character in his comic *Tortilla Flat*, "the curse of realism lay uneasily" on Steinbeck. Even *The Grapes of Wrath*, his most important fictional achievement, and arguably one of the world's great novels, owes as much to the mythopoeic legacy of nineteenth-century American romanticism and to the experimental techniques of modernist cinema as it does to the rigorous process of conducting field research among California's Dust Bowl migrants, upon which Steinbeck built his convincing vision.

It is worth recalling Steinbeck's early admission to his Stanford classmate and fellow novelist Carl Wilhelmson: *To a God Unknown*, he announced, "leaves realism farther and farther behind. I never had much ability for nor faith nor belief in realism." Realism is, he added, just another "form of fantasy." For Steinbeck, all modes of discourse, all enabling theories of writing, were equally fictive. Objectivity, which he adopted as a technical strategy, created narrative distance and control (which allowed him to establish irony and/or ambiguity). Like so many other American novelists who had an anxious, even subversive, relationship with literary realism (Mark Twain, Willa Cather, and William Faulkner are three he explicitly admired), Steinbeck always distrusted its naïve veneer. So he redefined realism for his own purposes, made it up as he went, so to speak, and consistently nudged his readers behind or beyond the exterior face of reality to the contextual and constitutive factors—whether biological, economic, social, historical, emotional, mythical, or psychological—that impinge on the way his fictional human beings act (he built a "wall of background," as he later called it). The "profound and dark and strong" libidinous "streams" of the unconscious in every human being had become the locus of his interest, he admitted to Wilhelmson in August 1933; in *The Pastures of Heaven* and *To a God Unknown,* Steinbeck defined reality to include seen and unseen, physical and metaphysical, quotidian and psychological, elements. His characters follow "a trail of innumerable meanings" toward what Joseph Wayne tells his wife is ". . . the undistorted real," the alluring reality behind reality. This novel, then, inscribes a related web in which the conscious life is affected by the unconscious, and the literal, denotative properties of language are interpenetrated by symbolic, connotative values. Steinbeck's goal, writes his biographer, Jackson Benson, was to make people "see the whole as it really is."

By striking through outward masks, of course, Steinbeck also frequently bent the formal rules of realistic writing. In a loose sense, all his fiction—even his most naturalistic—has an allegorical dimension and can be considered fabular. (His propensity for writing parables has ensured Steinbeck's popular success, but has hurt his reputation in the highest reaches of the critical academy; parables and fables, the argument goes, are not serious art.) His favorite metaphoric gambit was to choose a microcosm to represent the drama of the world: the fruit orchard in *In Dubious Battle*, the bunkhouse in *Of Mice and Men*, the Joad family's Hudson Super-Six in *The Grapes of Wrath*, and the pre–World War II industrial cannery section on Monterey's Ocean View Avenue in *Cannery Row* are perhaps his four most recognizable examples of contested sites.

But Steinbeck also saw the macrocosm represented in the geographical space of his native country—California's Monterey County—and especially in his home turf, the Salinas Valley. This entire region, which takes on a distinct life of its own in his fiction, was his equivalent of Faulkner's fictional Yoknapatawpha County in Mississippi, and the rugged Carmel/Big Sur landscape of neighbor Robinson Jeffers's poems. From an early stage of his career, Steinbeck exhibited a special affinity with and—like Joseph Wayne—an enormous hunger toward this unique part of his native state. In 1933 Steinbeck told Albee, "I think I would like to write the story of this whole valley, of all the little towns and all the farms and the ranches in the wilder hills. I can see how I would like to do it so that it would be the valley of the world." Steinbeck's gaze covered an area from Santa Cruz and Watsonville on the north, to King City and Jolon on the south; westward, Steinbeck's country was bounded by the Pacific Ocean and the Santa Lucia Mountains, and to the east by the Gabilan Mountains. That slice of northern California is now popularly known as "Steinbeck Country."

Steinbeck's hunger, his compulsion to tell the significant stories of people situated in and on, but not apart from, this land, became one of his recognizable signatures as a novelist. In a 1932 journal (addressed privately to former Stanford roommate and close friend Carlton "Duke" Sheffield), Steinbeck noted of *To a God Unknown*: "The story is a parable, Duke, the story of a race, growth and death. Each figure is a population, and the stones, the trees, the muscled mountains are the world—but not the world apart from man—the world *and* man—the one indescribable unit man plus his environment." Chronicling the lives of people in "the valley of the world" in such a way that they would be more than mere regional oddities, and so that they would represent an embedded part of the environment out of which they came, was Steinbeck's special achievement in *The Pastures of Heaven*, in the stories of *The Long Valley*, including *The Red Pony*, and of course in *To a God Unknown*—particularly in Chapter 21, where Steinbeck's ecological posture reaches a visionary level as he metaphorizes Joseph Wayne's body as a land mass, a "world-brain" with the power to destroy environmental "order" on a whim. Philosopher John Elof Boodin's axiom that "the laws of thought must be the laws of things"—one of Steinbeck's favorite quotations—has special resonance here and underscores the novelist's view of the human body as text, the text as body, on which are written the defining struggles of desire, as well as the intricate difficulties of representation.

When reading this unusual novel, then, with its oddly unsettling and sometimes strained combination of Christian and pagan, sacred and profane attributes—its earthiness and surreality, violence and pastoralism, pantheism and anthropomorphism, naturalism and lyricism—it is helpful to remember that Steinbeck invested his essential self in it, which is to say, he wrote it more like an extensive poem, or extended dream sequence, than like a traditionally mimetic or realistic novel. "I have the instincts of a minstrel rather than those of a scrivener," he informed Grove Day in late 1929. Thus, while *To a God Unknown* has an urgent, breathless fairy-tale quality, and is, as critic Howard Levant asserts, more "a series of detached . . . scenes" than "a unified . . . organic whole," it is not an incoherent concoction—"a rambling and improbable history," as Warren French calls it—that flies in the face of all sensible literary convention. During its long gestation through different versions and multiple drafts, Steinbeck worked hard to create a palpable factual dimension that gives this otherwise arcane book a recognizable texture in regard to its geographical setting and landmarks (the moss-covered rock actually existed in the northern California town of Laytonville), its unusual characters (some of whom, such as the seer, Steinbeck claimed were based on living persons), and in its feel for telling details of nature and social life in Monterey County in the early part of this century.

Although Steinbeck is not normally considered an autobiographical writer, the story of Joseph Wayne's pursuit is, up to a certain point, the story of Steinbeck; both are obsessed with tracing out destinies, and with seeking a generative place behind the reality of words and actions. To a God Unknown is driven by a kind of masculine poetics (symbolized by the totemic bull in Chapter 6), which thrives on competitiveness and prizes primacy and mastery. But it is also leavened by irony, and employment of a "new eye in the west." Steinbeck subverted California's populist image as a carefree golden land by pitilessly exposing its dichotomies, its mysteries, its unattainable felicities. Like those "twisted" madrone trees of Chapter 2, whose "bright green and shiny" leaves appear only at the end of "horrible limbs," Steinbeck's imagination, and his vision of himself as author, were thoroughly implicated in these paradoxical critiques. Indeed, Joseph's drive toward the ineffable functions as a parable of Steinbeck's own struggle with his art—but where Joseph's solipsistic fetish leads him back to the vortex of unconsciousness, which erases presence and the need for language, Steinbeck's expressive fetish thrusts him out of the unconscious toward a self-fashioned place in the vast geography of words. "You haven't any place you know until you make one," Steinbeck informed George Albee in 1932. "And if you make one, it will be a new one. Forget about genius and write books. Whatever you write will be you."

II

On September 12, 1933, John Steinbeck received from Robert O. Ballou, his financially beleaguered New York publisher, a small shipment of his newly printed *To a God Unknown*, with its dark green pictorial dust jacket designed by Steinbeck's artist friend Mahlon Blaine. Editor Ballou had gone out on his own after the rapid, successive bankruptcies of Jonathan Cape, and then Brewer, Warren, and Putnam (publisher of *The Pastures of Heaven*); although several houses eventually bid for *To a God Unknown* (including Simon and Schuster, which would have promised more money), Steinbeck had remained loyal to Ballou's fragile, shoestring operation while the publisher sought the cash necessary to bring out his two fall-list books—Steinbeck's and one by Julia Peterkin. "The books came this morning and I like them immensely. Thank you for doing such a fine job with them." They gave, Steinbeck confessed, "more pleasure than I have felt for a number of months." His casual reply has a restrained elegance that belies the protracted and difficult history of the book's development and eventual production. In fact, in one form or another under three different working titles (marking various and sometimes overlapping stages of its progress), *To a God Unknown* occupied Steinbeck's attention and tested his artistic mettle and resources for over four years. Except for the posthumously published *The Acts of King Arthur and His Noble Knights* (1976), Steinbeck labored longer on *To a God Unknown* than on any other book, including his two famous epics, *The Grapes of Wrath* and *East of Eden* (1952). "The book was hellish hard to write," he told Ballou succinctly in February 1933, and he admitted, without going into details, having worked toward it "for about five years."

The history of the making of *To a God Unknown* is worth elaborating upon, for the story behind the story (informed by a number of heretofore unpublished primary documents), makes an intriguing tale of its own, as well as a lesson in the felicities of endurance and dedication. Neither individual expression nor cultural construction alone can fully explain the source of the creative act, which eludes final categorization. John Steinbeck was nothing if not resolutely single-minded. The process by which the book grew was not so unitary, however, because forces of every kind from within and without kept entering his purview, altering his text, altering him. Even if all those factors were known—which is doubtful—it would still be impossible to establish their priority or present them fully, so what follows here is a working sketch, a narrative in and of process.

Steinbeck's novel had its roots in an unlikely source—an unfinished stage play called "The Green Lady" written in the midtwenties by his Stanford University undergraduate classmate and boon companion, Webster "Toby" Street. In the third and only extant draft of Street's play, the action "takes place in a front room of Andy Wane's ranch house in the hill country of Mendocino County, California." Street's main characters include Andy Wane, "a tall, well-knit man of about fifty-five, or more, with the characteristic stoop of one who has made his way with his hands"; Mrs. Ruth Wane, "a woman about fifty"; and their three children—two sons, Luke and John, and one daughter, Susan, "a girl of seventeen or eighteen." In addition, a neighbor, Milton, is a suitor for Susan's hand. The Wane family is gradually being torn apart by Andy Wane's pathological preoccupation with the trees on his land, which make up "her"—the female forest, the "green witch" of the natural world: "Seems like the whole outdoors was a green lady sometimes," Mrs. Wane complains bitterly. As the play progresses, the drama turns on Andy's nature worship, but also on his selfish refusal to sell timber rights to raise the money necessary to send his daughter back to the University of California at Berkeley. Moreover, Andy conceives an illicit, unseemly attraction to Susie, confusing one form of natural beauty for another: "Men loves things 'cause they're like a woman, or 'cause they're pretty. They git 'em mixed up sometimes, an' don't know which is which," her jealous mother explains. In the end Andy is supposed to die in a raging forest fire.

Even though Street was an active amateur playwright who "wrote all the time," by his own admission his work was "not very good." In the case of this unfinished play, his dialogue and gestures are wooden, his characterizations one-dimensional and unrealized. "I don't think it's anything like *To a God Unknown*, except that there is a pantheistic streak in it," he said in 1975. And yet, despite Street's disclaimer, in protagonist Andy Wane's pantheism, his fatal attraction to natural and sexual forces, this otherwise uninspired melodrama does indeed contain the essential germ of Steinbeck's *To a God Unknown*, though it would be left entirely to Steinbeck to raise Andy Wane's aberrant behavior to the level of Joseph Wayne's tragic obsession in this novel.

Street, on the path to becoming an attorney (LLB, Stanford, 1928), recognized his friend's artistic ambitions, and permitted Steinbeck to novelize the original treatment (which included a prologue and first act, but only written suggestions for acts two and three). Although Steinbeck may have given thought to revising the play as early as 1927, it wasn't until April 14, 1928, that he told their mutual friend, Robert Cathcart (another Stanford classmate), that he was "preparing to write a novel around" Street's play, which, he claimed, has "a fine thesis, and I do not know whether I have the power and acuteness and artistry to bring it out." From that point on, even though it may have been intended as a collaborative effort, Steinbeck himself worked sporadically and mostly alone at "The Green Lady" for the next two years, marking the manuscript's uneven progress in frequent letters to his close friends of the time—Albee, Cathcart, Sheffield, Wilhelmson, poet Katherine Beswick, and lawyer Amassa "Ted" Miller, who, until Steinbeck signed with literary agents Mavis McIntosh and Elizabeth Otis in 1931, served as the novelist's sole representative to New York publishing houses. All of them became sounding boards for Steinbeck's artistic concerns with this book.

In its first stage of composition, the book seems to have languished during much of 1928 and into 1929—that is, for about a year after Steinbeck announced his intention to adapt Street's play. In February 1929, he traveled with Street to Laytonville and its environs in Mendocino County (north of San Francisco) to visit the locale of the action, and hoped to finish a draft by September. But over the next two months, writing went very slowly, and in early March he reported to Kate Beswick that he had temporarily fled Pacific Grove, and headed for San Francisco, hoping to escape the "terror" of "The Green Lady," by which he probably meant his own inadequacy at executing an inherited story, no matter how sympathetic he was to its basic premise. His hiatus, however, accomplished positive ends, in that it allowed Steinbeck to reassess his obligation to Street's original, and to initiate important modifications, some of which would have long-range results. With fresh innovations in mind, around mid-April 1929, Steinbeck started "The Green Lady" again, this time so enthusiastically that by May 22, 1929, he reported to Beswick that he had finished eighty pages, and had set his eye confidently on completing one hundred pages by June 1:

> The Lady progresses pretty rapidly . . . and it seems to be improving in fluency and ease and in interest all the time. I am terribly anxious for you to have a look at it. I didn't make a carbon though. What shall I do? Shall I send you the first hundred pages heavily insured? Then if it were lost I would be repaid for doing it again. You see I write with a pen for five days of the week and on saturday and sunday I type and revise the pages I have written, so if the typed pages were lost all I would have to do would be to go through the typing and revising again. Or else I could wait and send you the third draft of which I shall make carbons. The only trouble is that I should like your criticism before I make the third draft.

In his new version, Steinbeck began with a key decision to move the setting from Mendocino County—about which he felt no emotional attachment, and with whose geography he was unfamiliar—to an area near Jolon, in southern Monterey County, the writer's home county, and thus a familiar landscape upon which to build his dynastic tale. (As a child Steinbeck had spent summers on his uncle Tom Hamilton's ranch in King City, not far from Jolon). The flat voice and slightly ironic tone registered in this characteristic early paragraph of "The Green Lady" indicates how declarative his approach was at this point. (Compare the following entry with its counterpart in *To a God Unknown*, the opening paragraph of Chapter 2): "Jolon is a large bowl in the earth in central California. It is watered in part by two large streams, the Naciemento and the San Antonio. It lies in the arms of the Coast Range mountains of which one rampart guards it from the ocean while a smaller ridge separates it from the long, fertile Salinas Valley. On one of the river's banks sat the old Mission San Antonio surrounded by its gardens and irrigation ditches, maintained by the Indians who, in return for their labor in making bricks, digging ditches and tilling the soil, received from the mission divine grace and cotton pants."

Furthermore, instead of following Street's plan to begin in medias res in the present, Steinbeck started in 1850 (when the lure of easy money in California's gold fields was drawing men "westward like Hamlin's rats")—which, he must have thought, would lend his version greater historical reach and sociological context. Steinbeck would also develop two generations of male Waynes: Joseph, the "strong" father, "born to be a patriarch," and husband to three successive wives, including his last, a Bible-reading woman named Carry, who never quite fits into the Wayne family regime; and Andy, Joseph's "strange," sensitive prodigal son (by his second wife, Beth Willets) who would become the protagonist of "The Green Lady" (and of "To the Unknown God"). The second half of the novel was probably intended to chronicle Andy's domestic life with his new bride, Julia Seib. (In the third and final version of the novel Steinbeck would abandon the second half; he would also transpose the fledgling story of the Lopez sisters to Chapter 7 of *The Pastures of Heaven*).

Another element not mentioned by Street but added by Steinbeck was climatological: Steinbeck's version of "The Green Lady" incorporated the cyclical return of the dry years, but did not elaborate upon its effect in determining characters' actions. (One of the handwritten editorial comments on the "Green Lady" manuscript—perhaps by Street, or Beswick, or Sheffield—reads, "Must show effect of heat and dryness on Andy.") The basis for one aspect of *To a God Unknown*'s wasteland motif is evident here in the precursor draft:

> About every thirty years there have come periods of rainlessness to Central and Southern California. These desolating years seem to come creeping up out of the white desert to warn the west that it will one day die as the desert has died. They are like the Reminders of Death at an Egyptian feast. . . .
>
> And now the periodic drought had settled on the land. Little by little, year on year the water was sucked from the ground. The hills looked gaunt and hungry and pale. The bones of many thousands of starved cattle were whitening on the ground. Two families of Waynes packed up their possessions and drove away. Joe watched his dying land with terror and with loathing.

Several other basic elements in this originating version of "The Green Lady" would eventually be developed more fully in *To a God Unknown*: Joseph Wayne's preoccupation with fertility; a haunting "green grotto" in the mountains would become the published book's mysterious glade, where much of the novel's key action occurs; Beth Willet's accidental death would be reprised in Elizabeth's death; and Andy's unconscious desire to "become one with the greenness" of the voluptuous forest would prefigure Joseph Wayne's attraction to the forest's "curious femaleness." Thus, from its roots in a circumscribed social and familial melodrama, Steinbeck was gradually broadening the work to a larger, more elemental scope.

Steinbeck's impulse to elaborate, to push the horizons of his vision to cosmogonic vistas, urged him on. Six months later, in November 1929, Steinbeck told Beswick that "The Green Lady" was nearly finished. Later that year he sent her part of the manuscript to read and comment upon, planning to cut the "bad parts" with her assistance, though there is no proof that this collaboration actually occurred. At some point Webster Street may have read the typescript and made editorial comments, but given his work schedule as an attorney, he probably had little time to do so, at least in any kind of sustained fashion. (Street made no mention whatsoever of being involved in the novelized version of "The Green Lady," and for that matter never mentioned the manuscript at all in his 1975 interview.) So even though the title page of the manuscript read "*THE GREEN LADY*, a novel by John Steinbeck and Webster Street," Steinbeck was in the venture alone, and he was beginning to envision further changes that would make the material more congenial to his own imaginative and psychological demands, particularly in emphasizing Andy Wayne's delusional behavior.

Through the winter of 1929–1930, Steinbeck kept at the book. His life meantime had changed significantly. In January 1930, he had married Carol Henning, a remarkably strong and independent-minded person, who not only encouraged his career as a writer, but willingly shared the hard financial times of their early years together. In an effort to save both time and money—and because Carol was an incisive and effective editor (further removing Steinbeck's need to depend on Beswick and Street)—in addition to her other jobs and duties (including a stint working at Ed Ricketts's lab), she typed

Steinbeck's books, which freed the novelist to concentrate mostly on writing and revising. "Carol is a good influence on my work," he informed Carl Wilhelmson. He agreed with her suggestion that this book was "melodramatic" in places, but felt that could be corrected in the next draft, for which, he told Wilhelmson, he would be "cutting several things out," including "all of that throw back about the childhood of Carry," which leads "off the interest from the main theme." Nevertheless, he continued, "I think it is a better book than I have done though that is not much to say for it. Certainly it has more effort in it than I have ever put in anything."

Part of his effort at "amplifying and clarifying" involved seeking the right title. As early as January 1930, Steinbeck had wanted a new name for the second stage of his manuscript; by March 10, he had titled his book "To the Unknown God." Writing from Eagle Rock, near Los Angeles, where the Steinbecks were living temporarily, he explained to Ted Miller that the novel—projected to be about 375 pages or 110,000 words in length—"will be done and ready in about a month." He had "given it the title TO THE UNKNOWN GOD and am using some verses from the Vedic hymn of that title as a forepiece." Steinbeck wasn't sure that Robert M. McBride's publishing company would want this book because, while it contained "nothing particularly sexual," it was "not a book that will please the great middle west." (In late March, Steinbeck told Miller that when his father read the manuscript he "was quite disgusted at the end," for he "expected Andy to recover and live happily ever after. . . . The American people demand miracles in their literature.") For the first time since he had begun working on the novel, he was able to follow Edith Mirrieliees's advice and reduce the novel's "thesis" to a single dispassionate statement: "It is a fairly close study of a paranoiac mind and of primitive instincts of a modern man. Whether or not there is any kind of race memory in paranoia is unimportant to me. I have recounted only that such a man reacted in a given manner. I have seen such reactions. And I have not drawn any conclusions from such reactions." And a few weeks later he admitted to Wilhelmson:

Everything has been in a haze pretty much for the past three weeks. I have been working to finish this ms. and the thing took hold of me so completely that I lost track of nearly everything else. Now the thing is done. I started rewriting this week and am not going to let it rest. Also I have a title which gives me the greatest of pleasure. For my title I have taken one of the Vedic Hymns, the name of the hymn—

TO THE UNKNOWN GOD

You surely remember the hymn with its refrain at the end of each invocation "Who is the god to whom we shall offer sacrifice?"

Steinbeck's employment of the ancient hymn to Prajapati, supreme lord of creation, indicates that his story was exceeding regional concerns into a more profound and universal arena. His statement of artistic belief, written around this time to George Albee, speaks to his evolving "ambitious" vision: "I'd rather underreach a large theme than wax redundant over a small one. I consider a magnitude of conception and paucity in execution far more desirable than a shallow conception with preciousness." Although the novel was becoming increasingly his own property, he was still mindful of its origins in Street's play, however, so when Steinbeck sent Miller his finished manuscript in April 1930, he instructed that, should McBride accept the book, Steinbeck would write a short foreword "in which some mention of Toby Street should be made. . . . He has decided that he didn't do as much on this as he at first thought he did. But such a foreword is really necessary." (When *To a God Unknown* appeared, Steinbeck inscribed a gift copy: "For Toby—This isn't much like our old story and yet it is the same story many generations later.")

As it turned out, however, his acknowledgment would not be needed because no publishing firm would take the novel, even though Steinbeck worked diligently in successive drafts to improve it by enlarging his characterization of the protagonist, another indication of the novel's growing reach: "I'm having a devil of a time with my new book," he wrote Albee on February 27, 1931, Steinbeck's twenty-ninth birthday: "It just won't seem to come right. Largeness of character is difficult. Never deal with an Olympian character." For fourteen months, from April 1930 to June 1931, Miller dutifully circulated "To the Unknown God" to numerous publishers, including McBride; John Day; Harper's; Farrar and Rinehart; Little, Brown; and others as well, all of whom rejected the manuscript. "The God must have been to ten publishers by now and has only received a decent note from one [John Day]," Steinbeck lamented. "That is a pretty fair indication of its appeal." Partway through this period, in a letter postmarked January 7, 1931, he registered his despair to Miller: "Rejection follows rejection. Haven't there ever been encouraging letters? Perhaps an agent with a thorough knowledge of markets would see that the mss. were not marketable at all and would return them on that ground. You see the haunting thought comes that perhaps I have been kidding myself all these years, myself and other people—that I have nothing to say or no art in saying nothing. It is two years since I have received the slightest encouragement and that was short lived."

Steinbeck got his wish: by May 1931 he signed on as a client with the new firm of McIntosh and Otis. "Carl Wilhelmson recommended me," he told Albee, and added humorously that if he had not known their method of doing business, he should be "very suspicious" of their "boundless enthusiasm. . . ." The upshot of this new arrangement on Steinbeck's side was a renewed vigor and confidence at a point when he most needed assurance, and an abiding appreciation of and trust in McIntosh and Otis's professional abilities. (They remained his agents throughout his life, and still represent his estate.) On August 18, 1931, Steinbeck confessed to Mavis McIntosh that "the imperfections of the Unknown God had bothered me ever since I first submitted the book for publication. In consequence of this uneasiness, your announcement of the book's failure to find a publisher is neither unwelcome nor unpleasant to me. If I were sure of the book, I should put it aside and wait. . . . But I know its faults. I know, though, that the story is good. I shall rewrite it immediately." Before he undertook his proposed rewriting, in late 1931 McIntosh submitted the manuscript of "To the Unknown God" one last time—to William Morrow (without success)—and Steinbeck, convinced more than ever of its unsalability, entered another "period of indecision and self-doubt," he told Wilhelmson. "I reread the Unknown God and was horrified at its badness as a whole." Between bouts of anger at his inadequacy with this book, and a growing entanglement with the stories that would comprise the linked chapters of *The Pastures of Heaven*, Steinbeck proposed a solution: "I guess I'll go back to the Unknown God," he informed Albee. "That title will have to be changed. Because the story will be cut to pieces and the pieces refitted and changed." It seems likely that, despite Steinbeck's repeated efforts at revision and elaboration, "To the Unknown God" was not substantively or stylistically different from its predecessor, and so something far deeper than mechanical patching and tinkering was necessary to keep it from reading "like a case history in an insane asylum," as he had once told Miller. During the following year, however, Steinbeck made his greatest leap forward when a number of unanticipated elements spurred him to complete the novel we now have.

III

Nineteen thirty-two was the breakthrough year for *To a God Unknown*. In the previous version, Steinbeck had treated Andy's paranoia, his "incurable ailment," too clinically, he told Miller, so that Andy's only options would be to commit "suicide" or to become a "homicidal maniac." Clearly, more complicated motivation was needed to make the new book succeed. Immediately, Steinbeck reconceived Joseph Wayne as chief character, and collapsed the former roles of patriarch (Joseph) and protagonist (Andy) into one. In so doing, Steinbeck created a character who resonated more deeply with aspects of the Old Testament Joseph (in Genesis), especially in his role as chosen brother and as dreamer and visionary; meanwhile, the epic cast of Joseph Wayne's westering journey to California's promised land echoed the biblical Joseph's removal to Egypt. As the book progressed, Joseph would increasingly—and rather heavy-handedly—recapitulate the overt symbology of Jesus Christ and covert symbology of a host of pagan sacrificial gods and primitive vegetation-myth deities. (Some critics have also drawn parallels between Joseph of Arimathea and Joseph Wayne.)

Eventually, Steinbeck also decided upon a new title: *To a God Unknown*. "The Unknown in this case meaning Unexplored," he said, so as not to confuse it with the "Unknown God of St. Paul" (in Acts 17:22–29). Steinbeck later admitted to Ballou that he was writing a "religious" book (using the "pure and effective religion" of Bach's *Art of the Fugue* for inspiration and accompaniment as he wrote). But Steinbeck was explicitly rejecting "mysticism," by which he meant "bad vague thinking" and "things that don't really happen." His new twist on the Vedic hymn was extremely important because, as he later confided to Los Angeles book critic Wilbur Needham, the "unknown god" he employed was "that powerful fruitful and moving Unconscious." In his new version, the god Joseph sought was not manifest in the exterior world, but resided inside himself. In directing Joseph's quest toward deep psychic recesses, Steinbeck was drastically changing the novel's thesis, altering its ground of being.

Steinbeck's new version would also be enhanced by a contemporary historical event. He had incorporated the cyclical dry years into the fabric of the early versions, but it functioned as backdrop rather than as a controlling metaphor. Here the Jolon drought and its effects would create ambience for Joseph's obsessive belief that only he can save the land, which would become the focus of the novel. (Joseph's brooding concern for the wasted land reflects the role of the mythological Fisher King of Frazer's *The Golden Bough* and Jessie Weston's *From Ritual to Romance*—two works which stand prominently behind T. S. Eliot's 1922 poem *The Waste Land* as well as *To a God Unknown*.) On January 25, 1932, a couple of weeks before launching his final version, Steinbeck told McIntosh he no longer intended to merely patch up his book. "It would surely show such surgery. . . . I shall cut it in two at the break and work only at the first half, reserving the last half for some future novel." The reason for emphasizing the first half was "suggested by recent, and, to me, tremendous events":

Do you remember the drought in Jolon that came every thirty five years? We have been going through one identical with the one of 1880. Gradually during the last ten years the country has been dying of lack of moisture. The dryness has peculiar effects. Diseases increase. . . . This winter started as usual—no rain. Then in December the thing broke. There were two weeks of downpour. The rivers overflowed and took away houses and cattle and land. I've seen decorous people dancing in the mud. They have laughed with a kind of crazy joy when their land was washing away. The disease is gone and the first delirium has settled to a steady jubilance. There will be no ten people a week taken to asylums from this county as there were last year. Anyway, there is the background. The new novel will be closely knit and I can use much of the material from the Unknown God, but the result will be no rewritten version.

. "No rewritten version" is the key statement. Three weeks later, on February 16, 1932, Steinbeck informed Ted Miller that he had changed "the place, characters, time, theme, and thesis and name" of his new novel so "it won't be much like the first book." On March 14, 1932, he again wrote Miller, saying that he was "about a third finished with the first draft of the new version," and that he liked it "pretty well this time." His writing still went slowly (after reading in Spengler's *Decline of the West*, he was unable to work for three weeks), but at least it was moving toward a final shape.

For two years, Steinbeck had enjoyed the company of an informal group of inquisitive, like-minded friends at Ricketts's Pacific Biological Laboratory. In early 1932, Carol started working for Ricketts, and the mutual relationship of all involved became more intense. Progressive, irreverent, freewheeling discussions on every conceivable subject, and a critical bohemian attitude toward life were the order of the day. As scholar Richard Astro has shown, Steinbeck and Ricketts were immediately compatible and launched the intellectual give-and-take that would eventually help Steinbeck formulate his phalanx, or group-man, theory, prominent in later works (there are moments of it in *To a God Unknown*, for instance when the dancers in Chapter 16 join into one unit), as well as the shared philosophical tenets of "breaking through" and nonteleological thinking (already evident in the novel's omniscient point of view and in Joseph Wayne's live-and-let-live attitude) that would propel their 1941 collaborative nonfiction book *Sea of Cortez*. (Ricketts would also become the model for Doc, the protagonist of *Cannery Row*, published four years later.) Besides his metaphysical discussions with Ricketts, Steinbeck also enjoyed the use of the lab's excellent library. Steinbeck had already researched Celtic and Arthurian lore, Sir James Frazer's *The Golden Bough*, and Carl Jung's treatises on psychology and the unconscious, to cite but a few examples, and he continued to build a legitimate personal foundation of knowledge regarding what he called "psychological and anthropological" sources. Into this dynamic nexus of people, books, forces, and ideas, rivals entered who would further transform the novel.

The first was Joseph Campbell. Later to become one of the world's most famous mythologists as a result of *The Hero with a Thousand Faces* (1949) and *The Masks of God* (1959–1968), Campbell arrived in the Carmel/Monterey area in February 1932, and quickly gravitated toward Ricketts and his freethinking cronies. Steinbeck had just started his revised manuscript, and Campbell recalled hearing Steinbeck read sections of his first four days' composition to him aloud. Campbell thought the opening lacked "a sensuous, visual quality," and Steinbeck, impressed with the younger man's erudition and insight, decided to start over again with those qualities in mind. For a while, Campbell and Steinbeck enthusiastically shared their parallel investigations into anthropology, ethnography, psychology, primitivism, mythology, comparative religions, and Arthurian romance. The hero's spiritual quest toward self-realization was to become one of Campbell's supreme subjects, so their discussions undoubtedly enlarged Steinbeck's view of Joseph Wayne's mythic dimension and the several stages of his progress, from his call to action through his transformation. In the poetical and by now more visual passages of the revised *To a God Unknown* that Steinbeck continued to read to him, and in Steinbeck's use of Joseph Wayne's rite of passage toward the sacred center of the world, Campbell discovered his and Steinbeck's mutual attraction to the "tendency" of "symbolism" as an essential way of apprehending and understanding reality. (Campbell later recalled that he had learned as much from Steinbeck as Steinbeck had from him).

In an ironic twist of life imitating art, both men shared an interest in the archetype of the eternal woman: Steinbeck's writing of Joseph Wayne's attraction to the "curious femaleness" of the forest of Our Lady paralleled in an uncanny way Joseph Campbell's belief in the importance of the feminine muse that leads the hero toward his destiny. This connection became extremely complicated for Campbell who fell in love with Carol. Their mutual attraction added yet another tangled dimension to Steinbeck's work. The ritual quest of the fictive Joseph became blurred by the flesh-and-blood Campbell, and once more slowed down Steinbeck's work on his book. And although Steinbeck, like his main character, wanted to conduct his life above pity and therefore beyond teleological categories of assigning praise and blame, he could also be jealous and manipulative. Ostensibly he accepted the dalliance between the two platonic lovers, but he talked Carol into moving away to Montrose, near Los Angeles, for the next seven months, and also wrote his true reaction into *To a God Unknown*. The gay, alluring, lustful interloper Benjy Wayne (who earlier had nearly sung his way into the heart of Elizabeth before she married Joseph) is killed by Juanito for seducing his wife, Alice. If writing well was Steinbeck's best revenge for dispatching a rival, it could also be argued that the strain of the affair gave his novel a charged quality, a sexual reverberation, that earlier drafts lacked. The scene in Chapter 21 when Rama and Joseph have intercourse out of "need" exemplifies this lusty dimension. Around the time Campbell exited the scene, in the summer of 1932, an invigorated Steinbeck was having "the most fun" writing eight pages a day, and considered the book "nearly half finished."

In this final phase, Steinbeck discovered something about himself that would mark his writing career for the rest of the decade: he needed to feel a sense of competitiveness, needed to feel something threatening or annoying pushing back at him, creating internal stress as he composed. Campbell's involvement with Carol was one such transactional event that injected a heightened sense of life into his novel, but a more lasting pressure on *To a God Unknown* came inadvertently from Robinson Jeffers. Beginning with *Tamar and Other Poems* in 1924, and continuing through six more volumes by 1932, Jeffers had created a unique poetry of enormous sweep and power centered around "continent's end," the California coastal landscape between Carmel and Big Sur. His long narrative poems, such as "Tamar," "Roan Stallion," "The Woman at Point Sur," and "Cawdor," dealt with the aberrant and often violent behavior of contemporary people whose dramatic lives and actions resonated with mythological symbolism and erotic pantheism. (Although he lacked direct "evidence," Lawrence Clark Powell was intuitively right in claiming "that Steinbeck was influenced by Jeffers.")

Again, it was Carol Steinbeck who acted as catalyst. The group was avidly reading and discussing Jeffers's work that spring when *Thurso's Landing and Other Poems* was published and the poet appeared on the cover of the April 4, 1932, issue of *Time*, establishing him as one of the most visible contemporary American writers. Because Jeffers drew attention to a nearby part of California, Steinbeck was bound to feel nervous, threatened, even betrayed. When Carol discovered the central message of Jeffers's earlier poem "Roan Stallion"—which states, "Humanity is the mold to break away from, the crust to break / through, the coal to break into fire. . . . Tragedy that breaks man's face and a white / fire flies out of it; vision that fools him / Out of his limits, desire that fools him out of his limits"—Ricketts and Campbell quickly realized the value of Jeffers's urge to push beyond the confines of the human ego. Jeffers was "one of the few poets that have ever really influenced my own thinking and style," Campbell admitted. And Ricketts, in developing two essays, "The Philosophy of Breaking Through," and "A Spiritual Morphology of Poetry," found that Jeffers penetrated to deep levels of "beyond," into realms of transhuman and natural beauty in his pessimistic poems. (Ricketts also found this "deep thing" in *To a God Unknown*.)

As a creative writer, not a scholar or scientist, Steinbeck's reaction differed from Ricketts's and Campbell's by being more affective. Where the others tended outward, Steinbeck tended inward. Highly respectful of Jeffers's ecological vision of the universe as an organic whole, he also felt keenly the competitive sense, the anxiety of influence, which the older man's poetry embodied. An "effusive" five-page letter Steinbeck wrote in late 1932 to Ballou is the vital corroborating link here which explains what was at stake. In it, Steinbeck pointed out three times that Jeffers was not a native Californian, but a transplanted Pennsylvanian, another interloper into his home country (Jeffers arrived in Carmel in 1914):

My country is different from the rest of the world. It seems to be one of those pregnant places from which come wonders. Lhasa is such a place. I am trying to translate my people and my country in this . . . book. The problem frightens me. Jeffers came into my country and felt the thing but he translated it into the symbols of Pittsburg[h]. I cannot write the poetry of Jeffers but I know the god better than he does for I was born to it and my father was. Our bodies came from this soil—our bones came . . . from the limestone of our own mountains and our blood is distilled from the juices of this earth. I tell you now that my country—a hundred miles long and about fifty wide—is unique in the world. . . . I've wanted to write this book for so long, and I've been afraid to. I've been too young, too ignorant, too thick headed. After the Roan Stallion, I thought Jeffers would do it but he hasn't. He got caught by Spengler and high school girls, and . . . Pittsburg[h] and the taboos of Pittsburg[h] to be rebelled against. He wrote the greatest poetry since Whitman but he didn't write my country. Perhaps he didn't want to.

It does not matter how accurate Steinbeck's assessment of Jeffers is; what matters is that Steinbeck believed it. At once an apology and a credo, a hope and a boast, Steinbeck's self-confessedly "humorless" letter registers the gravity of his reaction, the degree to which Jeffers was someone to be reckoned with, appropriated if necessary, and even "surpassed," as Joseph Campbell wrote in characterizing Steinbeck's attitude toward the poet.

At a crucial but undetermined point in his novel's development, Steinbeck began to experience Jeffers's poems in a haunting, visceral way (perhaps as much a challenge as a threat); consequently, prone to borrow like a "shameless magpie," he transmuted something essential from them into his own text. As both Lawrence Clark Powell and Joseph Fontenrose indicate, there are in *To a God Unknown* strong echoes of and parallels to Jeffers's overwrought and nearly unreadable 1927 epic *The Woman at Point Sur* (in which Arthur Barclay, self-created prophet of a new religion, sacrifices himself); but it wasn't simply Jeffers's subject matter, themes, characters, or setting that Steinbeck was after, for he had been marking those areas out for himself for a number of years, perhaps even before having read Jeffers at all. Instead, it was the example Jeffers's work and life set as a standard of commitment to his art. If, as Steinbeck believed, poets and artists were still suspect in the American West, here was one who appeared as tough-minded as the country he wrote about. (A few years later Steinbeck told Powell, their mutual friend, that Jeffers should be awarded the Nobel Prize—"I don't know any American who can compete with him for it.")

Although we can never fully isolate or understand the influences that pass from one writer to another, practically speaking, Jeffers's muscular style apparently appealed to Steinbeck and helped elevate this book to the next level of intensity. For instance, in their sustained lyricism the last five chapters of *To a God Unknown* frequently show that Steinbeck internalized Jeffers's rhythmic style, such as in this passage where Steinbeck's sentences easily break into the kind of sonorous line Jeffers favored:

The blades of the windmill shone faintly in the moonlight.
It was a view half obscured, for the white dust filled the air, and the wind
   drove fiercely down the valley.
Joseph turned up the hill to avoid the houses, and as he went up toward

the black grove,
the moon sank over the western hills and the land was blotted
   out of sight.
The wind howled down from the slopes and cried in the dry branches of
   the trees.
The horse lowered its head against the wind.

The cadence here creates a compelling tempo that reflects an inevitable march to the dark interior of Joseph's psyche. ("It's hardly the same book. Different feeling and rhythm," Steinbeck boasted to Kate Beswick.) Where Jeffers's Nietzschean inhumanism could be shrill, abrasive, and defiant, Steinbeck exposed the potential for power inside man, especially at that threshold where human being and landscape conjoin. In this controversial and much-debated climax, when Joseph sacrifices himself to restore vitality to the land, Joseph is more everyman than superman: "And yet he looked down the mountains of his body where the hills fell to an abyss. He felt the driving rain, and heard it whipping down, pattering on the ground. He saw his hills grow dark with moisture. Then a lancing pain shot through the heart of the world. 'I am the land,' he said, 'and I am the rain. The grass will grow out of me in a little while.'" And in that surreal epiphanic scene in Chapter 21, referred to earlier, Steinbeck imagines Joseph's body as an extended trope of the earth, achieved by a doubling of self and world: "And he thought in tones, in currents of movement, in color, and in slow prodding rhythm. He looked down at his slouched body, at his curved arms and hands resting in his lap. Size changed." The anatomy of the "world-brain" that follows is unlike anything else in Steinbeck's writing, or anything in Jeffers's for that matter. In these scenes Steinbeck attempts to surpass Jeffers by laying claim to the generative roots of "my country," and "my god" in a way that is indigenously organic, not philosophically superimposed. In this sense, Steinbeck's borrowing from Jeffers can be considered both an homage and a challenge, a return and a breakthrough, a relinquishment and a possession.

Meeting the challenge from Jeffers helped Steinbeck finish. In December, a month after *The Pastures of Heaven* was published, he claimed that Ballou had announced the book for spring release. Given the weak sales of *Pastures* (about 650 copies), Ballou's announcement was probably an incentive, and throughout January

1933, Steinbeck wrote quickly and steadily, completing the novel by February 11. He and Carol were so poor that a friend volunteered to pay postage to New York. This version displayed greater fascination for Joseph's stature as a "pattern breaker." Steinbeck had come a long way from his cold view of Andy Wane as a scientific oddity, a "close study of a paranoiac mind." This Joseph had fire because Steinbeck identified with him in a way he was unable to identify with Andy. In his private journal, he wrote: "Joseph is a giant shouldering his way among the ages, pushing the stars aside to make a passage to god. And this god—that is the thing. When god is reached—will anybody believe it [?] It really doesn't matter. I believe it and Joseph believes it."

Like Herman Melville, who had created in *Moby-Dick*'s Captain Ahab a "grand, ungodly, god-like man" (Ahab's motto was "I baptize you in the name of the devil")—and afterward, as he told Nathaniel Hawthorne, felt spotless as a lamb—so too Steinbeck was in the precarious position of presenting a character his readers might find zealous, imperious, and unlikable, and whose life presented a tragical dichotomy between means and end. Writing to Ballou on the day he had shipped the final manuscript, Steinbeck said: "It will probably be a hard book to sell. Its characters are not 'home folks.' They make no more attempt at being sincerely human than the people in the Iliad. Boileau [Nicolas Boileau-Despreaux, in *The Art of the Poetic* (1674)] . . . insisted that only gods, kings and heroes were worth writing about. I firmly believe that. The detailed accounts of the lives of clerks don't interest me much, unless, of course, the clerk breaks into heroism."

Joseph is monomaniacal, but he is also brave, energetic, inventive, and prophetic. As an ungodly, godlike hero, he has the courage of his convictions, even though they happen to fly in the face of normative social and institutional values. It isn't stretching too much to say that, as a type of the artist (a "self-character," as Steinbeck would later call such creations), Joseph reflects the young Steinbeck's sense of passionate commitment toward his own way of doing things, and of the necessity of sacrifice to break through to deeper levels of ecstasy or being. Of course, where Joseph is locked in the prison of self, and desires to reach the other side of reality ("the naked thing," he calls it in Chapter 22) where words are "ridiculous," Steinbeck, pregnant with words, is constrained by the very limitations of the genre in which he is bound to work (it takes words to describe the naked, unutterable presence). At one level, Joseph's act of emptying himself of blood as a way of saving nature symbolizes Steinbeck's own call to the complex improbabilities of working in a medium that required him to empty himself of life, and which, when he was emptied, made him feel dead and "uninhabited." Joseph's dilemma was Steinbeck's: the very thing that promised to sustain them also threatened to consume them, to defeat their aspirations. But as the two states are linked, one cannot exist without the other. Each thing is an index of everything else, as Steinbeck became fond of saying.

Never a thoroughgoing inhumanist (as his attitude toward Spengler and Jeffers shows), Steinbeck was nonetheless uninterested in—and actually discouraged—a reductive humanistic interpretation of his book; rather, he was interested in the saga of creation and the process of interior passage for its own sake: "What the thing will be I don't care," he told Albee. "The unspeakable joy of merging into this world I am building is more than enough." Given what Louis Owens calls the book's "brilliantly sustained ambiguity," however, readers are free to perceive Joseph's salvation either as patently heroic (as a priest of nature, his sacrifice causes the rain) or as ironic (as a confused mystic, his death cannot possibly have caused the rain). To choose the first is to choose an exotic, romantic reading in which Joseph's redemption is earned and Christianity is ridiculed, and which makes Steinbeck's artistic purpose seem silly, reductive, or naïve. To choose the latter is to choose a serviceable, empirical reading in which Joseph's resolution is misguided and irrational and Father Angelo's point of view, secured by common sense, prevails; this in turn makes Steinbeck's book a cautionary tale about the dangers of total immersion. Most scholarly appraisals of this novel fall into one of these camps.

But privileging one interpretation over another violates Steinbeck's equally balanced tensions. In fact, *To a God Unknown* is his version of Keats's negative capability in action. Before irritably reaching after the facts and reasons that we imagine will explain one reading or another, we must first accept that, for Steinbeck at that moment of his creative life, this poetical novel announced a new way of being in the world, one that was comfortable juggling uncertainty, mystery, even doubt. "The cult of so called realism is a recent one, and anyone who doesn't conform is looked on with suspicion. On the moral side, our moral system came in about two hundred years ago and will be quite gone in 25 more," he proclaimed. What Steinbeck proposed in language had a consecration and validity all its own, so he did not feel obligated to resolve things for his audience in a traditionally moral or realistic manner. In mid-May 1933, while proofreading galley sheets Ballou had sent, he wrote in another notebook: "I read a few pages and found them fairly effective. The detached quality is there undoubtedly. Here and there I could see a word I would like to change were I better known and the fear of proof correction costs less fearful to me. But I was not cast down by the prose. It is ambitious. Perhaps in its thousands of lines there are one or two of pure poetry. The critics will scream at me but I do not care about that."

For the most part, contemporary reviews were mixed. The loudest scream appeared in *The New York Times* (October 1, 1933). Virginia Barney called it a "symbolical novel conceived in mysticism and dedicated to the soil," which "attempts too much" and "achieves too little," and hence "fails to cohere." A reviewer for *The Nation* (October 18, 1933) found it "reads like a novelized version of a Robinson Jeffers poem, and its setting is what may be known to tourists of the future as the 'Robinson Jeffers country.'" He judged the novel "pitifully thin and shadowy." A writer in the *Christian Century* (September 20, 1933) considered it a "modern appendix to *The Golden Bough.*" A critic in *Saturday Review of Literature* (October 28, 1933) said it "is full of . . . worship of the sun, the land, nature, the sexual act. And yet . . . it is almost without religious feeling." Nevertheless, it painted "a fairly interesting and (apparently) accurate picture of the region and the life of the times." Margaret Cheney Dawson, writing in *New York Herald Tribune Books* (September 24, 1933), called it a "strange and mightily obsessed book" that would appeal only to readers "who are capable of yielding themselves completely to the huge embrace of earth-mysticism." When Wilbur Needham reviewed the book positively in the *Los Angeles Times*, Steinbeck thanked him for not branding it mystical: "all the devils . . . and all the mysticism and all the religious symbology in the world are children of the generalized unconscious. Can it be that most . . . critics . . . are sublimely unconscious of the investigations and experiments in human psychology which are marshalling not only a new knowledge of man but a new conception of realities?

You may judge then my relief on finding that you did know what I was trying to do, understood the foundation and found it valid in literature." Harry Thornton Moore found Steinbeck's premise valid, too; when he reviewed *To a God Unknown* in *The London Mercury* (March 1935), he refrained from calling it mystical, and instead praised it as a "powerful, earthy story" with "some of the finest prose yet written in America."

Good, bad, or indifferent, reviews didn't help move the book. Publisher Ballou printed 1,498 copies, of which 598 were bound and sold (at two dollars each)—not enough copies sold to recoup the small advance he had paid Steinbeck. Within a year Ballou, whom Steinbeck would eventually consider a "fine" and "sensitive" man, but too gentlemanly to fight New York publishing battles, remaindered both *The Pastures of Heaven* and *To a God Unknown* and rejected Steinbeck's *Tortilla Flat* manuscript as unsuitable. For a while Steinbeck was back in a familiar situation: writing under stressful circumstances (both his parents were seriously ill) and trying not to worry about publication. Arguably, the time he and Carol spent caring first for his mother, then for his father, probably did as much as anything else to end Steinbeck's interest in heroic, larger-than-life literary characters. Frequent interruptions to clean his mother's bedpans and wash loads of soiled sheets, and later to witness his father's decline into senility, refocused Steinbeck's attention on common life, on the realm of "clerks" who, when they broke through reality at all, broke into a far more limited, even dubious, kind of heroism than Henry Morgan's or Joseph Wayne's. Steinbeck had already struck that chord in *Pastures*, but it would be with *In Dubious Battle* and with *Of Mice and Men* that a gritty style and an uncompromising vision of beleaguered humans caught in overwhelming circumstances would carry his "new conception of realities" to yet another stage of achievement.

In 1934, Steinbeck signed with Covici-Friede, a small, progressive New York firm, which would not only publish the rejected *Tortilla Flat* (it became a best-seller and won the Commonwealth Club's Gold Medal as the best California novel of 1935), but would also reissue both *The Pastures of Heaven* and *To a God Unknown* in 1935, followed by *In Dubious Battle* and *Of Mice and Men* over the next two years. (In mid-1938, when the firm went bankrupt, Pascal Covici was hired as a senior editor by the Viking Press, which became Steinbeck's publisher for the rest of his life.) In April 1934, by the time Steinbeck thanked Needham for his prescient review in the *Los Angeles Times*, he was at the threshold of becoming not only the accomplished writer he had started out to be seven years earlier, but a popular one as well. If the remainder of Steinbeck's career after *Tortilla Flat* can be seen as an anguished dance with fame, he had here arrived at a transitional moment when his sense of himself as a writer was still driven by the private pleasures of his art. "A couple of years ago," he confessed in August 1933, "I realized that I was not the material of which great artists are made and that I was rather glad I wasn't. And since then I have been happier simply to do the work and to take the reward at the end of every day that is given for a day of honest work." His candor still strikes a resonant chord. *To a God Unknown* is not considered a great novel, though it is a quirky, memorable one. But because John Steinbeck may have learned more about crafting long fiction from it than from anything else he worked on during that period, this book laid the foundation for later artistic greatness.

SUGGESTIONS FOR
FURTHER READING

Note: Webster Street's play "The Green Lady"; the Steinbeck/Street novel draft of the same name; Steinbeck's undergraduate transcript; Street's inscribed copy of *To a God Unknown*; and various unpublished letters from Steinbeck to Katherine Beswick, Amassa Miller, and Carl Wilhelmson are in the Department of Special Collections and University Archives, Cecil H. Green Library, Stanford University, Stanford, California. Consult Susan F. Riggs, ed., *A Catalogue of the John Steinbeck Collection at Stanford University* (Stanford, Calif.: Stanford University Libraries, 1980), and for a more current and comprehensive view, log on to http://library.stanford.edu/depts/spc/findaids_sub.html#steinbeckjohn. Steinbeck's letters to Robert O. Ballou are in the Harry Ransom Humanities Research Center, University of Texas at Austin. For access to HRC's Steinbeck collection, log on to http://www.hrc.utexas.edu/research/ta/steinbeck.html. Steinbeck's *Long Valley Notebook* (1933–1937) is at the Martha Heasley Cox Center for Steinbeck Studies (formerly Steinbeck Research Center), Dr. Martin Luther King Jr. Library, San Jose State University, San Jose, California. The Center's collection is accessible at http://www.steinbeck.sjsu.edu/home/index.jsp.

Arvind, S. A. "Man-Land Relationships in Steinbeck's Novels." In *John Steinbeck: A Centennial Tribute*. Edited by M. A. Syed. Jaipur: Surabhi Publications, 2004, pp. 11–26.

Astro, Richard. *John Steinbeck and Edward F. Ricketts: The Shaping of a Novelist*. Minneapolis: University of Minnesota Press, 1973.

Beegel, Susan, Susan Shillinglaw, and Wesley N. Tiffney, eds. *Steinbeck and the Environment: Interdisciplinary Approaches*. Tuscaloosa: University of Alabama Press, 1997.

Benson, Jackson J. *The True Adventures of John Steinbeck, Writer*. New York: Viking Press, 1984.

Campbell, Joseph. [Excerpted personal diary (1932)]. In Stephen and Robin Larsen, *A Fire in the Mind: The Life of Joseph Campbell*. New York: Doubleday, 1991, pp. 173–200.

———. *The Hero with a Thousand Faces*. New York: Bollingen Foundation, 1949.

DeMott, Robert. *Steinbeck's Reading*. New York: Garland Publishing, 1984.

———. " 'Writing My Country': Making *To a God Unknown*." In *Steinbeck's Typewriter: Essays on His Art*. Troy, N.Y.: Whitston Publishing, 1996, pp. 108–145.

Ditsky, John. *John Steinbeck and the Critics*. Rochester, N.Y.: Camden House, 2000.

Everson, William. *Archetype West: The Pacific Coast as Literary Region*. Berkeley, Calif.: Oyez, 1976.

Fontenrose, Joseph. *John Steinbeck: An Introduction and Interpretation*. New York: Holt, Rinehart and Winston, 1963.

French, Warren. *John Steinbeck's Fiction Revisited*. New York: Twayne, 1994.

Jeffers, Robinson. *The Collected Poetry of Robinson Jeffers*. Vol. 1, *1920–1928*. Vol. 2, *1928–1938*. Edited by Tim Hunt. Stanford, Calif.: Stanford University Press, 1988, 1989.

Levant, Howard. *The Novels of John Steinbeck: A Critical Study*. Columbia: University of Missouri Press, 1974.

Lisca, Peter. *John Steinbeck: Nature and Myth*. New York: Thomas Y. Crowell, 1978.

Li, Luchen. ed. *Dictionary of Literary Biography, Volume 309: John Steinbeck: A Documentary Volume*. Detroit: Thomson Gale, 2005.

McElrath, Joseph, Jesse S. Crisler, and Susan Shillinglaw, eds. *John Steinbeck: The Contemporary Reviews*. New York: Cambridge University Press, 1996.

Moore, Harry. *The Novels of John Steinbeck: A First Critical Study*. Chicago: Normandie House, 1939.

Owens, Louis. *John Steinbeck's Re-Vision of America*. Athens: University of Georgia Press, 1985.

———. "Ways Out of the Waste Land: Steinbeck and Modernism, or Lighting Out for the Twenty-First Century Ahead of the Rest." *Steinbeck Studies* 13 (Fall 2001): 12–17.

Parini, Jay. *John Steinbeck: A Biography*. New York: Henry Holt, 1995.

Powell, Lawrence Clark. *"To a God Unknown."* In *California Classics: The Creative Literature of the Golden State*. Los Angeles: Ward Ritchie Press, 1971, pp. 220–230.

Prindle, Dennis. "The Pretexts of Romance: Steinbeck's Allegorical Naturalism from *Cup of Gold* to *Tortilla Flat*." In *The Steinbeck Question: New Eaasys in Criticism*. Edited by Donald R. Noble. Troy, N.Y.: Whitston Publishing, 1993, pp. 23–36.

Railsback, Brian. *Parallel Expeditions: Charles Darwin and the Art of John Steinbeck*. Moscow: University of Idaho Press, 1995.

Rickets, Edward F. *The Outer Shores. Part 2. Breaking Through*. Edited by Joel W. Hedgpeth. Eureka, Calif.: Mad River Press, 1978.

Rodger, Katharine A., ed. *Rennaissance Man of Cannery Row: The Life and Letters of Edward F. Ricketts*. Tuscaloosa: University of Alabama Press, 2002.

Sheffield, Carlton A. *John Steinbeck: The Good Companion*. Edited by Terry White. Berkeley, Calif.: Creative Arts Book Company, 2002.

Simmonds, Roy S. *A Biographical and Critical Introduction of John Steinbeck*. Lewiston, N.Y.: Edwin Mellen Press, 2000.

Steinbeck, John. Preface. In Edith Mirrielees, *Story Writing*. New York: Viking Press, 1962, pp. vi–viii.

———. *Steinbeck: A Life in Letters*. Edited by Elaine Steinbeck and Robert Wallsten. New York: Viking Press, 1975.

———. *To a God Unknown* Journal (1932). In Nelson Valjean, *John Steinbeck: An Intimate Biography of His California Years*. San Francisco: Chronicle Books, 1975, 119–124.

———. *Your Only Weapon Is Your Work: A Letter by John Steinbeck to Dennis Murphy*. Edited by Robert DeMott. San Jose, Calif.: Steinbeck Research Center, 1985.

Street, Webster. "John Steinbeck: A Reminiscence." In *Steinbeck: The Man and His Work*. Edited by Richard Astro and Tetsumaro Hayashi. Corvallis: Oregon State University Press, 1971, pp. 35–41.

———. "Remembering John Steinbeck." Interview with Martha H. Cox. *San Jose Studies* 1 (November 1975): 108–127.

Tamm, Eric Enno. *Beyond the Outer Shores: The Untold Odyssey of Ed Ricketts, the Pioneering Ecologist Who Inspired John Steinbeck and Joseph Campbell*. New York: Four Walls Eight Windows, 2004.

Timmerman, John. *John Steinbeck's Fiction: The Aesthetics of the Road Taken*. Norman: University of Oklahoma Press, 1986.

Werlock, Abby. " 'Am I My Brother's Keeper?' Fathers, Brothers and Wives in Steinbeck's *To a God Unknown*." In *The Betrayal of Brotherhood in the Work of John Steinbeck: Cain Sign*. Edited by Michael Meyer. Lewiston, N.Y.: Edwin Mellen Press, 2000, pp. 111–145.

Williams, Terry Tempest. [Personal response on *To a God Unknown*.] In *John Steinbeck: Centennial Reflections by American Writers*. Edited by Susan Shillinglaw. San Jose, Calif.: San Jose State University Center for Steinbeck Studies, 2002, pp. 98–103.

Wyatt, David. "Steinbeck's Lost Gardens." In *The Fall into Eden: Landscape and Imagination in California*. New York: Cambridge University Press, 1986.

A NOTE ON THE TEXT

This Penguin Classics edition of *To a God Unknown* reproduces the original text of the novel from the 1935 edition published by Covici-Friede Publishers.

TO A GOD UNKNOWN

He is the giver of breath, and strength is his gift.
The high Gods revere his commandments.
His shadow is life, his shadow is death;
Who is He to whom we shall offer our sacrifice?

Through His might He became lord of the living
and glittering world
And he rules the world and the men and the beasts
Who is He to whom we shall offer our sacrifice?

From His strength the mountains take being, and
the sea, they say,
And the distant river;
And these are his body and his two arms.
Who is He to whom we shall offer our sacrifice?

He made the sky and the earth, and His will
fixed their places,
Yet they look to Him and tremble.
The risen sun shines forth over Him.
Who is He to whom we shall offer our sacrifice?

He looked over the waters which stored His power
and gendered the sacrifice.
He is God over Gods.
Who is He to whom we shall offer our sacrifice?

May He not hurt us, He who made earth,
Who made the sky and the shining sea?
Who is the God to whom we shall offer sacrifice?

Veda

1

When the crops were under cover on the Wayne farm near Pittsford in Vermont, when the winter wood was cut and the first light snow lay on the ground, Joseph Wayne went to the wing-back chair by the fireplace late one afternoon and stood before his father. These two men were alike. Each had a large nose and high, hard cheekbones; both faces seemed made of some material harder and more durable than flesh, a stony substance that did not easily change. Joseph's beard was black and silky, still thin enough so that the shadowy outline of his chin showed through. The old man's beard was long and white. He touched it here and there with exploring fingers, turned the ends neatly under out of harm's way. A moment passed before the old man realized that his son was beside him. He raised his eyes, old and knowing and placid eyes and very blue. Joseph's eyes were as blue, but they were fierce and curious with youth. Now that he had come before his father, Joseph hesitated to stand to his new heresy.

"There won't be enough in the land now, sir," he said humbly.

The old man gathered his shawl of shepherd's plaid about his thin straight shoulders. His voice was gentle, made for the ordering of simple justice. "What do you wish to complain of, Joseph?"

"You've heard that Benjy has gone courting, sir? Benjy will be married when the spring comes; and in the fall there will be a child, and in the next summer another child. The land doesn't stretch, sir. There won't be enough."

The old man dropped his eyes slowly and watched his fingers where they wrestled sluggishly on his lap. "Benjamin hasn't told me yet. Benjamin has never been very dependable. Are you sure he has gone seriously courting?"

"The Ramseys have told it in Pittsford, sir. Jenny Ramsey has a new dress and she's prettier than usual. I saw her today. She wouldn't look at me."

"Ah; maybe it's so, then. Benjamin should tell me."

"And so you see, sir, there won't be enough in the land for all of us."

John Wayne lifted his eyes again. "The land suffices, Joseph," he said placidly. "Burton and Thomas brought their wives home and the land sufficed. You are the next in age. You should have a wife, Joseph."

"There's a limit, sir. The land will feed only so many."

His father's eyes sharpened then. "Have you an anger for your brothers, Joseph? Is there some quarrel I haven't heard about?"

"No sir," Joseph protested. "The farm is too small and—" He bent his tall body down toward his father. "I have a hunger for land of my own, sir. I have been reading about the West and the good cheap land there."

John Wayne sighed and stroked his beard and turned the ends under. A brooding silence settled between the two men while Joseph stood before the patriarch, awaiting his decision.

"If you could wait a year," the old man said at last, "a year or two is nothing when you're thirty-five. If you could wait a year, not more than two surely, then I wouldn't mind. You're not the oldest, Joseph, but I've always thought of you as the one to have the blessing. Thomas and Burton are good men, good sons, but I've always intended the blessing for you, so you could take my place. I don't know why. There's something more strong in you than in your brothers, Joseph; more sure and inward."

"But they're homesteading the western land, sir. You have only to live a year on the land and build a house and plough a bit and the land is yours. No one can ever take it away."

"I know, I've heard of that; but suppose you should go now. I'll have only letters to tell me how you are, and what you're doing. In a year, not more than two, why I'll go with you. I'm an old man, Joseph. I'll go right along with you, over your head, in the air. I'll see the land you pick out and the kind of house you build. I'd be curious about that, you know. There might even be some way I could help you now and then. Suppose you lose a cow, maybe I could help you to find her; being up in the air like that I could see things far away. If only you wait a little while I can do that, Joseph."

"The land is being taken," Joseph said doggedly. "The century is three years gone. If I wait, the good land might all be taken. I've a hunger for the land, sir," and his eyes had grown feverish with the hunger.

John Wayne nodded and nodded, and pulled his shawl close about his shoulders. "I see," he mused, "It's not just a little restlessness. Maybe I can find you later." And then decisively: "Come to me, Joseph. Put your hand here—no, here. My father did it this way. A custom so old cannot be wrong. Now, leave your hand there!" He bowed his white head, "May the blessing of God and my blessing rest on this child. May he live in the light of the Face. May he love his life." He paused for a moment. "Now, Joseph, you may go to the West. You are finished here with me."

The winter came soon, with deep snow, and the air was frozen to needles. For a month Joseph wandered about the house, reluctant to leave his youth and all the strong material memories of his youth, but the blessing had cut him off. He was a stranger in the house and he felt that his brothers would be glad when he was gone. He went away before the spring had come, and the grass was green on the hills in California when he arrived.

2

After a time of wandering, Joseph came to the long valley called Nuestra Señora, and there he recorded his homestead. Nuestra Señora, the long valley of Our Lady in central California, was green and gold and yellow and blue when Joseph came into it. The level floor was deep in wild oats and canary mustard flowers. The river San Francisquito flowed noisily in its bouldered bed through a cave made by its little narrow forest. Two flanks of the coast range held the valley of Nuestra Señora close, on one side guarding it against the sea, and on the other against the blasting winds of the great Salinas Valley. At the far southern end a pass opened in the hills to let out the river, and near this pass lay the church and the little town of Our Lady. The huts of Indians clustered about the mud walls of the church, and although the church was often vacant now and its saints were worn and part of its tile roof lay in a shattered heap on the ground, and although the bells were broken, the Mexican Indians still lived near about and held their festivals, danced La Jota on the packed earth and slept in the sun.

When his homestead was recorded, Joseph set out for his new home. His eyes glittered with excitement under his broad-brimmed hat and he sniffed at the valley hungrily. He wore new jeans with a circle of brass buttons around the waist, a blue shirt, and a vest for the sake of the pockets. His high-heeled boots were new and his spurs shone like silver. An old Mexican was trudging painfully in to Our Lady. His face lighted up with pleasure when Joseph drew near. He removed his hat and stepped aside. "Is there a fiesta some place?" he asked politely.

Joseph laughed with delight. "I have a hundred and sixty acres of land up the valley. I'm going to live on it."

The old walker's eyes lighted on the rifle which, in its scabbard, lay snugly under Joseph's leg. "If you see a deer, señor, and if you kill that deer, remember old Juan."

Joseph rode on, but he called back over his shoulder, "When the house is built I'll make a fiesta. I'll remember you, then, Old Juan."

"My son-in-law plays the guitar, señor."

"Then he'll come too, Old Juan."

Joseph's horse walked quickly along, swishing with its hoofs through the brittle oak leaves; the iron shoes rang against protruding stones. The path went through the long forest that bordered the river. As he rode, Joseph became timid and yet eager, as a young man is who slips out to a rendezvous with a wise and beautiful woman. He was half-drugged and overwhelmed by the forest of Our Lady. There was a curious femaleness about the interlacing boughs and twigs, about the long green cavern cut by the river through the trees and the brilliant underbrush. The endless green halls and aisles and alcoves seemed to have meanings as obscure and promising as the symbols of an ancient religion. Joseph shivered and closed his eyes. "Perhaps I'm ill," he said. "When I open my eyes I may find that all this is delirium and fever." As he rode on and on the fear came upon him that this land might be the figure of a dream which would dissolve into a dry and dusty morning. A manzanita branch whipped his hat off and dropped it on the ground, and, when Joseph dismounted he stretched his arms and leaned down to pat the earth with his hand. There was a need in him to shake off the mood that had fallen upon him. He looked up to the treetops where the sun flashed on trembling leaves, where the wind sang huskily. When he mounted his horse again he knew that he could never lose the feeling for the land. The crying leather of his saddle, the jingle of his spur chains, the rasping of the horse's tongue over the bit-roller sang the high notes over the land's throbbing. Joseph felt that he had been dull and now suddenly was sensitized; had been asleep and was awakened. Far in the back of his mind lay the feeling that he was being treacherous. The past, his home and all the events of his childhood were being lost, and he knew he owed them the duty of memory. This land might possess all of him if he were not careful. To combat the land a little, he thought of his father, of the calm and peace, the strength and eternal rightness of his father, and then in his thought the difference ended and he knew that there was no quarrel, for his father and this new land were one. Joseph was frightened then. "He's dead," he whispered to himself. "My father must be dead."

The horse had left the river's forest now to follow a smooth rounded track that might have been made by a python's body. It was an ancient game trail made by the hoofs and pads of lonely fearful animals that had followed the track as though they loved even the ghosts of company. It was a trail of innumerable meanings. Here it swung wide to avoid a large oak with one thick overhanging limb where long ago a lion had crouched and made its kill and left its scent to turn the trail aside: here the track went carefully around a smooth rock whereon a rattlesnake habitually sunned its cold blood. The horse kept to the center of the trail and heeded all its warnings.

Now the path broke into a broad grassy meadow, in the center of which a colony of live oaks grew like a green island in a lake of lighter green. As Joseph rode toward the trees he heard an agonized squealing, and turning the grove's shoulder he came in sight of a huge boar with curved tusks and yellow eyes and a mane of shaggy red hair. The beast sat on its haunches and tearingly ate the hind quarters of a still-squealing little pig. In the distance a sow and five other little pigs bounded away, crying their terror. The boar stopped eating and set its shoulders when Joseph rode into its line of scent. It snorted and then returned to the dying pig, which still squealed piercingly. Joseph jerked up his horse. His face contracted with anger and his eyes paled until they were almost white. "Damn you," he cried. "Eat other creatures. Don't eat your own people." He pulled his rifle from its scabbard and aimed between the yellow eyes of the boar. And then the barrel lowered and a firm thumb let down the hammer. Joseph laughed shortly at himself. "I'm taking too great power into my hands," he said. "Why he's the father of fifty pigs and he may be the source of fifty more." The boar wheeled and snorted as Joseph rode on by.

Now the trail skirted a long side hill densely protected by underbrush—blackberry, manzanita and scrub oak so thickly tangled that even the rabbits had to make little tunnels through it. The trail forced its way up the long narrow ridge and came to a belt of trees, tan oak and live oak and white oak. Among the branches of the trees a tiny white fragment of mist appeared and delicately floated along just over the treetops. In a moment another translucent shred joined it, and another and another. They sailed along like a half-materialized ghost, growing larger and larger until suddenly they struck a column of warm air and rose into the sky to become little clouds. All over the valley the flimsy little clouds were forming and ascending like the spirits of the dead rising out of a sleeping city. They seemed to disappear against the sky, but the sun was losing its warmth because of them. Joseph's horse raised its head and sniffed the air. On top of the ridge stood a clump of giant madrone trees, and Joseph saw with wonder how nearly they resembled meat and muscles. They thrust up muscular limbs as red as flayed flesh and twisted like bodies on the rack. Joseph laid his hand on one of the branches as he rode by, and it was cold and sleek and hard. But the leaves at the ends of the horrible limbs were bright green and shiny. Pitiless and terrible trees, the madrones. They cried with pain when burned.

Joseph gained the ridge-top and looked down on the grass lands of his new homestead where the wild oats moved in silver waves under a little wind, where the patches of blue lupins lay like shadows in a clear lucent night, and the poppies on the side hills were broad rays of sun. He drew up to look at the long grassy meadows in which clumps of live oaks stood like perpetual senates ruling over the land. The river with its mask of trees cut a twisting path down through the valley. Two miles away he could see, beside a gigantic lonely oak, the white speck of his tent pitched and left while he went to record his homestead. A long time he sat there. As he looked into the valley, Joseph felt his body flushing with a hot fluid of love. "This is mine," he said simply, and his eyes sparkled with tears and his brain was filled with wonder that this should be his. There was pity in him for the grass and the flowers; he felt that the trees were his children and the land his child. For a moment he seemed to float high in the air and to look down upon it. "It's mine," he said again, "and I must take care of it."

The little clouds were massing in the sky; a legion of them scurried to the east to join the army already forming on the hill line. From over the western mountains the lean grey ocean clouds came racing in. The wind started up with a gasp and sighed through the branches of the trees. The horse stepped lightly down the path toward the river again, and often it raised its head and sniffed at the fresh sweet odor of the coming rain. The cavalry of clouds had passed and a huge black phalanx marched slowly in from the sea with a tramp of thunder. Joseph trembled with pleasure in the promised violence.

The river seemed to hurry along down its course, to chatter excitedly over the stones as it went. And then the rain started, fat lazy drops splashing on the leaves. Thunder rolled like caissons over the sky. The drops grew smaller and thicker, raked through the air and hissed in the trees. Joseph's clothing was soaked in a minute and his horse shone with water. In the river the trout were striking at tumbled insects and all the tree trunks glistened darkly.

The trail left the river again, and as Joseph neared his tent the clouds rolled backward from the west to the east like a curtain of grey wool and the late sun sparkled on the washed land, glittered on the grass blades and shot sparks into the drops that lay in the hearts of wildflowers. Before his tent Joseph dismounted and unsaddled the horse and rubbed its wet back and shoulders with a cloth before he turned the tired beast loose to graze. He stood in the damp grass in front of his tent. The setting sun played on his brown temples and the evening wind ruffled his beard. The hunger in his eyes became rapaciousness as he looked down the long green valley. His possessiveness became a passion. "It's mine," he chanted. "Down deep it's mine, right to the center of the world." He stamped his feet into the soft earth. Then the exultance grew to be a sharp pain of desire that ran through his body in a hot river. He flung himself face downward on the grass and pressed his cheek against the wet stems. His fingers gripped the wet grass and tore it out, and gripped again. His thighs beat heavily on the earth.

The fury left him and he was cold and bewildered and frightened at himself. He sat up and wiped the mud from his lips and beard. "What was it?" he asked himself. "What came over me then? Can I have a need that great?" He tried to remember exactly what had happened. For a moment the land had been his wife. "I'll need a wife," he said. "It will be too lonely here without a wife." He was tired. His body ached as though he had lifted a great rock, and the moment of passion had frightened him.

Over a little fire before his tent he cooked his meager supper, and when the night came he sat on the ground and looked at the cold white stars, and he felt a throbbing in his land. The fire died down to coals and Joseph heard the coyotes crying in the hills, and he heard the little owls go shrieking by, and all about him he heard the field mice scattering in the grass. After a while the honey-colored moon arose behind the eastern ridge. Before it was clear of the hills, the golden face looked through bars of pine-trunks. Then for a moment a black sharp pine tree pierced the moon and was withdrawn as the moon arose.

3

Long before the lumber wagons came in sight Joseph heard the sweet harsh clangour of their bells, the shrill little bells perched above the hames, that warned other teams to turn out of the narrow road. Joseph was washed clean; his hair and beard were combed and his eyes were eager with expectation, for he had seen no one in two weeks. At last the big teams came into view from among the trees. The horses walked with little humping steps to pull the heavy loads of planks over the rough new road. The leading driver waved his hat to Joseph and the sun flashed on his hat buckle. Joseph walked down to meet the teams and climbed to the high seat beside the first driver, a middle-aged man whose cropped coarse hair was white, whose face was brown and seamed like a tobacco leaf. The driver shifted the lines to his left hand and extended his right.

"I thought you'd be here earlier," Joseph said. "Did you have trouble on the way?"

"No trouble, Mr. Wayne, that you could call trouble. Juanito had a hot box and my own son Willie dropped his front wheel into a bog-hole. He was asleep, I guess. It isn't much of a road these last two miles."

"It will be," Joseph said, "when enough teams like these go over it, it'll be a good road." He pointed a finger. "Over by that big oak we'll drop this lumber."

To the face of the driver there came an expression of half-foreboding. "Going to build under a tree? That's not good. One of those limbs might crack off and take your roof with it, and smash you, too, some night while you're asleep."

"It's a good strong tree," Joseph assured him. "I wouldn't like to build my house very far from a tree. Is your house away from a tree?"

"Well no, that's why I'm telling you. The damn thing is right smack under one. I don't know how I happened to build it there. Many a night I've laid awake and listened to the wind and thought about a limb as big around as a barrel coming through the roof." He pulled up his team and wound the handful of lines around the brake. "Pull up even, here," he shouted to the other drivers.

When the lumber lay on the ground and the horses, haltered head-inward about the wagons, munched barley from their nose-bags, the drivers unrolled their blankets in the wagon-beds. Joseph had already built a fire and started the supper. He held his frying pan high above the flame and turned the bacon constantly. Romas, the old driver, walked up and sat beside the fire. "We'll get an early start in the morning," he said. "We'll make good time with empty wagons."

Joseph held his pan from the fire. "Why don't you let the horses have a little grass?"

"When they are working? Oh, no. There's no guts in grass. Got to have something stronger to pull over a road like yours. Put your pan down in the fire and let it lay a minute if you want to cook that bacon."

Joseph scowled. "You people don't know how to fry bacon. Slow heat and turning, that's what makes it crisp without losing it all in grease."

"It's all food," said Romas. "Everything's food."

Juanito and Willie walked up together. Juanito had a dark, Indian skin and blue eyes. Willie's face was twisted and white with some unknown illness under its crusting of dirt, and Willie's eyes were furtive and frightened, for no one believed in the pains which shook his body in the night and no one believed the dark dreams which tortured him when he slept. Joseph looked up and smiled at the two.

"You are seeing my eyes," Juanito said boldly. "I am not Indian. I am Castillian. My eyes are blue. See my skin. It is dark, and that is the sun, but Castillians have blue eyes."

"He tells everybody that," Romas broke in. "He likes to find a stranger to tell that to. Everybody in Nuestra Señora knows his mother was a squaw, and only God knows who his father was."

Juanito glared and touched his fingers to a long knife in his belt, but Romas only laughed and turned to Joseph. "Juanito tells himself, 'Some time I'll kill somebody with this knife.' That's the way he keeps feeling proud. But he knows he won't, and that keeps him from being too proud. Sharpen a stick to eat your bacon with, Juan-ito," he said contemptuously, "and next time you tell about being a Castillian, be sure nobody knows you."

Joseph set down his frying pan and looked questioningly at Romas. "Why do you tell on him?" he asked. "What good do you do by it? He does no harm being a Castillian."

"It's a lie, Mr. Wayne. One lie is like another. If you believe that lie, he'll tell another lie. In a week he'd be the cousin of the Queen of Spain. Juanito, here, is a teamster, a damn good one. I can't let him be a prince."

But Joseph shook his head and took up the frying pan again. Without looking up, he said, "I think he is a Castillian. His eyes are blue, and there's something else besides. I don't know how I know it, but I think he is."

Juanito's eyes grew hard and proud. "Thank you, señor," he said. "It is true, what you say." He drew himself up dramatically. "We understand each other, señor. We are caballeros."

Joseph put the bacon on tin plates and poured the coffee. He was smiling gently. "My father thinks he is almost a god. And he is."

"You don't know what you're doing," Romas protested. "I won't be able to stand this caballero. He won't work now. He'll walk around admiring himself."

Joseph blew wrinkles in his coffee. "When he gets too proud, I can use a Castillian here," he said.

"But God damn it, he's a good skinner."

"I know it," Joseph said quietly. "Gentlemen usually are. They don't have to be made to work."

Juanito got up hastily and walked off into the growing darkness, but Willie explained for him. "A horse has got its foot over a halter-rope."

The western range was still edged with the silver of the after-glow, but the valley of Our Lady was filled to the mountain-rims with darkness. The cast stars in the steel-grey fabric of the sky seemed to struggle and wink against the night. The four men sat about the coals of the fire, their faces strong with shadows. Joseph caressed his beard and his eyes were brooding and remote. Romas clasped his knees with both his arms. His cigarette gleamed red and then disappeared behind its ash. Juanito held his head straight and his neck stiff, but his eyes, behind crossed lashes, did not leave Joseph. Willie's pale face seemed to hang in the air unconnected to a body; the mouth contracted to a nervous grimace now and then. His nose was pinched and bony and his mouth came to a curved point like a parrot's beak.

When the firelight had died down so that only the faces of the men were visible, Willie put out his lean hand and Juanito took it and clasped the fingers strongly, for Juanito knew how frightened Willie was of the darkness. Joseph threw a twig into the fire and started a little blaze. "Romas," he said, "the grass is good here, the soil is rich and free. It needs only lifting with a plow. Why was it left, Romas? Why didn't anyone take it before this?"

Romas spat his cigarette stump at the fire. "I don't know. People are coming slowly to this country. It's off the main road. This would have been taken, I guess, but for the dry years. They set the country back a long time."

"Dry years? When were the dry years?"

"Oh, between eighty and ninety. Why, all the land dried up and the wells went dry and the cattle died." He chuckled. "It was dry enough, I tell you. Half the people who lived here then had to move away. Those who could, drove the cattle inland to the San Joaquin, where there was grass along the river. The cows died along the road, too. I was younger then, but I remember the dead cows with swelled-up guts. We shot at them and they went down like punctured balloons, and the stink would knock you down."

"But the rain came again," Joseph said quickly. "The ground is full of water now."

"Oh, yes, the rain came after ten years. Floods of it came. Then the grass came up again and the trees were green. We were glad then, I still remember it. The people down in Nuestra Señora had a fiesta in the rain, only a little roof over the guitar players to keep the strings dry. And the people were drunk and dancing in the mud. They got drunk on the water. Not only Mexicans, either. Father Angelo came upon them, and he made them stop."

"What for?" Joseph demanded.

"Well, you don't know what the people were doing there in the mud. Father Angelo was pretty mad. He said we'd let the devil in. He drove out the devil and made the people wash themselves and stop rolling in the wallows. He put penances on everybody. Father Angelo was pretty mad. He stayed right there until the rain stopped."

"The people were drunk, you say?"

"Yes, they were drunk for a week, and they did bad things—took off their clothes."

Juanito interrupted him. "They were happy. The wells were dry before, señor. The hills were white like ashes. It made the people happy when the rain came. They couldn't bear it to be so happy, and they did bad things. People always do bad things when they are too happy."

"I hope it never comes again," Joseph said.

"Well, Father Angelo said it was a judgment, but the Indians said it had been before, twice in the memory of old men."

Joseph stood up nervously. "I don't like to think about it. It won't come again, surely. Feel how tall the grass is already."

Romas was stretching his arms. "Maybe not. But don't depend on that. It's time to go to bed. We'll be starting at daylight."

The night was cold with the dawning when Joseph awakened. He seemed to have heard a shrill cry while he slept. "It must have been an owl," he thought. "Sometimes the sound is warped and magnified by a dream." But he listened tensely and heard a choked sobbing outside his tent. He slipped on his jeans and boots and crept out between the tent flaps. The soft crying came from one of the wagons. Juanito was leaning over the side of the wagon in which Willie slept.

"What's the matter?" Joseph demanded. In the faint light he saw that Juanito was holding Willie's arm.

"He dreams," Juanito explained softly. "Sometimes he cannot awaken unless I help him. And sometimes when he wakes up he thinks that is the dream and the other true. Come, Willie," Juanito said. "See, you are awake now. He dreams terrible things, señor, and then I pinch him. He is afraid, you see."

Romas spoke from the wagon where he lay, "Willie eats too much," he said. "He's just had a nightmare. He always did have them. Go back to bed, Mr. Wayne."

But Joseph bent down and saw the terror on Willie's face. "There's nothing in the night to hurt you, Willie," he said. "You can come and sleep in my tent if you want to."

"He dreams he is in a bright place that is dry and dead, and people come out of holes and pull off his arms and legs, señor. Nearly every night he dreams it. See, Willie, I will stay with you now. See, the horses are here all around you, looking at you, Willie. Sometimes, señor, the horses help him in the dream. He likes to sleep with them around him. He goes to the dry dead place, but he's safe from the people when the horses are near. Go to bed, señor, I will hold him for a while."

Joseph laid his hand on Willie's forehead and found that it was cold as stone. "I'll build up a fire and get him warm," he said.

"No use, señor; he is always cold. He cannot be warm."

"You are a good boy, Juanito."

Juanito turned away from him. "He calls to me, señor."

Joseph drew his hand under the warm flank of a horse, and walked back to his tent. The pine grove on the eastern ridge made a jagged line across the faint light of the morning. The grass stirred restively in the awakening breeze.

4

The frame of the house was standing, waiting for its skin, a square house crossed by inner walls to make four equal rooms. The great lone oak tree stretched a protecting arm over its roof. The venerable tree was tufted with new, shiny leaves, glittering and yellow-green in the morning sunshine. Joseph fried his bacon over the campfire, turning the slices endlessly. Then, before he ate his breakfast, he went to his new buckboard, in which a barrel of water stood. He ladled out a basinful, and filling his cupped hands, flung water on his hair and beard and wiped the beads of sleep from his eyes. He scraped the water off with his hands and went to his breakfast with his face all shining with moisture. The grass was damp with dew, sprinkled with fire. Three meadowlarks with yellow vests and light grey coats hopped near the tent stretching their beaks, friendly and curious. Now and then they puffed their chests and raised their heads like straining prima donnas and burst into a rising ecstasy of song, then cocked their heads at Joseph to see whether he noticed or approved. Joseph raised his tin cup and swallowed the last of his coffee and flung the grounds into the fire. He stood up and stretched his body in the strong sunlight before he walked to his house frame and threw back the canvas that covered his tools, and the three larks scurried behind him, stopping to sing despairingly for his attention. Two hobbled horses hopped in from their pasturage and raised their noses and snorted in a friendly manner. Joseph picked up a hammer and an apron full of nails, then turned with irritation on the larks.

"Go out and dig worms," he said. "Stop your noise. You'll make me want to dig worms, too. Get along now." The three larks raised their heads in mild surprise and then sang in unison. Joseph took his black slouch hat from the pile of lumber and pulled it down over his eyes. "Go and dig worms," he growled. The horses snorted again and one of them nickered shrilly. Instantly Joseph dropped his hammer in relief. "Hello! Who's coming?" He heard an answering nicker from the trees far down the road, and while he watched, a horseman issued into sight, his beast traveling at a tired trot. Joseph walked quickly to the dying fire and built it to a flame again and put the coffee pot back. He smiled happily. "I didn't want to work today," he told the larks. "Go and dig worms, I won't have time for you now." And then Juanito rode up. He stepped gracefully down, with two movements slipped off the saddle and bridle, and then took off his sombrero and stood smiling, expectant of his welcome.

"Juanito! I am glad to see you! You haven't had breakfast, have you? I'll fry you some breakfast."

And Juanito's expectant smile broke wide with gladness. "I have been riding all night, señor. I have come to be your vaquero."

Joseph extended his hand. "But I haven't a single cow for you to ride herd on, Juanito."

"You will have, señor. I can do anything, and I am a good vaquero."

"Can you help to build a house?"

"Surely, señor."

"And your pay, Juanito—how much pay do you get?"

Juanito's lids drew down solemnly over his bright eyes. "Before now, señor, I have been a vaquero, a good one. Those men paid me thirty dollars every month, and they said I was Indio. I wish to be your friend, señor, and have no pay."

Joseph was puzzled for a moment. "I think I see what you mean, Juanito, but you'll want money to have a drink when you go to town. You'll need money to see a girl now and then."

"You shall give me a present when I go to town, señor. A present is not pay." The smile was back again. Joseph poured out a cup of coffee for him.

"You're a good friend, Juanito. Thank you."

Juanito reached into the peak of his sombrero and drew out a letter. "Since I was coming, I brought you this, señor."

Joseph took the letter and walked slowly away. He knew what it was. He had been expecting it for some time. And the land seemed to know what it was, too, for a hush had fallen over the grass flats, the meadowlarks had gone away, and even the linnets in the oak tree had stopped their twittering. Joseph sat down on a lumber pile under the oak and slowly tore open the envelope. It was from Burton.

"Thomas and Benjy have asked me to write to you," it said. "The thing we knew must happen has happened. Death shocks us even when we know it must come. Father passed to the Kingdom three days ago. We were all with him at the last, all except you. You should have waited.

"His mind was not clear at the last. He said some very peculiar things. He did not talk about you so much as he talked to you. He said he could live as long as he wanted, but he wished to see your new land. He was obsessed with this new land. Of course his mind was not clear. He said, 'I don't know whether Joseph can pick good land. I don't know whether he's competent. I'll have to go out there and see.' Then he talked a great deal about floating over the country, and he thought he was doing it. At last he seemed to go to sleep. Benjy and Thomas went out of the room then. Father was delirious. I really should shut up his words and never tell them, for he was not himself. He talked about the mating of animals. He said the whole earth was a—no, I can't see any reason for saying it. I tried to get him to pray with me, but he was too nearly gone. It has troubled me that his last words were not Christian words. I haven't told the other boys because his last words were to you, as though he talked to you."

The letter continued with a detailed description of the funeral. It ended—"Thomas and Benjy think we could all move to the West if there's still land to be taken. We shall want to hear from you before we make any move."

Joseph dropped the letter on the ground and put his forehead down in his hands. His mind was inert and numb, but there was no sadness in him. He wondered why he was not sad. Burton would reproach him if he knew that a feeling of joy and of welcome was growing up in him. He heard the sounds come back to the land. The meadowlarks built little crystal towers of melody, a ground squirrel chattered shrilly, sitting upright in the doorway of his hole, the wind whispered a moment in the grass and then grew strong and steady, bringing the sharp odors of the grass and of the damp earth, and the great tree stirred to life under the wind. Joseph raised his head and looked at its old, wrinkled limbs. His eyes lighted with recognition and welcome, for his father's strong and simple being, which had dwelt in his youth like a cloud of peace, had entered the tree.

Joseph raised his hand in greeting. He said very softly, "I'm glad you've come, sir. I didn't know until now how lonely I've been for you." The tree stirred slightly. "It *is* good land, you see," Joseph

went on softly. "You'll like to be staying, sir." He shook his head
to clear out the last of the numbness, and he laughed at himself,
partly in shame for the good thoughts, and partly in wonder at his
sudden feeling of kinship with the tree. "I suppose being alone is
doing it. Juanito will stop that, and I'll have the boys come out to
live. I am talking to myself already." Suddenly he felt guilty of trea-
son. He stood up, walked to the old tree and kissed its bark. Then
he remembered that Juanito must be watching him, and he turned
defiantly to face the boy. But Juanito was staring steadily at the
ground. Joseph strode over to him. "You must have seen—" he
began angrily.

Juanito continued to stare downward. "I did not see, señor."

Joseph sat down beside him. "My father is dead, Juanito."

"I am sorry, my friend."

"But I want to talk about that, Juanito, because you are my friend.
For myself I am not sorry, because my father is here."

"The dead are always here, señor. They never go away."

"No," Joseph said earnestly. "It is more than that. My father is
in that tree. My father is that tree! It is silly, but I want to believe
it. Can you talk to me a little Juanito? You were born here. Since I
have come, since the first day, I have known that this land is full of
ghosts." He paused uncertainly. "No, that isn't right. Ghosts are
weak shadows of reality. What lives here is more real than we are.
We are like ghosts of its reality. What is it, Juanito? Has my brain
gone weak from being two months alone?"

"The dead, they never go away," Juanito repeated. Then he
looked straight ahead with a light of great tragedy in his eyes. "I lied
to you, señor. I am not Castillian. My mother was Indian and she
taught me things."

"What things?" Joseph demanded.

"Father Angelo would not like it. My mother said how the earth
is our mother, and how everything that lives has life from the mother
and goes back into the mother. When I remember, señor, and when
I know I believe these things, because I see them and hear them, then
I know I am not Castillian nor caballero. I am Indio."

"But I am not Indian, Juanito, and now I seem to see it."

Juanito looked up gratefully and then dropped his eyes, and the
two men stared at the ground. Joseph wondered why he did not try
to escape from the power that was seizing upon him.

After a time Joseph raised his eyes to the oak and to the house-frame beside it. "In the end it doesn't matter," he said abruptly. "What I feel or think can kill no ghosts nor gods. We must work, Juanito. There's the house to build over there, and here's the ranch to put cattle on. We'll go on working in spite of ghosts. Come," he said hurriedly, "we haven't time to think," and they went quickly to work on the house.

That night he wrote a letter to his brothers:

"There's land untaken next to mine. Each of you can have a hundred and sixty acres, and then we'll have six hundred and forty acres all in one piece. The grass is deep and rich, and the soil wants only turning. No rocks, Thomas, to make your plough turn somersaults, no ledges sticking out. We'll make a new community here if you'll come."

5

The grass was summer brown, ready for cutting, when the brothers came with their families and settled on the land. Thomas was the oldest, forty-two, a thick strong man with golden hair and a long yellow mustache. His cheeks were round and red and his eyes a cold wintry blue between slitted lids. Thomas had a strong kinship with all kinds of animals. Often he sat on the edge of a manger while the horses ate their hay. The low moaning of a cow in labor could draw Thomas out of bed at any hour of the night to see that the calving was true, and to help if there were trouble. When Thomas walked through the fields, horses and cows raised their heads from the grass and sniffed the air and moved in toward him. He pulled dogs' ears until they cried with the pain his strong slender fingers induced, and, when he stopped, they put their ears up to be pulled again. Thomas had always a collection of half-wild animals. Before he had been a month on the new land he had collected a racoon, two half-grown coyote pups that slunk at his heels and snarled at everyone else, a box of ferrets and a red-tailed hawk, besides four mongrel dogs. He was not kind to animals; at least no kinder than they were to each other, but he must have acted with a consistency beasts could understand, for all creatures trusted him. When one of the dogs foolishly attacked the coon and lost an eye in the encounter, Thomas was unruffled. He scraped out the torn eye-ball with his pocket knife and pinched the dog's feet to make it forget the torture in its head. Thomas liked animals and understood them, and he killed them with no more feeling than they had about killing each other. He was too much an animal himself to be sentimental. Thomas never lost a cow, for he seemed to know instinctively where a straying beef would stray. He rarely hunted, but when he did go out for game, he marched straight to the hiding place of his prey and killed it with the speed and precision of a lion.

Thomas understood animals, but humans he neither understood nor trusted very much. He had little to say to men; he was puzzled and frightened by such things as trade and parties, religious forms and politics. When it was necessary to be present at a gathering of people he effaced himself, said nothing and waited with anxiety for release. Joseph was the only person with whom Thomas felt any relationship; he could talk to Joseph without fear.

Thomas' wife was Rama, a strong, full-breasted woman with black brows that nearly met over her nose. She was nearly always contemptuous of everything men thought or did. She was a good and efficient midwife and an utter terror to evildoing children; although she never whipped her three little daughters, they went in fear of her displeasure, for she could find a soft spot in the soul and punish there. She understood Thomas, treated him as though he were an animal, kept him clean and fed and warm, and didn't often frighten him. Rama had ways of making her field: cooking, sewing, the bearing of children, housecleaning, seem the most important things in the world; much more important than the things men did. The children adored Rama when they had been good, for she knew how to stroke the tender places in the soul. Her praise could be as delicate and sharp as her punishment was terrible. She automatically took charge of all children who came near her. Burton's two children recognized her authority as far more legally constituted than the changeable rules their own soft mother made, for the laws of Rama never changed, bad was bad and bad was punished, and good was eternally, delightfully good. It was delicious to be good in Rama's house.

Burton was one whom nature had constituted for a religious life. He kept himself from evil and he found evil in nearly all close human contacts. Once, after a service to the church, he had been praised from the pulpit, "A strong man in the Lord," the pastor called him, and Thomas bent close to Joseph's ear and whispered, "A weak man in the stomach." Burton had embraced his wife four times. He had two children. Celibacy was a natural state for him. Burton was never well. His cheeks were drawn and lean, and his eyes hungry for a pleasure he did not expect this side of heaven. In a way it gratified him that his health was bad, for it proved that God thought of him enough to make him suffer. Burton had the powerful resistance of the chronically ill. His lean arms and legs were strong as braided ropes.

Burton ruled his wife with a firm and scriptural hand. He parceled out his thoughts to her and pared down her emotions when they got out of line. He knew when she exceeded the laws, and when, as happened now and then, some weak thing in Harriet cracked and left her sick and delirious, Burton prayed beside her bed until her mouth grew firm again and stopped its babbling.

Benjamin, the youngest of the four, was a charge upon his brothers. He was dissolute and undependable; given a chance, he drank himself into a romantic haze and walked about the country, singing gloriously. He looked so young, so helpless and so lost that many women pitied him, and for this reason Benjamin was nearly always in trouble with some woman or other. For when he was drunk and singing and the lost look was in his eyes, women wanted to hold him against their breasts and protect him from his blunders. It always surprised those who mothered Benjamin when he seduced them. They never knew quite how it happened, for his was a deadly helplessness. He accomplished things so badly that everyone tried to help him. His new young wife, Jennie, labored to keep Benjamin from hurt. And when she heard him singing in the night and knew that he was drunk again she prayed he might not fall and hurt himself. The singing drew off into the dark and Jennie knew that before the night was out, some perplexed and startled girl would lie with him. She cried a little for fear he might be hurt.

Benjy was a happy man, and he brought happiness and pain to everyone who knew him. He lied, stole a little, cheated, broke his word and imposed upon kindnesses; and everyone loved Benjy and excused and guarded him. When the families moved West they brought Benjy with them for fear he might starve if he were left behind. Thomas and Joseph saw that his homestead was in good order. He borrowed Joseph's tent and lived in it until his brothers found time to build him a house. Even Burton, who cursed Benjy, prayed with him and hated his way of living, couldn't let him live in a tent. Where he got whiskey his brothers could never tell, but he had it always. In the valley of Our Lady the Mexicans gave him liquor and taught him their songs, and Benjy took their wives when they were not watching him.

6

The families clustered about the house Joseph had built. They put up little shacks on their own land as the law required, but never for a minute did they think of the land as being divided into four. It was one ranch, and when the technicalities of the homesteading were satisfied, it was the Wayne ranch. Four square houses clustered near to the great oak, and the big barn belonged to the tribe.

Perhaps because he had received the blessing, Joseph was the unquestioned lord of the clan. On the old farm in Vermont his father had merged with the land until he became the living symbol of the unit, land and its inhabitants. That authority passed to Joseph. He spoke with the sanction of the grass, the soil, the beasts wild and domesticated; he was the father of the farm. As he watched the community of cabins spring up on the land, as he looked down into the cradle of the firstborn—Thomas' new child—as he notched the ears of the first young calves, he felt the joy that Abraham must have felt when the huge promise bore fruit, when his tribesmen and his goats began to increase. Joseph's passion for fertility grew strong. He watched the heavy ceaseless lust of his bulls and the patient, untiring fertility of his cows. He guided the great stallion to the mares, crying, "There, boy, drive in!" This place was not four homesteads, it was one, and he was the father. When he walked bareheaded through the fields, feeling the wind in his beard, his eyes smouldered with lust. All things about him, the soil, the cattle and the people were fertile, and Joseph was the source, the root of their fertility; his was the motivating lust. He willed that all things about him must grow, grow quickly, conceive and multiply. The hopeless sin was barrenness, a sin intolerable and unforgivable. Joseph's blue eyes were growing fierce with this new faith. He cut off barren creatures mercilessly, but when a bitch crept about swollen with puppies, when a cow was fat with calf, that creature was holy to him. Joseph did not think these things in his mind, but in his chest and in the corded muscles of his legs. It was the heritage of a race which for a million years had sucked at the breasts of the soil and cohabited with the earth.

One day Joseph stood by the pasture fence, watching a bull with a cow. He beat his hands against the fence rail; a red light burned in his eyes. As Burton approached him from behind, Joseph whipped off his hat and flung it down and tore open the collar of his shirt. He shouted, "Mount, you fool! She's ready. Mount now!"

"Are you crazy, Joseph?" Burton asked sternly.

Joseph swung around. "Crazy? What do you mean?"

"You're acting queerly, Joseph. Someone might see you here." Burton looked about to see if it was true.

"I want calves," Joseph said sullenly. "Where's the harm in that, even to you?"

"Well, Joseph—" Burton's tone was firm and kind as he implanted his lesson, "—everyone knows such things are natural. Everyone knows such things must happen if the race is to go on. But people don't watch it unless it's necessary. You might be seen acting this way."

Joseph reluctantly tore his eyes from the bull and faced his brother. "What if they did?" he demanded. "Is it a crime? I want calves."

Burton looked down in shame for the thing he had to say. "People might say things if they heard you talking as I just did."

"And what could they say?"

"Surely, Joseph, you don't want me to say it. The Scripture mentions such forbidden things. People might think your interest was— personal." He looked at his hands and then hid them quickly in his pockets as though to keep them from hearing what he said.

"Ah—" Joseph puzzled. "They might say—I see." His voice turned brutal. "They might say I felt like the bull. Well, I do, Burton. And if I could mount a cow and fertilize it, do you think I'd hesitate? Look, Burton, that bull can hit twenty cows a day. If feeling could put a cow with a calf, I could mount a hundred. That's how I feel, Burton." Then Joseph saw the grey, sick horror that had come over his brother's face. "You don't understand it, Burton," he said gently. "I want increase. I want the land to swarm with life. Everywhere I want things growing up." Burton turned sulkily away. "Listen to me, Burton, I think I need a wife. Everything on the land is reproducing. I am the only sterile thing. I need a wife."

Burton had started to move away, but he turned around and spat his words, "You need prayer more than anything. Come to me when you can pray."

Joseph watched his brother walk away and he shook his head in bewilderment. "I wonder what he knows that I don't know," he said to himself. "He has a secret in him that makes everything I think or do unclean. I have heard the telling of the secret and it means nothing to me." He ran his fingers through his long hair, picked up his soiled black hat and put it on. The bull came near the fence, lowered its head and snorted. Then Joseph smiled and whistled shrilly, and at the whistle, Juanito's head popped out of the barn. "Saddle a horse," Joseph cried. "There's more in this old boy. Drive in another cow."

He worked mightily, as the hills work to produce an oak tree, slowly and effortlessly and with no doubt that it is at once the punishment and the heritage of hills to strive thus. Before the morning light came over the range, Joseph's lantern flashed across the yard and disappeared into the barn. There among the warm and sleepy beasts he worked, mending harness, soaping the leather, cleaning the buckles. His curry comb rasped over muscled flanks. Sometimes he found Thomas there, sitting on a manger in the dark, with a coyote pup sleeping in the hay behind him. The brothers nodded good-morning. "Everything all right?" Joseph asked.

And Thomas—"Pigeon has cast a shoe and cracked his hoof. He shouldn't go out today. Granny, the black devil, kicked Hell out of her stall. She'll hurt somebody some day if she doesn't kill herself first. Blue dropped a colt this morning, that's what I came out to see."

"How did you know, Tom? What made you know it would come this morning?"

Thomas grabbed a horse's forelock and pulled himself down from the manger. "I don't know, I can always tell when a colt will drop. Come and see the little son-of-a-bitch. Blue won't mind now. She's got him clean by now."

They went to the box-stall and looked over at the spider-legged colt, with knobby knees and a whisk-broom for a tail. Joseph put out his hand and stroked the damp shining coat. "By God!" he cried, "I wonder why I love the little things so much?" The colt lifted its head and looked up sightlessly out of clouded, dark-blue eyes, and then moved away from Joseph's hand.

"You always want to touch them," Thomas complained. "They don't like to be touched when they're little like that."

Joseph withdrew his hand. "I guess I'd better go to breakfast."

"Oh, say," Thomas cried, "I saw some swallows fooling around. There'll be mud nests in the barn eaves, and under the windmill tank next spring."

The brothers had been working well together, all except Benjy, and Benjy shirked when he could. Under Joseph's orders a long truck garden stretched out behind the houses. A windmill stood on its high stilts and flashed its blades every afternoon when the wind came up. A long, unwalled cowshed arose beside the big stable. The barbed-wire fences were edging out to encircle the land. Wild hay grew rankly on the flats and on the side-hills and the stock was multiplying.

As Joseph turned to leave the barn, the sun came over the mountains and sent warm white streaks through the square windows. Joseph moved into a shaft of light and spread his arms for a moment. A red rooster on the top of a manure pile outside the window looked in at Joseph, then squawked and retreated, flapping, and raucously warned the hens that something terrible would probably happen on so fine a day. Joseph dropped his arms and turned back to Thomas. "Get up a couple of horses, Tom. Let's ride out today and see if there are any new calves. Tell Juanito, if you see him."

After their breakfast, the three men rode away from their houses. Joseph and Thomas went side by side and Juanito brought up the rear. Juanito had ridden home from Nuestra Señora in the dawn, after spending a discreet and polite evening in the kitchen of the Garcia home. Alice Garcia had sat across from him, placidly watching the crossed hands in her lap, and the elder Garcias, guardians and referees, were placed on either side of Juanito.

"You see, I am not only the majordomo for Señor Wayne," Juanito explained into their admiring but slightly skeptical ears, "I am more like a son to Don Joseph. Where he goes, I go. He trusts only me with very important matters." Thus for a couple of hours he boasted mildly, and when, as decorum suggested, Alice and her mother retired, Juanito made formal words and prescribed gestures and was finally accepted by Jesus Garcia, with a comely reluctance, as son-in-law. Then Juanito rode back to the ranch, quite tired and very proud, for the Garcias could prove at least one true Spanish ancestor. And now he rode behind Joseph and Thomas, rehearsing to himself the manner of his announcement.

The sun blazed on the land as they rode up a grassy swell looking for calves to notch and cut. The dry grass made a whisking noise under the horses' hoofs. Thomas' horse skittered nervously, for in front of Thomas, perched on the saddle-horn, rode a villainous racoon, with beady, evil eyes looking out of a black mask. It kept its balance by grasping the horse's mane with one little black hand. Thomas looked ahead with eyes drooped against the sun. "You know," he said, "I was in Nuestra Señora Saturday."

"Yes," Joseph said impatiently, "Benjy must have been there too. I heard him singing late at night. Tom, that boy'll be getting into trouble. Some things the people here will not stand. Some day we'll be finding Benjy with a knife in his neck. I tell you, Tom, he'll get a knife some day."

Thomas chuckled. "Let him, Joe. He'll have had more fun than a dozen sober men, and he'll have lived longer than Methuselah."

"Well, Burton worries about it all the time. He's spoken to me about it over and over."

"I was telling you," said Thomas, "I sat in the store in Nuestra Señora Saturday afternoon, and the riders from Chinita were there. They got to talking about the dry years from eighty to ninety. Did you know about them?"

Joseph tied a new knot in the riata string on his saddle. "Yes," he said softly, "I've heard about them. Something was wrong. They won't ever come again."

"Well, the riders were talking about it. They said the whole country dried up and the cattle died and the land turned to powder. They said they tried to move the cows to the interior but most of them died on the way. The rain came a few years before you got here." He pulled the coon's ears until the fierce little creature slashed at his hand with its sharp teeth.

Joseph's eyes were troubled. He brushed his beard down with his hand and turned the ends under, as his father had done. "I heard about it, Tom. But it's all over now. Something was wrong, I tell you. It won't come again, ever. The hills are full of water."

"How do you know it won't come again? The riders said it had been before. How can you say it won't ever come again?"

Joseph set his mouth determinedly. "It can't come. The hill springs are all running. I won't—I can't see how it can come again."

Juanito urged his horse abreast of them. "Don Joseph, I hear a cowbell over the rise."

The three men swung their horses to the right and put them to a canter. The coon leaped to Thomas' shoulder and clung to his neck with its strong little arms. Over the rise they galloped. They came upon a little herd of red cows, and two young calves tottered among the cows. In a moment the calves were down. Juanito took a bottle of liniment from his pocket, and Thomas opened his broad-bladed knife. The shining knife snicked out the Wayne brand in the ears of both calves while they bawled hopelessly and their mothers stood by, bellowing with apprehension. Then Thomas knelt beside the bull calf. With two cuts he performed the castration and sloshed liniment on the wound. The cows snorted with fear when they smelled blood. Juanito untied the feet and the new steer scrambled up and hobbled lamely off to its mother. The men mounted and rode on.

Joseph had picked up the pieces of ear. He looked at the little brown fragments for a moment and then thrust them into his pocket.

Thomas watched the act. "Joseph," he said suddenly, "Why do you hang the hawks you kill in the oak tree beside your house?"

"To warn off other hawks from the chickens, of course. Everybody does that."

"But you know God-damned well it doesn't work, Joe. No hawk in the world will let the chance of a pullet go by just because his dead cousin is hanging up by the foot. Why, he'll eat his cousin if he can." He paused for a moment and then continued quietly, "You nail the ear notchings to the tree, too, Joseph."

His brother turned angrily in his saddle. "I nail up the notchings so I'll know how many calves there are."

Thomas looked puzzled. He lifted the coon to his shoulder again, where it sat and carefully licked the inside of his ear. "I almost know what you're doing, Joe. Sometimes it almost comes to me what you're getting at. Is it about the dry years, Joseph? Are you working already against them?"

"If it isn't for the reason I told you, it's none of your damn business, is it?" Joseph said doggedly. His eyes were worried and his voice grew soft with perplexity. "Besides, I don't understand it myself. If I tell you about it, you won't tell Burton, will you? Burton worries about all of us."

Thomas laughed. "Nobody tells Burton anything. He has always known everything."

"Well," Joseph said, "I'll tell you about it. Our father gave me a blessing before I came out here, an old blessing, the kind it tells about in the Bible, I think. But in spite of that I don't think Burton would have liked it. I've always had a curious feeling about father. He was so completely calm. He wasn't much like other fathers, but he was a kind of a last resort, a thing you could tie to, that would never change. Did you feel like that?"

Thomas nodded slowly, "Yes, I know."

"Well, then I came out here and I still felt safe. Then I got a letter from Burton and for a second I was thrown out of the world, falling, with nothing to land on, ever. Then I read on, where father said he was coming out to see me after he was dead. The house wasn't built then, I was sitting on a lumber pile. I looked up—and I saw that tree—" Joseph fell silent and stared down at his horse's mane. After a moment he looked over at his brother, but Thomas avoided his eyes. "Well, that's all. Maybe you can figure it out. I just do the things I do, I don't know why except that it makes me happy to do them. After all," he said lamely, "a man has to have something to tie to, something he can trust to be there in the morning."

Thomas caressed the coon with more gentleness than he usually bestowed on his animals, but still he did not look at Joseph. He said, "You remember once when I was a kid I broke my arm. I had it in a splint doubled up on my chest, and it hurt like Hell. Father came up to me and opened my hand, and he kissed the palm. That was all he did. It wasn't the kind of thing you'd expect of father, but it was all right because it was more like medicine than a kiss. I felt it run up my broken arm like cool water. It's funny how I remember that so well."

Far ahead of them a cowbell clanged. Juanito trotted up. "In the pines, señor. I don't know why they'd be in the pines where there's no feed."

They turned their horses up the ridge, which was crowned with the dark pines. The first trees stood deployed like outposts. Their trunks were as straight as masts, and the bark was purple in the shade. The ground under them, deep and spongy with brown needles, supported no grass. The grove was quiet except for a little whispering of the wind. Birds took no pleasure in the pines, and the brown carpet muffled the sound of walking creatures. The horsemen rode in among the trees, out of the yellow sunlight and into the purple gloom of the shade. As they went, the trees grew closer together, leaned for support and joined their tops to make one complete unbroken ceiling of needles. Among the trunks the undergrowth sprang up, brambles and blackberries, and the pale, light-hungry leaves of Guatras. The tangle grew thicker at every step until at last the horses stopped and refused to force their way farther into the thorn-armed barrier.

Then Juanito turned his horse sharply to the left. "This way, señores. I remember a path this way."

He led them to an old track, deep buried in needles but free of growth and wide enough for two to ride together. For a hundred yards they followed the path, and then suddenly Joseph and Thomas drew up and stared at the thing in front of them.

They had come to an open glade, nearly circular, and as flat as a pool. The dark trees grew about it, straight as pillars and jealously close together. In the center of the clearing stood a rock as big as a house, mysterious and huge. It seemed to be shaped, cunningly and wisely, and yet there was no shape in the memory to match it. A short, heavy green moss covered the rock with soft pile. The edifice was something like an altar that had melted and run down over itself. In one side of the rock there was a small black cave fringed with five-fingered ferns, and from the cave a little stream flowed silently and crossed the glade and disappeared into the tangled brush that edged the clearing. Beside the stream a great black bull was lying, his front legs folded under him; a hornless bull with shining black ringlets on his forehead. When the three men entered the glade the bull had been chewing his cud and staring at the green rock. He turned his head and looked at the men with red-rimmed eyes. He snorted, scrambled to his feet, lowered his head at them, and then, turning, plunged into the undergrowth and broke a passage free. The men saw the lashing tail for a moment, and the long, black swinging scrotum, which hung nearly to the knees; and then he disappeared and they heard him crashing in the brush.

It had all happened in a moment.

Thomas cried, "That's not our bull. I never saw it before." And then he looked uneasily at Joseph. "I never saw this place before. I don't think I like it, I can't tell." His voice was babbling. He held the coon tightly under his arm while it struggled and bit and tried to escape.

Joseph's eyes were wide, looking at the glade as a whole. He saw no single thing in it. His chin was thrust out. He filled his chest to a painful tightness and strained the muscles of his arms and shoulders. He had dropped the bridle and crossed his hands on the saddle-horn.

"Be still a moment, Tom," he said languidly. "There's something here. You are afraid of it, but I know it. Somewhere, perhaps in an old dream, I have seen this place, or perhaps felt the feeling of this place." He dropped his hands to his sides and whispered, trying the words, "This is holy—and this is old. This is ancient—and holy." The glade was silent. A buzzard swept across the circular sky, low over the treetops.

Joseph turned slowly. "Juanito, you knew this place. You have been here."

The light blue eyes of Juanito were wet with tears. "My mother brought me here, señor. My mother was Indian. I was a little boy, and my mother was going to have a baby. She came here and sat beside the rock. For a long time she sat, and then we went away again. She was Indian, señor. Sometimes I think the old ones come here still."

"The old ones?" Joseph asked quickly, "what old ones?"

"The old Indians, señor. I am sorry I brought you here. But when I was so close the Indian in me made me come, señor."

Thomas cried nervously, "Let's get the Hell out of here! We've got to find the cows." And Joseph obediently turned his horse. But as they rode out of the silent glade and down the path he spoke soothingly to his brother.

"Don't be afraid, Tom. There's something strong and sweet and good in there. There's something like food in there, and like cool water. We'll forget it now, Tom. Only maybe sometime when we have need, we'll go back again—and be fed."

And the three men fell silent and listened for the cowbells.

7

In Monterey there lived and worked a harness-maker and saddler named McGreggor, a furious philosopher, a Marxian for the sake of argument. Age had not softened his ferocious opinions, and he had left the gentle Utopia of Marx far behind. McGreggor had long deep wrinkles on his cheeks from constantly setting his jaw and pinching his mouth against the world. His eyes drooped with sullenness. He sued his neighbors for an infringement of his rights, and he was constantly discovering how inadequate was the law's cognizance of his rights. He tried to browbeat his daughter Elizabeth and failed as miserably as he had with her mother, for Elizabeth set her mouth and held her opinions out of reach of his arguments by never stating them. It infuriated the old man to think that he could not blast her prejudices with his own because he did not know what they were.

Elizabeth was a pretty girl, and very determined. Her hair was fluffy, her nose small and her chin firm from setting it against her father. It was in her eyes that her beauty lay, grey eyes set extremely far apart and lashed so thickly that they seemed to guard remote and preternatural knowledge. She was a tall girl; not thin, but lean with strength and taut with quick and nervous energy. Her father pointed out her faults, or rather faults he thought she had.

"You're like your mother," he said. "Your mind is closed. You have no single shred of reason. Everything you do is the way you feel about it. Take your mother, now, a highland woman and straight from home—her own father and mother believed in fairies, and when I put it up to her like a joke, she'd shoot her jaw and shut up her mouth like a window. And she'd say, 'There's things that won't stand reason, but are so, just the same.' I'll take a wager your mother filled you with fairies before she died."

And he modeled her future for her. "There's a time coming," he said prophetically, "when women will earn their own bread. There's no reason why a woman can't learn a trade. Take you, for instance," he said. "There's a time coming, and not far off, either, when a girl like you will be making her wage and be damned to the first man that wants to marry her."

McGreggor was shocked, nevertheless, when Elizabeth began studying for county examinations so she could be a teacher. McGreggor almost went soft. "You're too young, Elizabeth," he argued. "You're only seventeen. Give your bones a chance to get hard, at least." But Elizabeth smiled slightly in triumph and said nothing. In a house where the littlest statement automatically marshalled crushing forces of argument against itself, she had learned to be silent.

The profession of school teaching was something more than child-instructing to a girl of spirit. When she turned seventeen she could take county examinations and go adventuring; it was a decent means of leaving her home, and her town where people knew her too well; a means of preserving the alert and shatterable dignity of a young girl. To the community where she was sent she was unknown and mysterious and desirable. She knew fractions and poetry; she could read a little French and throw a word of it into conversation. Sometimes she wore underclothes of lawn or even silk, as could be seen when her laundry was on the line. These things which might have been considered uppish in an ordinary person were admired and expected in the school teacher, for she was a person of social as well as educational importance, and she gave an intellectual and cultural tone to her district. The people among whom she went to live did not know her baby name. She assumed the title "Miss". The mantle of mystery and learning enveloped her, and she was seventeen. If, within six months, she did not marry the most eligible bachelor in the district, she must be ugly as a gorgon, for a school teacher could bring social elevation to a man. Her children were thought to be more intelligent than ordinary children. School teaching could be, if the teacher wished to make it so, a subtle and certain move toward matrimony.

Elizabeth McGreggor was even more widely educated than most teachers. In addition to fractions and French she had read excerpts from Plato and Lucretius, knew several titles of Aeschylus, Aristophanes and Euripides, and had a classical background resting on Homer and Virgil. After she had passed the examinations she was assigned to the school at Nuestra Señora. The isolation of the place pleased Elizabeth. She wanted to think over all the things she knew, to arrange them in their places, and from their eventual arrangement to construct the new Elizabeth McGreggor. In the village of Our Lady she went to board with the Gonzales family.

Word flew through the valley that the new teacher was young and very pretty, and thereafter, when Elizabeth went out, when she walked to school or hurried to the grocery, she met young men who, though idle, were intensely preoccupied with their watches, with the rolling of a cigarette or with some vague but vital spot in the distance. But occasionally there was one strange man among the loiterers who was preoccupied with Elizabeth; a tall man, black-bearded and with sharp blue eyes. This man bothered Elizabeth, for he stared at her when she passed, and his eyes pierced through her clothing.

When Joseph heard about the new teacher he drew in upon her in lessening circles until at last he sat in the Gonzales parlor, a carpeted, respectable place, and he stared across at Elizabeth. It was a formal call. Elizabeth's soft hair was puffed on her head, but she was the teacher. Her face wore a formal expression, almost stern. Except that she smoothed down her skirt over her knees again and again, she might have been composed. At intervals she looked up into the searching eyes of Joseph and then looked away again.

Joseph wore a black suit and new boots. His hair and beard were trimmed, and his nails were as clean as he could get them.

"Do you like poetry?" Elizabeth asked, looking for a moment into the sharp, unmoving eyes.

"Oh, yes—yes, I like it; what I have read of it."

"Of course, Mr. Wayne, there are no modern poets like the Greeks, like Homer."

Joseph's face became impatient. "I remember," he said, "of course I remember. A man went to an island and got changed into a pig."

Elizabeth's mouth pinched at the corners. In an instant she was the teacher, remote and above the pupil. "That is the Odyssey," she said. "Homer is thought to have lived about nine hundred, B.C. He had a profound effect on all Greek literature."

"Miss McGreggor," Joseph said earnestly, "there's a way to do this thing, but I don't know it. Some people seem to know by instinct, but I don't. Before I came I tried to think what I'd say to you, but I couldn't discover a way, because I've never done anything like this before. There's a time of fencing to go through and I don't know how to do it. Besides it all seems useless to me."

Elizabeth was caught by his eyes now, and she was startled by his intensity of speech. "I don't know what you're talking about, Mr. Wayne." She had been flung from her seat of learning, and the fall frightened her.

"I know I'm doing it all wrong," he said. "I don't know any other way. You see, Miss McGreggor, I'm afraid I might get confused and embarrassed. I want you to be my wife, and you must know it. My brothers and I own six hundred and forty acres of land. Our blood is clean. I think I should be good to you if I could know what you want."

He had dropped his eyes while he talked. Now he looked up and saw that she was flushing and looking very miserable. Joseph jumped to his feet. "I suppose I've done it wrong. Now I'm confused, but I got it out first. And now I'll go, Miss McGreggor. I'll come back after we've stopped being embarrassed." He hurried out without saying good-bye, leaped on his horse and galloped away into the night.

There was a burn of shame and of exultance in his throat. When he came to the wooded river bottom he pulled up his horse, rose in his stirrups and shouted to ease the burn, and the echo blatted back at him. The night was very black and a high mist dulled the sharpness of the stars and muffled the night noises. His cry had blasted a thick silence and frightened him. For a moment he sat dumbly in his saddle and felt the swell and fall of his panting horse.

"This night is too still," he said, "too unimpressed. I must do something." He felt that the time required a sign, an act to give it point. Somehow an act of his must identify him with the moment that was passing or it would slip away, taking no part of him with it. He whipped off his hat and flung it away into the dark. But this was not enough. He felt for his quirt where it hung from the saddle-horn, and plucking it off, lashed his own leg viciously to make a moment of pain. The horse plunged aside, away from the whistle of the blow, and then reared. Joseph threw his quirt away into the brush, controlled the horse with a powerful pressure of his knees, and when it was quieted, trotted the nervous animal toward the ranch. Joseph opened his mouth to let the cool air into his throat.

Elizabeth watched the door close behind him. "There is too big a crack under that door," she thought. "When the wind blows, a draft will come in under the door. I wonder if I should move to another house." She spread her skirt tightly down, and then drew her finger up the center so that the cloth adhered to her legs and defined their shape. She inspected her fingers carefully.

"Now I am ready," she went on. "Now I am all ready to punish him. He is a bumpkin, a blundering fool. He has no manners. He doesn't know how to do things politely. He wouldn't know manners if he saw them. I don't like his beard. He stares too much. And his suit is pitiful." She thought over the punishment and nodded her head slowly. "He said he didn't know how to fence. And he wants to marry me. I'd have to bear those eyes all my life. His beard is probably coarse, but I don't think so. No, I don't think so. What a fine thing to go straight to a point. And his suit—and he would put his hand on my side." Her mind bolted away. "I wonder what I will do." The person who must act in the future was a stranger whose reactions Elizabeth did not quite understand. She walked up the stairs to her bedroom and slowly took off her clothes. "I must look at his palm next time. That will tell." She nodded gravely, and then threw herself face-downward on the bed and cried. Her crying was as satisfying and as luxurious as a morning's yawn. After a while she got up and blew out her lamp and dragged a little velvet-seated rocking chair to the window. Resting her elbows on the window-sill, she looked out into the night. There was a heavy misty dampness in the air now; a lighted window down the rutted street was fringed with light.

Elizabeth heard a stealthy movement in the yard below and leaned out to look. There was a pounce, a hissing, rasping cry, and then the crunch of bone. Her eyes pierced the grey darkness and made out a long, low, shadowy cat creeping away with some little creature in its mouth. A nervous bat circled her head, gritting as it looked about. "Now I wonder where he is," she thought. "He'll be riding now, and his beard will be blowing. When he gets home he'll be very tired. And I'm here, resting, doing nothing. It serves him right." She heard a concertina playing, coming nearer, from the other end of the village, where the saloon was. As it drew close, a voice joined, a voice as sweet and hopeless as a tired sigh.

"*Maxwellton's braes are bonnie—*"

Two lurching figures were passing by. "Stop! You're not playing

the right tune. Keep your damn Mexican tunes out of this. Now—
Maxwellton's braes are bonnie—wrong again!" The men paused. "I
wish I could play the blasted squeeze-organ."

"You can try, señor."

"Try, Hell. I have tried. It only belches when I try." He paused.
"Shall we try again, señor, this Maxwellton?" One of the men
moved close to the fence. Elizabeth could see him looking up at her
window.

"Come down," he pleaded. "Please come down." Elizabeth sat
very still, afraid to move. "I'll send the cholo along home."

"Señor, no 'cholos' to me!"

"I'll send the gentleman along home if you'll come down. I am
lonely."

"No," she said, and her voice startled her.

"I'll sing to you if you'll come down. Listen how I can sing. Play,
Pancho, play *Sobre las Olas*." His voice filled the air like vaporized
gold, and his voice was filled with delicious sorrow. The song finished so softly that she leaned forward to hear. "Now will you come
down? I'm waiting for you."

She shuddered violently and reaching up, pulled the window
down, but even through the glass she could hear the voice. "She
won't, Pancho. How about the next house?"

"Old people, señor; eighty, nearly."

"And the next house?"

"Well, maybe—a little girl, thirteen."

"We'll try the little girl thirteen, then. Now—*Maxwellton's braes
are bonnie*—"

Elizabeth had pulled the covers over her head, and she was shivering with fright. "I would have gone," she said miserably. "I'm
afraid I would have gone if he had asked again."

8

Joseph allowed two weeks to pass before he went again to call on Elizabeth. The fall was coming hazily, greying the sky with high mist. Huge puffy cotton clouds sailed in from the ocean every day and sat on the hilltops for a while, and then retired to the sea again like reconnoitering navies of the sky. The red-wing blackbirds massed their squadrons and practiced at maneuvering over the fields. The doves, unseen in the spring and summer, came from their hiding and sat in clusters on fences and dead trees. The sun, in its rising and setting, was red behind the autumn veil of air-borne dust.

Burton had taken his wife and gone to a camp meeting in Pacific Grove. Thomas said, wryly, "He's eating God the way a bear eats meat against the winter."

Thomas was sad with the coming winter. He seemed to fear the wet and windy time when he could find no cave to crawl into.

The children on the ranch began to consider Christmas as not too far buried in the future for anticipation. They addressed guarded questions to Rama concerning the kind of conduct most admired by the saints of the solstice, and Rama made the most of their apprehension.

Benjy was lazily ill. His young wife tried to understand why no one paid much attention.

There was little to be done on the ranch. The tall dry grass on the foothills was thick enough to feed the stock all winter. The barns were full of hay for the horses. Joseph spent a great deal of time sitting under the oak tree thinking of Elizabeth. He could remember how she sat, with her feet close together and her head held high, as though it was only restrained from flying upward by being attached to her body. Juanito came and sat beside him and looked secretly at Joseph's face to read his temper and to imitate it.

"I might be having a wife before the spring, Juanito," Joseph said. "Right in my house here, living here. She'd ring a little bell when it came dinnertime—not a cowbell. I would buy a little silver bell. I guess you'd like to hear a little bell like that, Juanito, ringing at dinnertime."

And Juanito, flattered at the confidence, uncovered his own secret. "I, too, señor."

"A wife, Juanito? You, too?"

"Yes, señor, Alice Garcia. They have a paper to prove their grandfather was Castillian."

"Why I'm glad of that, Juanito. We'll help you to build a house here, and then you won't be a rider any more. You'll live here."

Juanito giggled with happiness. "I'll have a bell, señor, hanging beside the porch; but a cowbell, me. It wouldn't be good to hear your bell and come for my dinner."

Joseph tilted back his head and smiled up at the twisted branches of the tree. Several times he had thought of whispering about Elizabeth, but a shame at doing a thing so silly had forbidden it. "I'm going to drive to town day after tomorrow, Juanito. I guess you'll want to go with me."

"Oh yes, señor. I'll sit in the buckboard and you can say, 'He is my driver. He is good with horses. Of course I never drive myself.' "

Joseph laughed at the rider. "I guess you'd like me to do the same for you."

"Oh no, señor, not I."

"We'll go in early, Juanito. You should have a new suit for a time like this."

Juanito stared at him incredulously. "A suit, señor? Not overalls? A suit with a coat?"

"Why, a coat and a vest, and for a wedding present a watch-chain for the vest."

It was too much. "Señor," Juanito said, "I have a broken cincha to fix," and he walked away toward the barn, for it would be necessary to think a good deal about a suit and a watch-chain. His manner of wearing such a costume would require consideration and some practice.

Joseph leaned back against the tree, and the smile slowly left his eyes. He looked again into the branches. A colony of hornets had made a button on a limb above his head and around this nucleus they were beginning to construct their papery nest. To Joseph's mind there leaped the memory of the round glade among the pines. He remembered every detail of the place, the curious moss-covered rock, the dark cave with its fringe of ferns and the silent clear water flowing out and hurrying stealthily away. He saw how the cress grew in the water and how it moved its leaves in the current. Suddenly Joseph wanted to go to that place, to sit by the rock and to stroke the soft moss.

"It would be a place to run to, away from pain or sorrow or disappointment or fear," he thought. "But I have no such need now. I have none of these things to run from. I must remember this place, though. If ever there's need to lose some plaguing thing, that will be the place to go." And he remembered how the tall trunks grew up and how peacefulness was almost a touchable thing in the glade. "I must look inside the cave some time to see where the spring is," he thought.

Juanito spent the whole next day working on the harness, the two bay driving-horses and the buckboard. He washed and polished, curried and brushed. And then, fearing he had missed some potential brightness, he went through the whole process again. The brass knob on the pole glittered fiercely; every buckle was silver; the harness shone like patent-leather. A bow of red ribbon fluttered from the middle of the whip.

Before noon on the great day he had the equipage out, to listen for squeaks in the newly-greased wagon. At length he slipped the bridle and tied the horses in the shade before he went in to lunch with Joseph. Neither of them ate very much, a slice or two of bread torn in pieces and dropped in milk. They finished, nodded at each other and rose from the table. In the buckboard, patiently waiting for them was Benjy. Joseph grew angry. "You shouldn't go, Benjy. You've been sick."

"I'm well again," said Benjy.

"I'm taking Juanito. There won't be room for you."

Benjy smiled disarmingly. "I'll sit in the box," he said, and he climbed over the seat and half reclined on the boards.

They started off over the rough wheel-tracks, and their spirits were a little damped by Benjy's presence. Joseph leaned back over the seat. "You mustn't drink anything, Benjy. You've been sick."

"Oh no, I'm going in to get a new clock."

"Remember what I say, Benjy. I don't want you to drink."

"I wouldn't swallow a drop, Joe, not even if it was in my mouth."

Joseph gave him up. He knew that Benjy would be drunk within an hour of his arrival, and there was nothing he could do to prevent it.

The sycamores along the creek were beginning to drop their leaves on the ground. The road was deep in the crisp brown fragments. Joseph lifted the lines and the horses broke into a trot, and their hoofs crashed softly in the leaves.

Elizabeth heard Joseph's voice on the porch and hurried upstairs so she could come down again. She was afraid of Joseph Wayne. Since his last visit she had thought of him nearly all the time. How could she refuse to marry him even though she hated him? Some terrible thing might happen if she should refuse—he might die; or perhaps he might strike her with his fist. In her room, before she went down to the parlor, she brought out all her knowledge to protect her—her algebra and when Caesar landed in England and the Nicene council and the verb être. Joseph didn't know things like that. Probably the only date he knew was 1776. An ignorant man, really. Her mouth pinched at the corners with contempt. Her eyes grew stern. She would put him in his place as she would a smart-alec boy in school. Elizabeth ran her fingers around her waist, inside her skirt, to make sure that her shirt-waist was tucked in. She patted her hair, rubbed her lips harshly with her knuckles to bring the blood to the surface, and last, blew out the lamp. She came majestically into the parlor where Joseph stood.

"Good evening," she said. "I was reading when they told me you were here. *Pippa Passes*, Browning. Do you like Browning, Mr. Wayne?"

He raked a nervous hand through his hair and destroyed the careful part. "Have you decided yet?" he demanded. "I must ask you that first. I don't know who Browning is." He was staring at her with eyes so hungry, so beseeching, that her superiority dropped away from her and her facts crawled back into their cells.

Her hands made a helpless gesture. "I—I don't know," she said.

"I'll go away again. You aren't ready now. That is, unless you'd like to talk about Browning. Or maybe you might like to go for a drive. I came in the buckboard."

Elizabeth stared downward at the green carpet with its brown footpath where the pile had been worn through, and her eyes moved to Joseph's boots, glittering with daubed polish which was not black but iridescent, green and blue and purple. Elizabeth's mind fastened on the shoes and felt safe for a moment. "The polish was old," she thought. "He probably had the bottle for a long time and left the cork out. That always makes the colors in it. Black ink does the same thing when it's left open. He doesn't know that, I guess, and I won't tell him. If I told him, I wouldn't have any privacy any more." And she wondered why he didn't move his feet.

"We could drive down by the river," Joseph said. "The river is fine, but it's very dangerous to cross on foot. The stones are slippery, you see. You must not cross on foot. But we could drive down there." He wanted to tell her how the wheels would sound, crushing the crisp leaves, and how a long blue spark with a head like a serpent's tongue, would leap from the crash of iron and stone now and then. He wanted to say how the sky was low this night, so low that one bathed one's head in it. There seemed no way to say such things. "I'd like you to go," he said. He took a short step toward her, and destroyed the safety her mind had found.

Elizabeth had a quick impulse to be gay. She put her hand timidly on his arm and then patted his sleeve. "I'll go," she said, hearing an unnecessary loudness in her voice. "I think I'll like to go. Teaching is a strain. I need to be out in the air." She ran upstairs for her coat, humming under her breath, and at the top of the stairs she pointed her toe twice, as little girls do in a Maypole dance. "Now I am committing myself," she thought. "People will see us driving alone at night, and that will mean we are engaged."

Joseph stood at the bottom of the stairs and looked upward, waiting for her to reappear. He felt a desire to open his body for her inspection, so that she could see all the hidden things in him, even the things he did not know were there.

"That would be right," he thought. "Then she would know the kind of man I am; and if she knew that she would be a part of me."

She paused on the landing and smiled down on him. Over her shoulders she wore a long blue cape, and some of her hair was loose from its puff and caught in the nap of the blue wool. A rush of tenderness came over Joseph for the loose hairs. He laughed sharply. "Come quickly before the horses fade," he said, "or the moment goes. Oh, of course I mean the polish Juanito put on the harness."

He opened the door for her, and when they reached the buckboard he helped her to the near seat before he untied the horses and fastened the ivory loops of their check reins. The horses danced a little, and Joseph was glad of that.

"Are you warm?" he asked.

"Yes, warm."

The horses broke into a trot. Joseph saw how he could make a gesture with his arms and hands, that would sweep in and indicate and symbolize the ripe stars and the whole cup of the sky, the land, eddied with black trees, and the crested waves that were the mountains, an earth storm, frozen in the peak of its rushing, or stone breakers moving eastward with infinite slowness. Joseph wondered whether there were any words to say these things.

He said, "I like the night. It's more strong than day."

From the first moment of her association with him, Elizabeth had been tensed to repel his attack upon her boundaried and fortified self, but now a strange and sudden thing had happened. Perhaps the tone, the rhythm, perhaps some personal implication in his words had done it, had swept her walls cleanly away. She touched his arm with her fingertips, and trembled with delight and drew away. Her throat tightened above her breathing. She thought, "He will hear me panting, like a horse. This is disgraceful," and she laughed nervously under her breath, knowing she didn't care. Those thoughts she had kept weak and pale and hidden in the recesses of her brain, just out of thinking vision, came out into the open, and she saw that they were not foul and loathesome like slugs, as she had always believed, but somehow light and gay and holy. "If he should put his lips upon my breast I would be glad," she thought. "The pressure of gladness in me would be more than I could stand. I would hold my breast to his lips with both hands." She saw herself doing it and she knew how she would feel, pouring the hot fluid of herself toward his lips.

The horses snorted loudly and swung to one side of the road, for a dark figure stood in front of them. Juanito walked quickly beside the wagon to talk to Joseph.

"Are you going home, señor? I was waiting."

"No, Juanito, not for some time."

"I'll wait again, señor. Benjy is drunk."

Joseph twisted nervously in his seat. "I guess I knew he would be."

"He is out on this road, señor. I heard him sing a little while ago. Willie Romas is drunk too. Willie is happy. Willie will kill someone tonight, maybe."

Joseph's hands were white in the starlight, holding the lines taut, jerking forward a little when the horses flung their heads against the bits.

"Find Benjy," Joseph said bitterly. "I'll be ready to go in a couple of hours." The horses leaped forward and Juanito sank away into the darkness.

Now that her wall was down, Elizabeth could feel that Joseph was unhappy. "He will tell me, and then I will help him."

Joseph sat rigid, and the horses, feeling the uncompromising weight of his clenched hands on the lines, slowed their trot to a careful, picking walk. They were nearing the ragged black barrier of the river trees when suddenly the voice of Benjy sounded from the cover of the brush.

"Estando bebiendo de vino,
"Pedro, Rodarte y Simon—"

Joseph tore the whip from its socket and lashed the horses ferociously, and then he had to put all his force on the lines to check their leaping. Elizabeth was crying miserably because of the voice of Benjy. Joseph pulled up the horses until the crashing of their hoofs on the hard road subsided to the intricate rhythm of a trot.

"I have not told you my brother is a drunkard. You'll have to know the kind of family I have. My brother is a drunkard. I do not mean he goes out and gets drunk now and then the way any man will. Benjy has the disease in his body. Now you know." He stared ahead of him. "That was my brother singing there." He felt her body jerking against his side as she wept. "Do you want me to take you home now?"

"Yes."

"Do you want me to stay away?" When she made no reply, he turned the horses sharply and started them back. "Do you want me to stay away from you?" he demanded.

"No," she said. "I'm being silly. I want to go home and go to bed. I want to try to know what it is I'm feeling. That is an honesty."

Joseph felt an exultance rising again in his throat. He leaned toward her and kissed her on the cheek and then touched up the horses again. At the gate he helped her down and walked to the door with her.

"I will go now to try to find my brother. In a few days I will come back. Good-night."

Elizabeth didn't wait to see him go. She was in bed almost before the sound of the wheels died out. Her heart pounded so that it shook her head against the pillow. It was hard to listen over the pounding of her heart, but at last she made out the sound she was waiting for. It came slowly toward her house, the drunken beautiful voice. Elizabeth gathered her spirit to resist the flaming pain that was coming with the voice.

She whispered to herself, "He is useless, I know! A drunken, useless fool. I have something to do, almost a magic thing." She waited until the voice came in front of the house. "Now I must do this. It is the only chance." She put her head under her pillow and whispered, "I love this singing man, useless as he is, I love him. I have never seen his face and I love him more than anything. Lord Jesus help me to my desire. Help me to have this man."

Then she lay quietly, listening for the response, for the answer to her magic. It came after a last splash of pain. A hatred for Benjy drove out the pain, a hatred so powerful that her jaws tightened and her lips drew snarlingly back from her teeth. She could feel how her skin tingled with the hatred and how her nails ached to attack him. And then the hatred floated off and away. She heard without interest the voice of Benjy growing fainter in the distance. Elizabeth lay on her back and rested her head on crossed wrists.

"Now I will be married soon," she said quietly.

9

The year had darkened to winter and the spring had come, and another fall, before the marriage took place. There was term-end to think of, and after that, in the heat of the summer, when the white oaks sagged under the sun and the river shrank to a stream, Elizabeth had dealings with dressmakers. The hills were rich with heavy-seeded grain; the cattle came out of the brush at night to eat, and when the sun was up, retired into the sage-scented shade to chew sleepily through the day. In the barn the men were piling the sweet wild hay higher than the rafters.

Once a week during the year Joseph went in to Nuestra Señora and sat in the parlor with Elizabeth or took her driving in the buckboard. And he asked, "When will we be married, Elizabeth?"

"Why, I must serve out my year," she said; "there are a thousand things that must be done. I should go home to Monterey for a little. Of course my father will want to see me once more before I am married."

"That is true," said Joseph soberly. "You might be changed afterwards."

"I know." She clasped her hands around his wrist and regarded her clasped fingers. "Look, Joseph, how hard it is to move the finger you want to move. You lose track of which is which." He smiled at the way her mind caught at things to escape thinking. "I am afraid to change," she said. "I want to, and I am afraid. Will I get stout, do you think? All in a moment will I be another person, remembering Elizabeth as an acquaintance who's dead?"

"I don't know," he said, edging his finger into a pleat at the shoulder of her shirtwaist. "Perhaps there isn't any change, ever, in anything. Perhaps unchangeable things only pass."

One day she went to the ranch and he led her about, boasting a little by implication. "Here is the house. I built it first. And at first there wasn't a building within miles, just the house under the oak tree."

Elizabeth leaned against the tree and stroked its trunk. "There could be a seat up in the tree, you see, Joseph, where those limbs start out from the trunk. Will you mind if I climb the tree, Joseph?" She looked up into his face and found that he was staring at her with a strange intensity. His hair had blown forward over his eyes. Elizabeth thought suddenly, "If only he had the body of a horse I might love him more."

Joseph moved quickly toward her and held out his hand. "You must climb the tree, Elizabeth. I want you to. Here, I'll help you." He cupped his hands for her foot and steadied her until she sat in the crotch from which the great limbs grew. And when he saw how she fitted in the hollow and how the grey arms guarded her, "I'm glad, Elizabeth," he cried.

"Glad, Joseph? You look glad! Your eyes are shining. Why are you so glad?"

He lowered his eyes and laughed to himself. "Strange things one is glad of. I am glad that you are sitting in my tree. A moment back I thought I saw that my tree loved you."

"Stand away a little," she called. "I'm going up to the next limb so I can see beyond the barn." He moved aside because her skirts were full. "Joseph, I wonder why I hadn't noticed the pines on the ridge. Now I can feel at home. I was born among the pines in Monterey. You'll see them, Joseph, when we go there to be married."

"They are strange pines; I'll take you there some time after we are married."

Elizabeth climbed carefully down from the tree and stood beside him again. She pinned her hair and patted it with dexterous fingers that went inquisitively about searching for loose strands and shaping them to their old course. "When I am homesick, Joseph, I can go up to those pines and it will be like going home."

10

The wedding was in Monterey, a sombre boding ceremony in a little Protestant chapel. The church had so often seen two ripe bodies die by the process of marriage that it seemed to celebrate a mystic double death with its ritual. Both Joseph and Elizabeth felt the sullenness of the sentence. "You must endure," said the church; and its music was a sunless prophecy.

Elizabeth looked at her bent father, where he glared at the furniture of Christianity because it insulted what he was calling his intelligence. There was no blessing in the leather fingers of her father. She glanced quickly at the man beside her who was becoming her husband second by second. Joseph's face was set and hard. She could see how his jaw muscles quivered tensely. And suddenly Elizabeth was sorry for Joseph. She thought with a little frantic sadness, "If my mother were here, she could say to him, 'Here is Elizabeth and she is a good girl because I love her, Joseph. And she will be a good wife when she learns how to be. I hope you will get outside the hard husk you're wearing, Joseph, so you may feel tenderly for Elizabeth. That's all she wants and it's not an impossible thing.'"

Elizabeth's eyes glittered suddenly with bright tears. "I will," she said aloud, and, silently, "I must pray a little. Lord Jesus, make things easy for me because I am afraid. In all the time I've had to learn about myself, I have learned nothing. Be kind to me, Lord Jesus, at least until I learn what kind of thing I am." She wished there were a crucifix some place in the church, but it was a Protestant church, and when she drew a picture of the Christ in her mind, He had the face, the youthful beard, the piercing puzzled eyes of Joseph, who stood beside her.

Joseph's brain was tight with a curious fear. "There's a foulness here," he thought. "Why must we go through this to find our marriage? Here in the church I've thought there lay a beauty if a man could find it, but this is only a doddering kind of devil worship." He was disappointed for himself and for Elizabeth. He was embarrassed that Elizabeth must witness the maculate entrance to the marriage.

49

Elizabeth tugged at his arm and whispered, "It's over now. We must walk out. Turn toward me slowly." She helped him to turn, and as they took the first step down the aisle, the bells broke forth in the belfry above them. Joseph sighed shudderingly. "Here's God come late to the wedding. Here's the iron god at last." He felt that he would pray if he knew some powerful way to do it. "This ties in. This is the marriage—the good iron voice!" And he thought, "This is my own thing and I know it. Beloved bells, pounding your bodies with your frantic hearts! It is the sun sticks, striking the bell of the sky in the morning; and it's the hollow beating of rain on the earth's full belly—of course, I know—the thing that whips the tortured air with lightning. And sometimes the hot sweet wind plucks at the treetops in a yellow afternoon."

He looked sidewise and down and whispered, "The bells are good, Elizabeth. The bells are holy."

She started and peered up at him in wonder, for her vision had not changed; the Christ's face was still the face of Joseph. She laughed uneasily and confessed to herself, "I'm praying to my own husband."

McGreggor, the saddler, was wistful when they went away. He kissed Elizabeth clumsily on the forehead. "Don't forget your father," he said. "But it wouldn't be an unusual thing if you did. It's almost a custom in these days."

"You'll come to the ranch to see us, won't you, father?"

"I visit no one," he replied angrily. "A man takes only weakness and a little pleasure from an obligation."

"We'll be glad to see you if you come," said Joseph.

"Well, you'll wait a long time, you and your thousand acre ranches. I'd see you both in Hell before I'd visit you."

After a time he drew Joseph aside, out of hearing of Elizabeth, and he said plaintively, "It's because you're stronger than I am that I hate you. Here I'm wanting to like you, and I can't because I'm a weak man. And it's the same about Elizabeth and about her crazy mother. Both of them knew I was a weak man, and I hated both of them."

Joseph smiled on the saddler and felt pity and love for him. "It's not a weak thing you're doing now," he observed.

"No," McGreggor cried, "it's a good strong thing. Oh, I know in my head how to be strong, but I can't learn to do it."

Joseph patted him roughly on the arm. "We'll be glad to see you when you come to visit." And instantly McGreggor's lip stiffened in anger.

They went by train from Monterey and down the long Salinas Valley, a grey-and-gold lane between two muscular mountain lines. From the train they could see how the wind blew down the valley, toward the sea, how its dry force bent the grain against the ground until it lay like the coat of a sleek-haired dog, how it drove the herds of rolling tumbleweeds toward the valley mouth and how it blew the trees lopsided and streaming until they grew that way. At the little stations, Chualar, Gonzales and Greenfield, they saw the grain teams standing in the road, waiting to store their fat sacks in the warehouses. The train moved beside the dry Salinas river with its broad yellow bed where blue herons stalked disconsolately over the hot sand, searching for water to fish in, and where now and then a grey coyote trotted nervously away, looking back apprehensively at the train; and the mountains continued on with them on either side like huge rough outer tracks for a tremendous juggernaut.

In King City, a small railroad town, Joseph and Elizabeth left the train and walked to the livery barn where Joseph's horses had been stabled while they were gone. They felt new and shiny and curiously young as they drove out of King City on the road to the valley of Our Lady. New clothes were in the traveling baskets in the wagon box. Over their clothes they wore long linen dusters to protect them from the road dirt, and Elizabeth's face was covered with a dark blue veil, behind which her eyes darted about, collecting data for memory. Joseph and Elizabeth were embarrassed, sitting shoulder to shoulder and looking ahead at the tan road, for it seemed a presumptuous game they were playing. The horses, four days rested and full of fat barley, flung their heads and tried to run, but Joseph tightened the brake a little and held them down, saying, "Steady, Blue. Steady, Pigeon. You'll be tired enough before we get home."

A few miles ahead they could see the willow boundary of their own home stream where it strode out to meet the broad Salinas river. The willows were yellow in this season, and the poison-oak that climbed into the branches had turned scarlet and menacing. Where the rivers joined, Joseph pulled up to watch how the glittering water from Nuestra Señora sank tiredly and disappeared into the white sand of its new bed. It was said the river ran pure and sweet under the ground, and this could be proved by digging a few feet into the sand. Even within sight of the juncture there were broad holes dug in the river bed so the cattle might drink.

Joseph unbuttoned his duster, for the afternoon was very hot, and he loosened the neckerchief designed to keep his collar free from dust, and removing his black hat he wiped the leather head-band with a bandana. "Would you like to get down, Elizabeth?" he asked. "You could bathe your wrists in the water and that would make you cool."

But Elizabeth shook her head. It was strange to see the swathed head shake. "No, I am comfortable, dear. It will be very late when we get home. I am anxious to go on."

He slapped the flat lines on the horses' buttocks and they moved on beside the river. The tall willows along the road whipped at their heads and sometimes drew a long pliant switch caressingly over their shoulders. The crickets in the hot brush sang their head-piercing notes, and flying grasshoppers leaped up with a flash of white or yellow wings, rattled a moment through the air and dropped to safety in the dry grass. Now and then some little blue brush rabbit skittered in panic off the road, and once safe, perched on its haunches and peeked at the wagon. There was a smell of toasting grass-stems in the air, and the bitter of willow bark, and the perfume of river bay trees.

Joseph and Elizabeth leaned loosely back against the leather seat, caught in the rhythm of the day and drowsed by the pounding hoofs. Their backs and shoulders supply absorbed the vibrations of the buckboard. Theirs was a state close to sleep but more withdrawn to thoughtlessness, more profound than sleep. The road and the river pointed straight at the mountains now. The dark sage covered the higher ridges like a coarse fur, except in the water scars, which were grey and bare like healed saddle sores on a horse's back. The sun was quartering to the westward and the road and the river pointed the place of its setting. For the two riding behind the plodding horses, clock time dissolved into the inconstant interval between thought and thought. The hills and the river pass swept toward them grandly, and then the road began to ascend and the horses hunched along stiffly, pounding the air with heads that swung up and down like hammers. Up a long slope they went. The wheels grated on shattered flakes of limestone, of which the hills were made. The iron tires ground harshly on the rock.

Joseph leaned forward and shook his head to be rid of the spell, as a dog shakes water from its ears. "Elizabeth," he said, "we're coming to the pass."

She untied her veil and laid it back over her hat. Her eyes came slowly to life. "I must have been asleep," she said.

"I too. My eyes were open and I was asleep. But here is the pass."

The mountain was split. Two naked shoulders of smooth limestone dropped cleanly down, verging a little together, and at the bottom there was only room for the river bed. The road itself was blasted out of the cliffside, ten feet above the surface of the water. Midway in the pass where the constrained river flowed swift and deep and silently, a rough monolith rose out of the water, cutting and mangling the current like a boat prow driving speedily upstream, making an angry swirling whisper. The sun was behind the mountain now, but through the pass they could see the trembling light of it falling on the valley of Our Lady. The wagon had driven into the chill blue shade of the white cliffs. The horses, having reached the top of the long foothill slope, walked easily enough, but they stretched their necks and snorted at the river far below them, under the road.

Joseph took a shorter grip on the lines and his right foot moved out and rested lightly on the brake. He looked down on the serene water and he felt a gush of pure warm pleasure in anticipation of the valley he would see in a moment. He turned to look at Elizabeth, for he wanted to tell her of the pleasure. He saw that her face had gone haggard and that her eyes were horrified.

She cried, "I want to stop, dear. I'm afraid." She was staring through the cleft into the sunlit valley.

Joseph pulled up the horses and set the brake. He looked at her questioningly. "I didn't know. Is it the narrow road and the stream below?"

"No, it is not."

He stepped to the ground, then, and held out a hand to her; but when he tried to lead her toward the pass she pulled her hand away from him and stood shivering in the shade. And he thought, "I must try to tell her. I've never tried to tell her things like this. It's seemed too difficult a thing, but now I'll have to try to tell her," and he practiced in his mind the thing he must try to say. "Elizabeth," he cried in his mind, "can you hear me? I am cold with a thing to say, and prayerful for a way to say it." His eyes widened and he was entranced. "I have thought without words," he said in his mind. "A man told me once that was not possible, but I have thought—Elizabeth, listen to me. Christ nailed up might be more than a symbol of all pain. He might in very truth contain all pain. And a man standing on a hilltop with his arms outstretched, a symbol of the symbol, he too might be a reservoir of all the pain that ever was."

For a moment she broke into his thinking, crying, "Joseph, I'm afraid."

And then his thought went on, "Listen, Elizabeth. Do not be afraid. I tell you I have thought without words. Now let me grope a moment among the words, tasting them, trying them. This is a space between the real and the clean, unwavering real, undistorted by the senses. Here is a boundary. Yesterday we were married and it was no marriage. This is our marriage—through the pass—entering the passage like sperm and egg that have become a single unit of pregnancy. This is a symbol of the undistorted real. I have a moment in my heart, different in shape, in texture, in duration from any other moment. Why, Elizabeth, this is all marriage that has ever been, contained in our moment." And he said in his mind, "Christ in his little time on the nails carried within his body all the suffering that ever was, and in him it was undistorted."

He had been upon a star, and now the hills rushed back and robbed him of his aloneness and of his naked thinking. His arms and hands felt heavy and dead, hanging like weights on thick cords from the shoulders that were tired of supporting them.

Elizabeth saw how his mouth had gone loose with hopelessness and how his eyes had lost the red gleaming of a moment before. She cried, "Joseph, what is it you want? What are you asking me to do?"

Twice he tried to answer, but a thickness in his throat prohibited speech. He coughed the passage free. "I want to go through the pass," he said hoarsely.

"I'm afraid, Joseph. I don't know why, but I'm terribly afraid."

He broke his lethargy then and coiled one of the swinging weights about her waist. "There's nothing to be afraid of, dear. This is nothing. I have been far too much alone. It seems to mean something to me to go through the pass with you."

She shivered against him and looked fearfully at the dismal blue shadow of the pass. "I'll go, Joseph," she said miserably. "I'll have to go, but I'll be leaving myself behind. I'll think of myself standing here looking through at the new one who will be on the other side."

She remembered sharply how she had served cambric tea in tiny tin cups to three little girls, how they had reminded each other, "We-'re ladies now. Ladies always hold their hands like this." And she remembered how she had tried to catch her doll's dream in a handkerchief.

"Joseph," she said. "It's a bitter thing to be a woman. I'm afraid to be. Everything I've been or thought of will stay outside the pass. I'll be a grown woman on the other side. I thought it might come gradually. This is too quick." And she remembered how her mother said, 'When you're big, Elizabeth, you'll know hurt, but it won't be the kind of hurt you think. It'll be a hurt that can't be reached with a curing kiss.'

"I'll go now, Joseph," she said quietly. "I've been foolish. You'll have to expect so much foolishness from me."

The weight left Joseph then. His arm tightened about her waist and he urged her forward tenderly. She knew, although her head was bent, how he gazed down on her and how his eyes were gentle. They walked slowly through the pass, in the blue shade of it. Joseph laughed softly. "There may be pains more sharp than delight, Elizabeth, like sucking a hot peppermint that burns your tongue. The bitterness of being a woman may be an ecstasy."

His voice ceased and their footsteps rang on the stone road and clashed back and forth between the cliffs. Elizabeth closed her eyes, relying on Joseph's arm to guide her. She tried to close her mind, to plunge it into darkness, but she heard the angry whisper of the monolith in the river, and she felt the stone chill in the air.

And then the air grew warm; there was no longer rock under her feet. Her eyelids turned black-red and then yellow-red over her eyes. Joseph stopped and drew her tightly against his side. "Now we are through, Elizabeth. Now it is done."

She opened her eyes and looked about on the closed valley. The land was dancing in the shimmer of the sun and the trees, clannish little families of white oaks, stirred slightly under the wind that brought excitement to a sloping afternoon. The village of Our Lady was before them, houses brown with weathering and green with rose vines, picket fences burning with a soft fire of nasturtiums. Elizabeth cried out sharply with relief, "I've been having a bad dream. I've been asleep. I'll forget the dream now. It wasn't real."

Joseph's eyes were radiant. "It's not so bitter, then, to be a woman?" he asked.

"It isn't any different. Nothing seems changed. I hadn't realized how beautiful the valley is."

"Wait here," he said. "I'll go back and bring the horses through."

But when he was gone, Elizabeth cried sadly, for she had a vision of a child in short starched skirts and with pigtails down her back, who stood outside the pass and looked anxiously in, stood on one foot and then on the other, hopped nervously and kicked a stone into the stream. For a moment the vision waited as Elizabeth remembered waiting on a street corner for her father, and then the child turned miserably away and walked slowly toward Monterey. Elizabeth was sorry for her, "For it's a bitter thing to be a child," she thought. "There are so many clean new surfaces to scratch."

11

The team came through the pass, the horses lifting their feet high, moving diagonally, cocking their heads at the stream while Joseph held tight reins on them and set the brake to shrieking. Once off the narrow place, the horses settled down and their long journey reasserted itself. Joseph pulled up and helped Elizabeth to her seat. She settled herself primly, drew her duster about her knees and dropped the veil over her face.

"We'll be going right through town," she said. "Everyone will see us."

Joseph clucked to the horses and relaxed the lines. "Will you mind that?"

"Of course I won't mind. I'll like it. I'll feel proud, as though I had done an unusual thing. But I must be sitting right and looking right when they see me."

Joseph chuckled. "Maybe no one will look."

"They'll look, all right. I'll make them look."

They drove down the one long street of Our Lady, where the houses clung to the side of the road as though for warmth. As they went, the women came from their houses, shamelessly to stare, to wave fat hands and to say the new title gently because it was a new word. *"Buenas tardes, señora,"* and over their shoulders they called into the houses, *"Ven aca, mira! mira! La nueva señora Wayne viene."* Elizabeth waved back happily and tried to look dignified. Farther along the street they had to stop for gifts. Old Mrs. Gutierrez stood in the middle of the road, waving a chicken by the legs while she shrieked the advantages of this particular chicken. But when the bird lay croaking in the wagon box, Mrs. Gutierrez was overcome with self-consciousness. She fixed her hair and nursed her hands, and finally scuttled back to her yard waving her arms and crying, *"No le hace."*

Before they got through the street the wagon box was loaded with trussed livestock: two little pigs, a lamb, an evil-eyed nanny goat with udders suspiciously shrunken, four hens and a gamecock. The saloon belched forth its customers as the wagon went by, and the men raised their glasses. For a little while they were surrounded by cries of welcome, and then the last house was gone and the river road was before them.

Elizabeth settled back in the seat and relaxed her primness. Her hand crept through the crook of Joseph's arm and pressed for a moment and then remained in quiet there. "It was like a circus," she said. "It was like being the parade."

Joseph took off his hat and laid it on his lap. His hair was tangled and damp, and his eyes tired. "They are good people," he said. "I'll be glad to get home, won't you?"

"Yes, I'll be glad." And she said suddenly, "There are some times, Joseph, when the love for people is strong and warm like a sorrow."

He looked quickly at her in astonishment at her statement of his own thought. "How did you think that, dear?"

"I don't know. Why?"

"Because I was thinking it at that moment—and there are times when the people and the hills and the earth, all, everything except the stars, are one, and the love of them all is strong like a sadness."

"Not the stars, then?"

"No, never the stars. The stars are always strangers—sometimes evil, but always strangers. Smell the sage, Elizabeth. It's good to be getting home."

She raised her veil as high as her nose and sniffed long and hungrily. The sycamores were yellowing and already the ground was thick with the first fallen leaves. The team entered the long road that hid the river, and the sun was low over the seaward mountains.

"It'll be 'way in the middle of the night when we get home," he said. The light in the wood was golden-blue, and the stream rattled among the round rocks.

With evening the air grew clear with moisture, so that the mountains were as hard and sharp as crystal. After the sun was gone, there was a hypnotic time when Joseph and Elizabeth stared ahead at the clear hills and could not take their eyes away. The pounding hoofs and the muttering of water deepened the trance. Joseph looked unblinkingly at the string of light along the western mountain rim. His thoughts grew sluggish, but with their slowness they became pictures, and the figures arranged themselves on the mountain tops. A black cloud sailed in from the ocean and rested on the ridge, and Joseph's thought made it a black goat's head. He could see the yellow, slanting eyes, wise and ironic, and the curved horns. He thought, "I know that it is really there, the goat resting his chin on a mountain range and staring in on the valley. He should be there. Something I've read or something I've been told makes it a fitting thing that a goat should come out of the ocean." He was endowed with the power to create things as substantial as the earth. "If I will admit the goat is there, it will be there. And I will have made it. This goat is important," he thought.

A flight of birds rolled and twisted high overhead, and they caught the last light on their flickering wings, and twinkled like little stars. A hunting owl drifted over and shrieked his cry, designed to make small groundling creatures start uneasily and betray themselves against the grass. The valley filled quickly with dark, and the black cloud, as though it had seen enough, withdrew to the sea again. Joseph thought, "I must maintain to myself that it was the goat. I must never betray the goat by disbelieving it."

Elizabeth shivered slightly and he turned around to her. "Are you cold, dear? I'll get the horseblanket to go over your knees." She shivered again, not quite so well, because she was trying to.

"I'm not cold," she said, "but it's a queer time. I wish you'd talk to me. It's a dangerous time."

He thought of the goat. "What do you mean, dangerous?" He took her clasped hands and laid them on his knee.

"I mean there's a danger of being lost. It's the light that's going. I thought I suddenly felt myself spreading and dissipating like a cloud, mixing with everything around me. It was a good feeling, Joseph. And then the owl went over, and I was afraid that if I mixed too much with the hills I might never be able to collapse into Elizabeth again."

"It's only the time of day," he reassured her. "It seems to affect all living things. Have you ever noticed the animals and the birds when its evening?"

"No," she said, turning eagerly toward him, for it seemed to her that she had discovered a communication. "I don't think I've ever noticed anything very closely in my life," she said. "Just now it seems to me that the lenses of my eyes have been wiped clean. What do the animals do at evening?" Her voice had grown sharp and had broken through his reverie.

"I don't know," he said sullenly. "I mean—I know, but I'll have to think. These things aren't always ready to hand, you know," he apologized. And he fell silent and looked into the gathering darkness. "Yes," he said at last, "it's like that—why all the animals stand still when it comes dark evening. They don't blink their eyes at all and they go dreaming." He fell silent again.

"I remember a thing," Elizabeth said. "I don't know when I noticed it, but just now—you said yourself it's the time of day, and this picture is important in this time of day."

"What?" he asked.

"Cats' tails lie flat and straight and motionless when they're eating."

"Yes," he nodded, "yes, I know."

"And that's the only time they're ever straight, and that's the only time they're ever still." She laughed gaily. Now that the foolish thing was said, she realized it might be taken as a satire on Joseph's dreaming animals, and she was glad it might. She felt rather clever to have said it.

He did not notice what construction might be put on the cats' tails. He said. "Over a hill and then down to the river wood again, and then across the long plain and we'll be home. We should see the lights from the hilltop." It was very dark by now, a thick night and silent. The wagon moved up the hill in the darkness, a stranger to the hushed night.

Elizabeth pressed her body against Joseph. "The horses know the road," she said. "Do they smell it?"

"They see it, dear. It is only dark to us. To them it is a deep twilight. We'll be on top of the hill in a little, and then we may see the lights. It's too quiet," he complained. "I don't like this night. Nothing is stirring about." It seemed an hour before they breasted the hill and Joseph stopped the team to rest from its climb. The horses sank their heads low and panted rhythmically. "See," Joseph said, "there are the lights. Late as it is, my brothers are expecting us. I didn't tell them when we would come, but they must have guessed. Look, some of the lights are moving. That's a lantern in the yard, I guess. Tom has been out to the barn to see the horses."

The night was thick on them again. Ahead, they could hear a heavy sigh, and then it rode up to them—a warm wind out of the valley. It whisked gently in the dry grass. Joseph muttered uneasily. "There's an enemy out tonight. The air's unfriendly."

"What do you say, dear?"

"I say there's a change of weather coming. The storms will be here soon."

The wind strengthened and bore to them the long deep howling of a dog. Joseph sat forward angrily. "Benjy has gone to town. I told him not to go while I was gone. That's his dog howling. It howls all night every time he goes away." He lifted the lines and clucked the horses up. For a moment they plodded, but then their necks arched and their ears pivoted forward. Joseph and Elizabeth could hear it now, the even clattering of a galloping horse. "Someone coming," Joseph said. "Maybe it's Benjy on his way to town. I'll head him off if I can."

The running horse came near, and suddenly its rider pulled it down almost to its haunches. A shrill voice cried, "Señor, is it you, Don Joseph?"

"Yes, Juanito, what's the matter? What do you want?"

The saddled horse was passing now, and the shrill voice cried, "You will want me in a little while, my friend. I'll be waiting for you at the rock in the pines. I did not know, señor. I swear I did not know."

They could hear the thud as the spurs drove in. The horse coughed and leaped ahead. They heard it running wildly over the hill. Joseph took the whip from its socket and flicked the horses to a trot.

Elizabeth tried to see into his face. "What's the matter, dear? What did he mean?"

His hands were rising and falling as he kept tight rein on the horses and yet urged them on. The tires cried on the rocks. "I don't know what it is," Joseph said. "I knew this night was bad."

Now they were in the level plain and the horses tried to slow to a walk, but Joseph whipped them sharply until they broke into a ragged run. The wagon lurched and pitched over the uneven road so that Elizabeth braced her feet and grasped the arm handle with both her hands.

They could see the buildings now. A lantern was standing on the manure pile and its light reflected outward from the new whitewash on the barn. Two of the houses were lighted, and as the wagon drew near, Joseph could see people moving about restlessly behind the windows. Thomas came out and stood by the lantern as they drove up. He took the horses by the bits and rubbed their necks with his palm. He wore a set smile that did not change. "You've been coming fast," he said.

Joseph jumped down from the wagon. "What has happened here? I met Juanito on the road."

Thomas unhooked the check reins and went back to loosen the tugs. "Why we knew it would happen some time. We spoke about it once."

Out of the darkness Rama appeared beside the wagon. "Elizabeth, I think you'd better come with me."

"What's the matter?" Elizabeth cried.

"Come with me, dear, I'll tell you."

Elizabeth looked questioningly at Joseph. "Yes, go with her," he said. "Go to the house with her."

The pole dropped and Thomas skinned the harness from the horses' wet backs. "I'll leave them here for a little," he apologized, and he threw the harness over the corral fence. "Now come with me."

Joseph had been staring woodenly at the lantern. He picked it up and turned. "It's Benjy, of course," he said. "Is he badly hurt?"

"He's dead," said Thomas. "He's been dead a good two hours."

They went into Benjy's little house, through the dark living-room and into the bedroom, where a lamp was burning. Joseph looked down into Benjy's twisted face, caught in a moment of ecstatic pain. The lips grinned off the teeth, the nose was flared and spread. Half-dollars lying on his eyes shone dully.

"His face will settle some after a while," Thomas said.

Joseph's eyes wandered slowly to a blood-stained knife which lay on a table beside the bed. He seemed to be looking down from a high place, and he was filled with a strange powerful calmness, and with a curious sense of omniscience. "Juanito did this?" he said with a half-question.

Thomas picked up the knife and held it to his brother. And when Joseph refused to take it, he set it back on the table. "In the back," Thomas said. "Juanito rode to Nuestra Señora to borrow a dehorner for that long-horned bull that's been raising so much Hell. And Juanito made the trip too quickly."

Joseph looked up from the bed. "Let's cover him up. Let's spread something over him. I met Juanito on the road. He said he didn't know."

Thomas laughed brutally. "How could he know? He couldn't see his face. He just saw, and stabbed. He wanted to give himself up, but I told him to wait for you. Why," Thomas said, "the only punishment of a trial would be on us."

Joseph turned away. "Do you suppose we'll have to have a coroner out? Have you changed anything, Tom?"

"Well, we brought him home. And we pulled up his pants."

Joseph's hand rose to his beard and he stroked it down and turned the ends under. "Where is Jennie now?" he asked.

"Oh, Burton took her home with him. Burton's praying with her. She was crying when she left. She must be nearly hysterical by now."

"We'll send her home to the East," Joseph said. "She'll never do, out here." He turned to the door. "You'll have to ride in and report it, Tom. Make it an accident. Maybe they'll never question. And it was an accident." He turned quickly back to the bed and patted Benjy's hand before he went out of the house.

He walked slowly across the yard toward where he could see the black tree against the sky. When he was come to it, he leaned his back against the trunk and looked upward, where a few pale misty stars glittered among the branches. His hands caressed the bark. "Benjamin is dead," he reported softly. For a moment he breathed deeply, and then turning, he climbed into the tree and sat between the great arms and laid his cheek against the cool rough bark. He knew his thought would be heard when he said in his mind, "Now I know what the blessing was. I know what I've taken upon me. Thomas and Burton are allowed their likes and dislikes, only I am cut off. I am cut off. I can have neither good luck nor bad luck. I can have no knowledge of any good or bad. Even a pure true feeling of the difference between pleasure and pain is denied me. All things are one, and all a part of me." He looked toward the house from which he had come. The light from the window alternately flashed and was cut off. Benjy's dog howled again, and in the distance the coyotes heard the howl and took it up with their maniac giggling. Joseph put his arms around the tree and hugged it tight against him. "Benjy is dead, and I am neither glad nor sorry. There is no reason for it to me. It is just so. I know now, my father, what you were—

lonely beyond feeling loneliness, calm because you had no contact." He climbed down from the tree and once more reported, "Benjamin is dead, sir. I wouldn't have stopped it if I could. Nothing is required in satisfaction."

And he walked toward the barn, for he must saddle a horse to ride toward the great rock where Juanito was awaiting him.

12

Rama took Elizabeth by the hand and led her across the farm yard. "No crying, now," she said. "There's no call for it. You didn't know the man that's dead, so you can't miss him. And I'll promise you won't ever see him, so there's no call for fear." She led the way up the steps and into her comfortable sitting-room where rocking-chairs were fitted with quilted pads and where the Rochester lamps wore china shades with roses painted on them. Even the braided rag rugs on the floor were made of the brightest underskirts.

"You have a comfortable place," Elizabeth said, and she looked up at the wide face of Rama, a full span between the cheekbones; the black brows nearly met over the nose; the heavy hair grew far down on her forehead in a widow's peak.

"I make it comfortable," Rama said. "I hope you can do as well."

Rama had dressed for the occasion in a tight-bodiced, full-skirted black taffeta which whispered sharply when she moved. Around her neck, upon a silver chain, she wore an amulet of ivory brought by some sailor ancestor from an island in the Indian Ocean. She seated herself in a rocking-chair of which the seat and back were covered with little flowers in petit point. Rama stretched her white strong fingers on her knees like a pianist sounding a practice chord. "Sit down," she said. "You'll have a time to wait."

Elizabeth felt the strength of Rama and knew she should resent it, but it was a safe pleasant thing to have this sure woman by her side. She seated herself daintily and crossed her hands in her lap. "You haven't told me yet what has happened."

Rama smiled grimly. "Poor child, you are come at a bad time. Any time would have been bad, but this is a shameful time." She stiffened her fingers on her lap again. "Benjamin Wayne was stabbed in the back tonight," she said. "He died in ten minutes. In two days he'll be buried." She looked up at Elizabeth and smiled mirthlessly, as though she had known all this would happen, even to the smallest detail. "Now you know," she continued. "Ask anything you want tonight. There's a strain on us and we are not ourselves. A thing like this breaks down our natures for a time. Ask anything you wish tonight. Tomorrow we may be ashamed. When we have buried him, we'll never mention Benjy any more. In a year we will forget he ever lived."

Elizabeth sat forward in her chair. This was so different from her picture of homecoming, in which she received the homage of the clan and made herself gracious to them. The room was swimming in a power beyond her control. She sat on the edge of a deep black pool and saw huge pale fishes moving mysteriously in its depth.

"Why was he stabbed?" she asked. "I heard Juanito did it."

A little smile of affection grew on Rama's lips. "Why Benjy was a thief," she said. "He didn't want the things he stole very much. He stole the precious little decency of girls. Why, he drank to steal a particle of death—and now he has it all. This had to happen, Elizabeth. If you throw a great handful of beans at an upturned thimble, one is pretty sure to go in. Now do you see?

"Juanito came home and found the little thief at work.

"We all loved Benjy," Rama said. "There's not a frightful span between contempt and love."

Elizabeth felt lonely and shut out and very weak before Rama's strength. "I've come such a long way," she explained. "And I've had no dinner. I haven't even washed my face." Her lips began to tremble as she remembered, one by one, the things she was suffering. Rama's eyes softened and looked at her, seeing the bride Elizabeth now. "And where's Joseph?" Elizabeth complained. "It's our first night at home and he's gone. I haven't even had a drink of water."

Rama stood up then, and smoothed down her whispering skirt. "Poor child, I'm sorry; I didn't think. Come into the kitchen and wash yourself. I'll make some tea and slice some bread and meat for you."

The teakettle breathed huskily in the kitchen. Rama cut pieces of roast beef and bread and poured a cup of scalding yellow tea.

"Now come back to the sitting-room, Elizabeth. You can have your supper there where it's more comfortable."

Elizabeth made thick sandwiches and ate them hungrily, but it was the hot tea, strong and bitter, that rested her and removed her complaints. Rama had gone back to her chair again. She sat stiffly upright, watching Elizabeth fill her cheeks too full of bread and meat.

"You're pretty," Rama said critically. "I wouldn't have thought Joseph could pick a pretty wife."

TO A GOD UNKNOWN

Elizabeth blushed. "What do you mean?" she asked. There were streams of feeling here she couldn't identify, methods of thinking that wouldn't enter the categories of her experience or learning. It frightened her and so she smiled amusedly. "Of course he knows that. Why he told me."

Rama laughed quietly. "I didn't know him as well as I thought I did. I thought he'd pick a wife as he'd pick a cow—to be a good cow, perfect in the activity of cows—to be a good wife and very like a cow. Perhaps he is more human than I thought." There was a little bitterness in her voice. Her strong white fingers brushed her hair down on each side of the sharp part. "I think I'll have a cup of tea. I'll put more water in. It must be poisonously strong."

"Of course he's human," Elizabeth said. "I don't see why you seem to say he isn't. He is self-conscious. He's embarrassed, that is all." And her mind reverted suddenly to the pass in the hills and the swirling river. She was frightened and put the thought away from her.

Rama smiled pityingly. "No, he isn't self-conscious," she explained. "In all the world I think there isn't a man less self-conscious, Elizabeth." And then she said compassionately, "You don't know this man. I'll tell you about him, not to frighten you, but so you won't be frightened when you come to know him."

Her eyes filled with thoughts and her mind ranged for a way to say them. "I can see," she said, "that you are making excuses already—why—excuses like bushes to hide behind, so you need not face the thoughts you have." Her hands had lost their sureness; they crawled about like the searching tentacles of a hungry sea creature. "'He is a child,' you say to yourself. 'He dreams.'" Her voice turned sharp and cruel. "He is no child," she said. "And if he dreams, you will never know his dreams."

Elizabeth flared angrily. "What are you telling me? He married me. You are trying to make a stranger of him." Her voice faltered uncertainly. "Why of course I know him. Do you think I would marry a man I didn't know?"

But Rama only smiled at her. "Don't be afraid, Elizabeth. You've seen things already. There's no cruelty in him, Elizabeth, I think. You can worship him without fear of being sacrificed."

The picture of her marriage flashed into Elizabeth's mind, when, as the service was going on, and the air was filled with its monotone, she had confused her husband with the Christ. "I don't know what you mean," she cried. "Why do you say *'worship'*? I'm tired, you know; I've been riding all day. Words have meanings that change as I change. What do you mean by 'worship'?"

Rama drew her chair forward so that she could put her hands on Elizabeth's knee. "This is a strange time," she said softly. "I told you at the beginning that a door is open tonight. It's like an All Souls' Eve, when the ghosts are loose. Tonight, because our brother has died, a door is open in me, and partly open in you. Thoughts that hide deep in the brain, in the dark, underneath the bone can come out tonight. I will tell you what I've thought and held secret. Sometimes in the eyes of other people I've seen the same thought, like a shadow in the water." She patted softly on Elizabeth's knee as she spoke, patted out a rhythm to her words, and her eyes shone with intensity until there were red lights in them. "I know men," she continued. "Thomas I know so well that I feel his thought as it is born. And I know his impulse before it is strong enough to set his limbs in motion. Burton I know to the bottom of his meager soul, and Benjy—I knew the sweetness and the laziness of Benjy. I knew how sorry he was to be Benjy, and how he couldn't help it." She smiled in reminiscence. "Benjy came in one night when Thomas was not here. He was so lost and sad. I held him in my arms until nearly morning." Her fingers doubled under, making a loose fist. "I knew them all," she said hoarsely. "My instinct was never wrong. But Joseph I do not know. I did not know his father."

Elizabeth was nodding slowly, caught in the rhythm.

Rama continued: "I do not know whether there are men born outside humanity, or whether some men are so human as to make others seem unreal. Perhaps a godling lives on earth now and then. Joseph has strength beyond vision of shattering, he has the calm of mountains, and his emotion is as wild and fierce and sharp as the lightning and just as reasonless as far as I can see or know. When you are away from him, try thinking of him and you'll see what I mean. His figure will grow huge, until it tops the mountains, and his force will be like the irresistible plunging of the wind. Benjy is dead. You cannot think of Joseph dying. He is eternal. His father died, and it was not a death." Her mouth moved helplessly, searching for words. She cried as though in pain, "I tell you this man is not a man, unless he is all men. The strength, the resistance, the long and stumbling thinking of all men, and all the joy and suffering, too, cancelling each other out and yet remaining in the contents. He is all these, a repository for a little piece of each man's soul, and more than that, a symbol of the earth's soul."

Her eyes dropped and her hand withdrew. "I said a door was open."

Elizabeth rubbed the place on her knee where the rhythm had been. Her eyes were wet and shining. "I'm so tired," she said. "We drove through the heat, and the grass was brown. I wonder if they took the live chickens and the little lamb and the nanny goat out of the wagon. They should be turned loose, else their legs might swell." She took a handkerchief out of her bosom and blew her nose and wiped it harshly and made it red. She would not look at Rama. "You love my husband," she said in a small, accusing voice. "You love him and you are afraid."

Rama looked slowly up and her eyes moved over Elizabeth's face and then dropped again. "I do not love him. There is no chance of a return. I worship him, and there's no need of a return in that. And you will worship him, too, with no return. Now you know, and you needn't be afraid."

For a moment more she stared at her lap, and then her head jerked up and she brushed down the hair on each side of the part. "It's closed now," she said. "It's all over. Only remember it for a time of need. And when that time comes, I'll be here to help you. I'll make some new tea now, and maybe you'll tell me about Monterey."

13

Joseph went into the dark barn and walked down the long gallery behind the stalls, toward the lantern hanging on its wire. As he passed behind the horses, they stopped their rhythmic chewing and looked over their shoulders at him, and one or two of the more lively ones stamped their feet to draw his attention. Thomas was in the stall opposite the lantern, saddling a mare. He paused in cinching and looked over the saddle at Joseph. "I thought I'd take Ronny," he said. "She's soft. A good fast go will harden her up. She's surest footed in the dark, too."

"Make up a story," Joseph said. "Say he slipped and fell on a knife. Try to get through with it without having a coroner out. We'll bury Benjy tomorrow if we can." He smiled wearily. "The first grave. Now we're getting someplace. Houses and children and graves, that's home, Tom. Those are the things to hold a man down. What's in the box-stall, Tom?"

"Only Patch," Thomas said. "I turned the other saddle-horses out yesterday to get some grass and to stretch their legs. They weren't being worked enough. Why, are you riding out tonight?"

"Yes, I'm riding out."

"You're riding after Juanito? You'll never catch him in these hills. He knows the roots of every blade of grass and every hole even a snake might hide in."

Joseph threw back cinch and stirrup over a saddle on the rack, and lifted it down by horn and cantle. "Juanito is waiting for me in the pines," he said.

"But Joe, don't go tonight. Wait until tomorrow when it's light. And take a gun with you."

"Why a gun?"

"Because you don't know what he'll do. These Indians are strange people. There's no telling what he'll do."

"He won't shoot me," Joseph reassured him. "It would be too easy, and I wouldn't care enough. That's better than a gun."

Thomas untied his halter rope and backed the sleepy mare out of the stall. "Anyway, wait until tomorrow. Juanito will keep."

"No, he's waiting for me now. I won't keep him waiting."

Thomas moved on out of the barn, leading his horse. "I still think you'd better take a gun," he said over his shoulder.

Joseph heard him mount and trot his horse away, and immediately there was a panting rush. Two young coyotes and a hound dashed out to follow him.

Joseph saddled big Patch and led him out into the night and mounted. When his eyes cleared from the lantern light he saw that the night was sharper. The mountain flanks, rounded and flesh-like, stood out softly in shallow perspective and a deep purple essence hung on their outlines. All of the night, the hills, the black hummocks of the trees were as soft and friendly as an embrace. But straight ahead, the black arrow-headed pines cut into the sky.

The night was aging toward dawn, and all the leaves and grasses whispered and sighed under the fresh morning wind. Whistle of ducks wings sounded overhead, where an invisible squadron started over-early for the south. And the great owls swung restlessly through the air at the last of the night's hunting. The wind brought a pine smell down from the hills, and the penetrating odor of tarweed and the pleasant bouquet of a skunk's anger, smelling, since it was far away, like azaleas. Joseph nearly forgot his mission, for the hills reached out tender arms to him and the mountains were as gentle and insistent as a loving woman who is half asleep. He could feel the ground's warmth as he rode up the slope. Patch flung up his big head and snorted out of stretched nostrils and shook his mane, lifted his tail and danced, kicked a few times and threw his feet high like a racehorse.

Because the mountains were womanly, Joseph thought of Elizabeth and wondered what she was doing. He had not thought of her since he saw Thomas standing by the lantern, waiting for him, "But Rama will take care of her," he thought.

The long slope was past now, and a harder, steeper climb began. Patch ceased his foolishness and bent his head over his climbing legs. And as they moved on, the sharp pines lengthened and pierced higher and higher into the sky. Beside the track there was a hissing of a little water, rushing downward toward the valley, and then the pine grove blocked the way. The black bulk of it walled up the path. Joseph turned right and tried to remember how far it was to the broad trail that led to the grove's center. Now Patch nickered shrilly and stamped and shook his head. When Joseph tried to head into the grove path, the horse refused to take it and spurs only made him rear and thresh his front feet, and the quirt sent him whirling down the hill. When Joseph dismounted and tried to lead him into the path, he set his hoofs and refused to stir. Joseph walked to his head and felt the quivering muscles of the neck.

"All right," he said. "I'll tie you out here. I don't know what you're afraid of, but Thomas fears it too, and Thomas knows you better than I could." He took the tie rope from the horn and threw two half-hitches around a sapling.

The pathway through the pines was black. Even the sky was lost behind the interlacing boughs, and Joseph, as he walked along, took careful, feeling steps and stretched his arms ahead to keep from striking a tree trunk. There was no sound except the muttering of a tiny stream somewhere beside the track. Then ahead, a little patch of grey appeared. Joseph dropped his arms and walked quickly toward it. The pine limbs whirred under a wind that could not penetrate down into the forest, but with the wind a restlessness came into the grove—not sound exactly, and not vibration, but a curious half-way between these two. Joseph moved more cautiously, for there was a breath of fear in the slumbering grove. His feet made no sound on the needles, and he came at last to the open circle in the forest. It was a grey place, filled with particles of light and roofed with the dull slaty mirror of the sky. Above, the winds had freshened so that the tall pine-tops moved sedately, and their needles hissed. The great rock in the center of the glade was black, blacker even than the tree trunks, and on its side a glow-worm shed its pale blue luminance.

When Joseph tried to approach the rock he was filled with foreboding and suspicion, as a little boy is who enters an empty church and cuts a wide path around the altar and keeps his eyes upon it for fear some saint may move his hand or the bloody Christ groan on the cross. So Joseph circled widely, keeping his head turned toward the rock. The glow-worm disappeared behind a corner and was lost.

The rustling increased. The whole round space became surcharged with life, saturated with furtive movement. Joseph's hair bristled on his head. "There's evil here tonight," he thought. "I know now what the horse feared." He moved back into the shadow of the trees and seated himself and leaned back against a pine trunk. And as he sat, he could feel a dull vibration on the ground. Then a soft voice spoke beside him. "I am here, señor."

Joseph half leaped to his feet. "You startled me, Juanito."

"I know, señor. It is so quiet. It is always quiet here. You can hear noises, but they're always on the outside, shut out and trying to get in."

They were silent for a moment. Joseph could only see a blacker shadow against the black before him. "You asked me to come," he said.

"Yes, señor, my friend, I would have no one do it but you."

"Do what, Juanito? What do you want me to do?"

"What you must, señor. Did you bring a knife?"

"No," Joseph said wonderingly. "I have no knife."

"Then I will give you my pocket knife. It is the one I used on the calves. The blade is short, but in the right place it will do. I will show you where."

"What are you talking about, Juanito?"

"Strike with the blade flat, my friend. Then it will go between the ribs, and I will show you where, so the blade will reach."

Joseph stood up. "You mean I am to stab you, Juanito."

"You must, my friend."

Joseph moved closer to him and tried to see his face, and could not. "Why should I kill you, Juanito?" he asked.

"I killed your brother, señor. And you are my friend. Now you must be my enemy."

"No," Joseph said. "There's something wrong here." He paused uneasily, for the wind had died out of the trees, and silence, like a thick fog, had settled into the glade so that his voice seemed to fill up the air with unwanted sound. He was uncertain. His voice went on so softly that part of the words were whispered, and even then the glade was disturbed by his speaking. "There's something wrong. You did not know it was my brother."

"I should have looked, señor."

"No, even if you had known, it would make no difference. This thing was natural. You did what your nature demanded. It is natural and—it is finished." Still he could not see Juanito's face, although a little grey of dawn was dropping into the glade.

"I do not understand this, señor," Juanito said brokenly. "It is worse than the knife. There would be a pain like fire for a moment, and then it would be gone. I would be right, and you would be right, too. I do not understand this way. It is like prison all my life." The trees stood out now with a little light between them, and they were like black witnesses.

Joseph looked to the rock for strength and understanding. He could see the roughness of it now, and he could see the straight line of silver light where the little stream cut across the glade.

"It is not punishment," he said at last. "I have no power to punish. Perhaps you must punish yourself if you find that among your instincts. You will act the course of your breed, as a young bird dog does when it comes to point where the birds are hidden, because that is in its breed. I have no punishment for you."

Juanito ran to the rock, then, and scooped up water and drank it from his hands. And he walked quickly back. "This water is good, señor. The Indians take it away with them, to drink when they are sick. They say it comes out of the center of the world." He wiped his mouth on his sleeve. Joseph could see the outline of his face, and the little caves where his eyes were.

"What will you do now?" Joseph asked.

"I will do what you say, señor."

Joseph cried angrily, "You put too much on me. Do what you wish!"

"But I wished you to kill me, my friend."

"Will you come back to work?"

"No," Juanito answered slowly, "It is too near the grave of an unrevenged man. I can't do that until the bones are clean. I will go away for a while, señor. And when the bones are clean I will come back. Memory of the knife will be gone when the flesh is gone."

Joseph was suddenly so filled with sorrow that it hurt his chest to contain it. "Where will you go, Juanito?"

"I know. I will take Willie. We will go together. Where there are horses we will be all right. If I am with Willie, helping him to fight off the dreams of the lonely place and the men who came out of the holes to tear him, then the punishment will not be so hard." He turned suddenly in among the pines and disappeared, and his voice came back from behind the wall of trees, "My horse is here, señor. I will come back when the bones are clean." A moment later Joseph heard the complaint of stirrup leather, and then the pounding of hoofs on pine needles.

The sky was bright now, and high over the center of the glade one little fragment of fiery cloud hung, but the glade was dark and grey yet, and the great rock brooded in its center.

Joseph walked to the rock and drew his hand over the heavy fur of moss. "Out of the center of the world," he thought, and he remembered the poles of a battery. "Out of the heart of the world." He walked away slowly, hating to turn his back on the rock, and as he rode down the slope the sun arose behind him and he could see it flashing on the windows of the farm houses below. The yellow grass glittered with dew. But now the hillsides were getting thin and worn and ready for the winter. A little band of steers watched him go by, turning slowly to keep their heads toward him.

Joseph felt very glad now, for within him there was arising the knowledge that his nature and the nature of the land were the same. He lifted his horse to a trot, for he remembered suddenly that Thomas was gone to Nuestra Señora and there was no one but himself to build a coffin for his brother. For a moment, while the horse hurried on, Joseph tried to think what Benjy had been like, but soon he gave it up, for he couldn't remember very well.

A column of smoke was drifting out of the chimney of Thomas' house as he rode into the corral. He turned Patch loose and hung up the saddle. "Elizabeth will be with Rama," he thought. And he walked eagerly in to see his new wife.

14

The winter came in early that year. Three weeks before Thanksgiving the evenings were red on the mountain tops toward the sea, and the bristling, officious wind raked the valley and sang around the house corners at night and flapped the window shades, and the little whirlwinds took columns of dust and leaves down the road like reeling soldiers. The blackbirds swarmed and flew away in twinkling clouds and doves sat mourning on the fences for a while and then disappeared during a night. All day the flocks of ducks and geese were in the sky, aiming their arrows unerringly at the south, and in the dusk they cried tiredly, and looked for the shine of water where they could rest the night. The frost came into the valley of Our Lady one night and burned the willows yellow and the dogwood red.

There was a scurrying preparation in the sky and on the ground. The squirrels worked frantically in the fields, storing ten times the food they needed in the community rooms under the ground, while in the hole-mouths the grey grandfathers squeaked shrilly and directed the harvest. The horses and cows lost their shiny coats and grew rough with new winter hair, and the dogs dug shallow holes to sleep in against the ground winds. And in spite of the activity, throughout the whole valley sadness hung like the blue smoky mist on the hills. The sage was purple-black. The live oaks dropped leaves like rain and still were clad with leaves. Every night the sky burned over the sea and the clouds massed and deployed, charged and retreated in practice for the winter.

On the Wayne ranch there was preparation, too. The grass was in and the barns piled high with hay. The crosscut saws were working on oak wood and the splitting mauls were breaking up the sticks. Joseph supervised the work, and his brothers labored under him. Thomas built a shed for the tools and oiled the plow shares and the harrow points. And Burton saw to the roofs and cleaned all the harness and saddles. The community woodpile rose up as high as a house.

Jennie saw her husband buried on a side-hill a quarter-mile away. Burton made a cross and Thomas built a little white paling fence around the grave, with a gate on iron hinges. Every day for a while Jennie took some green thing to put on the grave, but in a short time even she could not remember Benjy very well, and she grew homesick for her own people. She thought of the dances and the rides in the snow, and she thought how her parents were getting old. The more she thought about them, the greater their need seemed. And besides, she was afraid of this new country now that she had no husband. And so one day Joseph drove away with her, and the other Waynes watched them go. All her possessions were in a traveling-basket along with Benjy's watch and chain and the wedding pictures.

In King City Joseph stood with Jennie at the railway station, and Jennie cried softly, partly because she was leaving, but more because she was frightened at the long train trip. She said, "You'll all come home to visit, won't you."

And Joseph, anxious to be back on the ranch for fear the rain might come and he not there to see it, answered, "Yes, of course. Some time we'll go back to visit."

Juanito's wife, Alice, mourned much more deeply than Jennie did. She did not cry at all, but only sat on her doorstep sometimes and rocked her body back and forth. She was carrying a child, and besides, she loved Juanito very much, and pitied him. She sat too many hours there, rocking and humming softly to herself and never crying, and at last Elizabeth brought her to Joseph's house and put her to work in the kitchen. Alice was happier then. She chattered a little sometimes, while she washed the dishes, standing far out from the sink to keep from hurting the baby.

"He is not dead," she explained very often to Elizabeth. "Some time he will come back, and after a night, it'll be just as it always was. I will forget he ever went away. You know," she said proudly, "My father wants me to go home, but I will not. I will wait here for Juanito. Here is where he will come." And she questioned Joseph over and over about Juanito's plans. "Do you think he will come back? You are sure you think that?"

Joseph always seriously answered, "He said he would."

"But when, when do you think it will be?"

"In a year, perhaps, or maybe two years. He has to wait."

And she went back to Elizabeth, "The baby can walk, perhaps, when he comes back."

Elizabeth took on the new life and changed to meet it. For two weeks she went about her new house frowning, peering into everything, and making a list of furniture and utensils to be ordered from Monterey. The work of the house quickly drove away the memory of the evening with Rama. Only at night, sometimes, she awakened cold and fearful, feeling that a marble image lay in bed with her, and she touched Joseph's arm to be sure that it was warm. Rama had been right. A door was open on that night, and now it was closed. Rama never spoke in such a mood again. She was a teacher, Rama, and a tactful woman, for she could show Elizabeth methods of doing things about the house without seeming to criticize Elizabeth's method.

When the walnut furniture arrived, and all the graniteware kettles, and when everything had been arranged or hung up—the hatrack with diamond mirrors, and the little rocking-chairs; the broad maple bed, and the high bureau, then the shining airtight stove was set up in the living room, with a coat of stove black on its sides and nickel polish on the silver parts. When it was all done, the worried look went out of Elizabeth's eyes, and the frown left her brows. She sang, then, Spanish songs she had learned in Monterey. When Alice came to work with her they sang the songs together.

Every morning Rama came to talk, always in secrets, for Rama was full of secrets. She explained things about marriage that Elizabeth, having no mother, had not learned. She told how to have boy children and how to have girl children—not sure methods, true enough; sometimes they failed, but it did no harm to try them; Rama knew a hundred cases where they had succeeded. Alice listened too, and sometimes she said, "That is not right. In this country we do it another way." And Alice told how to keep a chicken from flopping when its head is cut off.

"Draw a cross on the ground first," Alice explained. "And when the head is off, lay the chicken gently on the cross, and it will never flop, because the sign is holy." Rama tried it later and found it true, and ever after that she had more tolerance for Catholics than she had before.

These were good times, filled with mystery and with ritual. Elizabeth watched Rama seasoning a stew. She tasted, smacking her lips and with a stern question in her eyes, "Is this just right? No, not quite." Nothing Rama ever cooked was as good as it should have been.

On Wednesdays, Rama came with a big mending basket on her arm, and behind her trooped those children who had been good. Alice and Rama and Elizabeth sat at three corners of a triangle, and the darning-eggs went searching in and out of socks.

In the center of the triangle the good children sat. (The bad ones were at home doing nothing, for Rama knew how idleness is a punishment to a child.) Rama told stories then, and after a while Alice grew brave and explained a good many miraculous things. Her father had seen a fiery goat crossing the Carmel Valley one night at dusk. Alice knew at least fifty ghost-stories, too; things not far away, but here in Nuestra Señora. She told how the Valdez family was visited All Souls' Eve by a great-great grandmother with a cough in her chest, and how Lieutenant-Colonel Murphy, killed by a troop of sad Yaquis on their way home to Mexico, rode through the valley holding his breast open to show he had no heart. The Yaquis had eaten it, Alice thought. These things were true and could be proved. Her eyes grew wide and frightened when she told the things. And at night the children had only to say, "He had no heart," or "The old lady coughed" to set themselves squealing with fear.

Elizabeth told some stories she had from her mother, tales of the Scotch fairies with their everlasting preoccupation with gold or at least some useful handicraft. They were good stories, but they hadn't the effect of Rama's stories, or Alice's, for they had happened long ago and in a far country which itself had little more reality than the fairies. You could go down the road and see the very place where Lieutenant-Colonel Murphy rode every three months, and Alice could promise to take you to a canyon where every night swinging lanterns plodded along with no one carrying them.

These were good times, and Elizabeth was very happy. Joseph didn't talk much, but she never passed him that his hand wasn't outstretched to caress her, and she never looked at him and failed to receive a slow calm smile that made her warm and happy. He seemed never to sleep completely, for no matter what time she awakened in the night and stretched an exploring hand toward him, he took her immediately in his arms. Her breasts filled out in these few months, and her eyes grew deep with mystery. It was an exciting time, for Alice was going to have a baby, and the winter was coming.

Benjy's house was vacant now. Two new Mexican riders moved out of the barn and occupied it. Thomas had caught a grizzly-bear cub in the hills and he was trying to tame it with very little success. "It's more like a man than an animal," Thomas said. "It doesn't want to learn." And although it bit him as often as he came near it, he was pleased to have the little bear, because everyone said there were no more grizzlies in the Coast Range mountains.

Burton was busy with inner preparation, for he was planning to go to the camp-meeting town of Pacific Grove and to spend the following summer. He rejoiced in advance at the good emotions to be found there. And he found within himself an exultation when he thought of the time when he would find Christ again and recite sins before a gathering of people.

"You can go to the common house in the evening," he told his wife. "Every evening the people will sing in the common house and eat ice-cream. We'll take a tent and stay a month, or maybe two." And he saw in advance how he would praise the preachers for the message.

15

It was early in November when the rain came. Every day in the morning Joseph searched the sky, studying the bulky rearing clouds, and again at evening he watched the sinking sun reddening the sky. And he thought of those prophetic nursery rhymes:

> "Red sky at morning,
> "Sailors take warning.
> "Red sky at night,
> "Sailors' delight."

and the other way around:

> "Red sky at morning,
> "Rain before dawning.
> "Red sky at night,
> "Clear days in sight."

He looked at the barometer more often than the clock, and when the needle swung down and down he was very happy. He went into the yard and whispered to the tree, "Rain in a few days now. It'll wash the dust off the leaves."

One day he shot a chicken hawk and hung it head downward high in the branches of the oak tree. And he took to watching the horses and the chickens closely.

Thomas laughed at him. "You won't bring it any quicker. You're watching the kettle, Joe. You may keep the rain away if you're too anxious." And Thomas said, "I'm going to kill a pig in the morning."

"I'll hang a cross-bar in the oak tree by my house to hang him on," said Joseph. "Rama will make the sausage, won't she?"

Elizabeth hid her head under a pillow while the pig was screaming, but Rama stood by and caught the throatblood in a milk bucket. And they weren't too soon, for the sides and hams were hardly in the new little stone smoke house before the rain came. There was no maneuvering this time. The wind blew fiercely for a morning, out of the southwest and the ocean, and the clouds rolled in and spread and dropped low until the mountain tops were hidden, and then the fat drops fell. The children stood in Rama's house and watched from the window. Burton gave thanks and helped his wife to give thanks, too, although she wasn't well. Thomas went to the barn and sat on a manger and listened to the rain on the barn roof. The piled hay was still warm with the sun of the summer slopes. The horses moved their feet restlessly and, twisting their heads against the halter ropes, tried to sniff the outside air through the little manure windows.

Joseph was standing under the oak tree when the rain started. The pig's blood he had dabbled on the bark was black and shiny. Elizabeth called to him from the porch, "It's coming now. You'll get wet," and he turned a laughing face to her.

"My skin is dry," he called. "I want to get wet." He saw the first big drops fall, thudding up dust in little spurts, then the ground was peppered with black drops. The rain thickened and a fresh wind slanted it. The sharp smell of dampened dust rose into the air, and then the first winter storm really began, raking through the air and drumming the roofs and knocking the weak leaves from the trees. The ground darkened; little rivulets started to edge out across the yard. Joseph stood with his head uplifted while the rain beat on his cheeks and on his eyelids and the water coursed into his beard and dripped into his open shirt collar, and his clothes hung heavily against him. He stood in the rain a long time to make sure it was not a little piddling shower.

Elizabeth called again: "Joseph, you'll take cold."

"No cold in this," he said. "This is healthy."

"You'll sprout weeds, then, out of your hair. Joseph, come in, there's a good fire going. Come in and change your clothes."

But still he stood in the rain, and only when the streaks of water were running down the oak trunk did he go in. "It will be a good year," he said. "The canyon streams will be flowing before Thanksgiving."

Elizabeth sat in the big leather chair; she had put a stew to simmering on the airtight stove. She laughed when he came in, there was such a feeling of joy in the air. "Why, you're dripping water on the floor, all over the clean floor."

"I know," he said. And he felt such a love for the land and for

Elizabeth that he strode across the room and rested his wet hand on her hair in a kind of benediction.

"Joseph, you're dripping water down my neck!"

"I know," he said.

"Joseph, your hand is cold. When I was confirmed, the bishop laid his hand on my head as you are doing, and his hand was cold. It ran shivers down my back. I thought it was the Holy Spirit." She smiled happily up at him. "We talked about it afterwards and all the other girls said it was the Holy Spirit. It was a long time ago, Joseph." She thought back to it, and in the middle of her long narrow picture of time lay the white pass in the mountains, and even it was a long way back in the picture of time.

He leaned over quickly and kissed her on the cheek. "The grass will be up in two weeks," he said.

"Joseph, there's nothing in the world as unpleasant as a wet beard. Your dry clothes are laid out on the bed, dear."

During the evening he sat in his rocking-chair beside the window. Elizabeth stole glances at his face, saw him frown with apprehension when the rain's drumming lightened, and smile slightly with reassurance when it continued again, harder than ever. Late in the evening Thomas came in, kicking and scraping his feet on the front porch.

"Well, it came all right," Joseph said.

"Yes, it came. Tomorrow we'll have to dig some ditches. The corral is under water. We'll have to drain it."

"There's good manure in that water, Tom. We'll run it down over the vegetable-flat."

The rain continued for a week, sometimes thinning to a mist and then pouring again. The drops bent down the old dead grass, and in a few days the tiny new spears came out. The river rumbled out of the western hills and rose over its banks, combing the willows down into the water and growling among the boulders. Every little canyon and crease in the hills sent out a freshet to join the river. The water-cuts deepened and spread in all the gullies.

The children, playing in the houses and in the barn, grew heartily sick of it before it was done; they plagued Rama for methods of amusement. The women had begun to complain about damp clothes hung up in their kitchens.

Joseph dressed in an oilskin and spent his days walking about the farm, now twisting a post-hole digger into the earth to see how deep the wet had gone, now strolling by the riverbank, watching the brush and logs and limbs go bobbing by. At night he slept lightly, listening to the rain or dozing, only to awaken when its force diminished.

And then one morning the sky was clean and the sun shone warmly. The washed air was sweet and clear, and all the leaves on the live oaks glittered with polish. And the grass was coming; anyone could see it, a richness in the color of the farther hills, a shade of blue in the near distance, and right at hand, the tiny green needles poking through the soil.

The children broke out of their cages like animals and played so furiously that they became feverish and had to go to bed.

Joseph brought out a plow and turned over the soil of the vegetable flat, and Thomas harrowed it and Burton rolled it. It was like a procession, each man eager to get his claws into the soil. Even the children begged a bit of dirt for radishes and carrots. Radishes were quickest, but carrots made the finest looking garden, if only they could wait that long. And all the time the grass pushed up and up. Needles became blades, and each blade sprang apart and made two blades. The ridges and flanks of the hills grew soft and smooth and voluptuous again, and the sage lost its dour darkness. In all the country, only the pine grove on the eastern ridge kept to its brooding.

Thanksgiving came with a great feast, and well before Christmas the grass was ankle-high.

One afternoon an old Mexican peddler walked into the farmyard, and he had good things in his pack; needles and pins and thread and little lumps of beeswax and holy pictures and a box of gum and harmonicas and rolls of red and green crêpe paper. He was an old bent man and carried only little things. He opened his pack on Elizabeth's front porch and then stood back, smiling apologetically, now and then turning over a card of pins to make it show to better advantage or prodding the gum gently with his forefinger to gain the attention of the gathered women. Joseph, from the barn door, saw the little crowd and sauntered over. Only then did the old man take off his tattered hat. "Buenas tardes, señor," he said.

"—Tardes," said Joseph.

The peddler grinned in extreme embarrassment. "You do not remember me, señor?"

Joseph searched the dark, lined face. "I guess I don't."

"One day," the old man said, "you rode by on the way from Nuestra Señora. I thought you were going hunting and I begged a piece of venison."

"Yes," Joseph said slowly. "I remember now. You are Old Juan."

The peddler tipped his head like an aged bird. "And then, señor—and then we spoke of a fiesta. I have been way down the country, below San Luis Obispo. Did you make that fiesta, señor?"

Joseph's eyes opened delightedly. "No, I did not, but I will. What would be a good time, Old Juan?"

The peddler spread his hands and pulled his neck between his shoulders at having so much honor put on him. "Why, señor—why in this country any time is good. But some days are better. There is Christmas, the Natividad."

"No," Joseph said. "It's too soon. There won't be time."

"Then there is the New Year, señor. That is the best time, because then everyone is happy and people go about looking for a fiesta."

"That's it!" Joseph cried. "On New Year's Day we'll have it."

"My son-in-law plays the guitar, señor."

"He shall come too. Who shall I invite, Old Juan?"

"Invite?" The old man's eyes filled with astonishment. "You do not 'invite,' señor. When I go back to Nuestra Señora I will tell that you make a fiesta on the New Year, and the people will come. Maybe the priest will come, with his altar in the saddle-bags, and hold the mass. That would be beautiful."

Joseph laughed up into the oak tree. "The grass will be so high by then," he said.

16

The day after Christmas, Martha, Rama's oldest girl, gave the other children a bad fright. "It will rain for the fiesta," she said, and because she was older than the others, a serious child who used her age and seriousness as a whip on the other children, they believed her and felt very badly about it.

The grass was deep. A spell of warm weather had sent it shooting up, and there were millions of mushrooms in the field, and puff-balls and toadstools too. The children brought buckets of mushrooms in, which Rama fried in a pan containing a silver spoon to test them for poison. She said that silver would turn black if a toadstool was present.

Two days before New Year, Old Juan appeared along the road, and his son-in-law, a smiling shiftless Mexican boy, walked directly behind him, for the son-in-law, Manuel, did not even like to take the responsibility of keeping out of ditches. The two of them stood smiling in front of Joseph's porch, caressing their hats against their chests. Manuel did everything Old Juan did, as a puppy imitates a grown dog.

"He plays the guitar," Old Juan said, and in proof, Manuel shifted the battered instrument around from his back and displayed it while he grinned agonizingly. "I told about the fiesta," Old Juan continued. "The people will come—four more guitars, señor, and father Angelo will come," (Here was the fine successful thing) "and he will hold mass right here! And I," he said proudly, "I am to build the altar. Father Angelo said so."

Burton's eyes grew sullen then. "Joseph, you won't have that, will you? Not on our ranch, not with the name we've always had."

But Joseph was smiling joyfully. "They are our neighbors, Burton, and I don't want to convert them."

"I won't stay to see it," Burton cried angrily. "I'll give no sanction to the Pope on this land."

Thomas chuckled. "You stay in the house, then, Burton. Joe and I aren't afraid of being converted, so we'll watch it."

There were a thousand things to be done. Thomas drove a wagon to Nuestra Señora and bought a barrel of red wine and a keg of whiskey. The vaqueros butchered three steers and hung the meat in the trees, and Manuel sat under the trees to keep the vermin off. Old Juan built an altar of boards under the great oak, and Joseph leveled and swept a dancing place in the farmyard. Old Juan was every place, showing the women how to make a tub of *salsa pura*. They had to use preserved tomatoes and chili and green peppers and some dried herbs that Old Juan carried in his pocket. He directed the digging of the cooking pits and carried the seasoned oak wood to the edges. Under the meat trees Manuel sat tiredly plucking the strings of his guitar, now and then breaking into a feverish melody. The children inspected everything, and were good, for Rama had let it be known that a bad child would stay in the house and see the fiesta from a window, a punishment so staggering that the children carried wood to the barbecue pits and offered to help Manuel watch the meat.

The guitars arrived at nine o'clock on New Year's Eve, four lank brown men with black straight hair and beautiful hands. They could ride forty miles, play their guitars for a day and a night and ride forty miles home again. They staggered with exhaustion after fifteen minutes behind a plow. With their arrival, Manuel came to life. He helped them to hang their precious saddle-bags out of harm and he spread their blankets for them in the hay, but they didn't sleep long; at three o'clock in the night, Old Juan built the fires in the pits, and then the guitars came out carrying their saddle-bags. They set four posts around the dancing place and took the fine things out of the saddle-bags: red and blue bunting and paper lanterns and ribbons. They worked in the leaping light from the barbecue pits, and well before day had built a pavilion.

Before daylight Father Angelo arrived on a mule, followed by a hugely packed horse and two sleepy altar boys riding together on a burro. Father Angelo went directly to work. He spread the service on Old Juan's altar, set up the candles, slapped the altar boys and set them running about. He laid the vestments out in the tool-shed and, last of all, brought out his figures. They were wonderful things, a crucifix and a mother and child. Father Angelo had carved and painted them himself and he had invented their peculiarities. They folded in the middle on hinges so carefully hidden that when they were set up the crack could not be seen; their heads screwed on, and the Child fitted into the Mother's arms with a peg that went into a slot. Father Angelo loved his figures, and they were very famous. Although they were three feet high, when folded both could fit into a saddle-bag. Besides being interesting mechanically, they were blessed and had the complete sanction of the archbishop. Old Juan had made separate stands for them, and he himself had brought a thick candle for the altar.

Before sunup the guests began to arrive, some of the richer families in surreys with swaying top fringes, the others in carts, buggies, wagons and on horseback. The poor whites came down from their scrabble ranch on King's Mountain on a sled half filled with straw and completely filled with children. The children arrived in droves and for a time stood about and stared at each other. The Indians walked up quietly and stood apart with stolid incurious faces, watching everything and never taking part in anything.

Father Angelo was a stern man where the church was concerned, but once out of the church, and with the matters of the church out of the way, he was a tender and a humorous man. Let him get a mouthful of meat, and a cup of wine in his hand, and there were no eyes that could twinkle more brightly than his. Promptly at eight o'clock he lighted the candles, drove out the altar boys and began the mass. His big voice rumbled beautifully.

Burton, true to his promise, remained in his house and held prayer with his wife, but even though he raised his voice he could not drown out the penetrating Latin.

As soon as the mass was done, people gathered close to watch Father Angelo fold up the Christ and the Mary. He did it well, genuflecting before each one before he took it down and unscrewed its head.

The pits were rosy with coals by now and the pit-sides glowed under the heat. Thomas, with more help than he needed, rolled the wine barrel up on a cradle and set a spiggot in its end and knocked the bung out. The huge pieces of meat hung over the fire and dripped their juices, and the coals jetted up white fire. This was prime beef, killed on the range and hung. Three men brought the tub of salsa out and went back for a wash boiler full of beans. The women carried sour bread like armloads of wood and stacked the golden loaves on a table. The Indians on the outskirts edged in closer, and the children, playing by now but still diffident, became a little insane with hunger when the meat smells began to fill the air.

To start the fiesta Joseph did a ceremonial thing Old Juan had told him about, a thing so ancient and so natural that Joseph seemed to remember it. He took a tin cup from the table and went to the wine cask. The red wine sang and sparkled into it. When it was full, he raised the cup level with his eyes and then poured it on the ground. Again he filled the cup, and this time drank it, in four thirsty gulps. Father Angelo nodded his head and smiled at the fine way in which the thing was done. When his ceremony was finished, Joseph walked to the tree and poured a little wine on its bark, and he heard the priest's voice speaking softly beside him: "This is not a good thing to do, my son."

Joseph whirled on him. "What do you mean?—There was a fly in the cup!"

But Father Angelo smiled wisely and a little sadly at him. "Be careful of the groves, my son. Jesus is a better saviour than a hamadryad." And his smile became tender, for Father Angelo was a wise as well as a learned man.

Joseph started to turn rudely away but then, uncertainly, he swung back. "Do you understand everything, Father?"

"No, my son," the priest said. "I understand very little, but the Church understands everything. Perplexing things become simple in the Church, and I understand this thing you do," Father Angelo continued gently. "It is this way: The Devil has owned this country for many thousands of years, Christ for a very few. And as in a newly conquered nation, the old customs are practiced a long time, sometimes secretly and sometimes changing slightly to comply with the tenor of the new rule, so here, my son, some of the old habits persist, even under the dominion of Christ."

Joseph said, "Thank you. The meat is ready now, I think."

At the pits the helpers were turning chunks of beef with pitchforks, and the guests, holding tin cups in their hands, had formed a line to the wine cask. First to be served were the guitars, and they drank whiskey, for the sun was high and their work was to be done. They wolfed their food, and while the other people were still eating, the guitars sat on boxes in a half-circle and played softly, bringing their rhythms together, feeling for a mood, so that when the dancing started they might be one passionate instrument. Old Juan, knowing the temper of music, kept their cups full of whiskey.

Now two couples entered the dancing place and stepped sedately through a formal dance, all bowings and slow turnings. The guitars ran trilling melodies into the throb of the beat. The line to the wine barrel formed again, and more couples entered the dancing space, these not so clever as the first few. The guitars sensed the change and took more heavily to the bass strings, and the rhythm grew stout and pounding. The space was filling now with guests who took little care to dance, but, standing arm in arm, thudded their feet on the earth. At the pits the Indians moved up and thanklessly took the bread and meat that was offered. They moved closer to the dancers, then, and gnawed the meat and tore at the hard bread with their teeth. As the rhythm grew heavy and insistent, the Indians shuffled their feet in time and their faces remained blank.

The music did not stop. On it went, and on, pounding and unchanging. Now and then one of the players plucked the unstopped strings while his left hand sought his whiskey cup. Now and then a dancer left the space to move to the wine barrel, toss off a cup and hurry back. There was no dancing in couples any more. Arms were outstretched to embrace everyone within reach, and knees were bent and feet pounded the earth to the slow beating of the guitars. The dancers began in low humming, one note struck deep in the throat, and in off-beat. A quarter-tone came in. More and more voices took up the beat and the quarter-tone. Whole sections of the packed dancing space were bobbing to the rhythm. The humming grew savage and deep and vibrant where at first there had been laughter and shouted jokes. One man had been notable for his height, another for the deepness of his voice; one woman had been beautiful, another ugly and fat, but that was changing. The dancers lost identity. Faces grew rapt, shoulders fell slightly forward, each person became a part of the dancing body, and the soul of the body was the rhythm.

The guitars sat like demons, slitted eyes glittering, conscious of their power yet dreaming of a greater power. And the strings rang on together. Manuel, who had grinned and smirked from embarrassment in the morning, threw back his head and howled a high shrill minor bar with meaningless words. The dancers chanted a deep refrain. The next player added his segment and the chant answered him.

The sun wheeled past meridian and slanted toward the hills, and a high wind soughed out of the west. The dancers, one by one, went back for meat and wine.

Joseph, with glowing eyes, stood apart. His feet moved slightly with the throbbing, and he felt tied to the dancing body, but he did not join it. He thought exultantly: "We have found something here, all of us. In some way we've come closer to the earth for a moment." He was strong with a pleasure as deep as the pounding bass strings, and he began to feel a strange faith arising in him. "Something will come of this. It's a kind of powerful prayer." When he looked at the western hills and saw a black cloud-head, high and ominous, coming over from the sea, he knew what was to come. "Of course," he said, "It will bring the rain. Something must happen when such a charge of prayer is let loose." He watched with confidence while the towering cloud grew over the mountains and stalked upward toward the sun.

Thomas had gone into the barn when the dancing started, for he was afraid of the wild emotion as an animal is afraid of thunder. The rhythm came into the barn to him now, and he stroked a horse's neck to soothe himself. After a time he heard a soft sobbing near him and, walking toward it, found Burton kneeling in a stall, whimpering and praying. Then Thomas laughed and caught himself back from fear. "What's the matter, Burton, don't you like the fiesta?"

Burton cried angrily, "It's devil-worship, I tell you! It's horrible! On our own place! First the devil-worshiping priest and his wooden idols, and then this!"

"What does it remind you of, Burton?" Thomas asked innocently.

"Remind me of? It reminds me of witchcraft and the Black Sabbath. It reminds me of all the devilish heathen practices in the world."

Thomas said, "Go on with your praying, Burton. Do you know what it puts me in mind of? Why only listen with your ears half open. It's like a camp meeting. It's like a great evangelist enlightening the people."

"It's devil-worship," Burton cried again. "It's unclean devil-worship, I tell you. If I had known, I would have gone away."

Thomas laughed harshly and went back to sit on his manger, and he listened to Burton's praying. It pleased Thomas to hear how Burton's supplication fell into the rhythm of the guitars.

As Joseph watched the swollen black cloud it seemed not to move, and yet it was eating up the sky, and all suddenly it caught and ate the sun. And so thick and powerful was the cloud that the day went to dusk and the mountains radiated a metallic light, hard and sharp. A moment after the sun had gone, a golden lance of lightning shot from the cloud, and the thunder ran, stumbling and falling, over the mountain tops—another quiver of light and a plunge of thunder.

The music and the dancing stopped instantly. The dancers looked upward with sleepy startled eyes, like children awakened and frightened by the grind of an earthquake. They stared uncomprehendingly for a moment, half-awake and wondering, before their reason came back. And then they scurried to the tied horses and began hooking up the surreys, fastening traces and tugs, backing their teams around the poles. The guitars stripped down the buntings and the unused lanterns and slipped them into the saddle-bags out of danger of the wet.

In the barn Burton arose to his feet and shouted triumphantly, "It's God's voice in anger!"

And Thomas answered him, "Listen again, Burton. It's a thunderstorm."

The glancing fires fell like rain from the great cloud now, and the air shook with the impact of thunder. In a few minutes the conveyances were moving out, a line of them toward the village of Our Lady and a few toward the hill ranches. Canvases were up against the coming rain. The horses snorted at the battering of the air and tried to run.

Since the beginning of the dance the Wayne women had sat on Joseph's porch holding a little aloof from the guests, as hostesses should. Alice had been unable to resist, and she had gone down to the dancing flat. But Elizabeth and Rama sat in rocking-chairs and watched the fiesta.

Now that the cloud had put a cap over the sky, Rama stood up from her chair and prepared to go. "It was a curious thing," Rama said. "You've been quiet today, Elizabeth. Be sure you don't take cold."

"I'm all right, Rama. I've felt a little dull today, with the excitement and the sadness. Ever since I can remember, parties have made me sad." All afternoon she had been watching Joseph where he had stood apart from the dancers. She had seen him looking at the sky. "Now he feels the rain." And when the thunder rolled over, "Joseph will like that. Storms make him glad." Now that the people were gone and the thunder had walked on over their heads, she continued to watch furtively the lonely figure of her husband.

The vaqueros were hustling the utensils and the remaining food under cover. Joseph watched until the first rain began to fall, and then he sauntered to the porch and sat on the top step, in front of Elizabeth; his shoulders slumped forward and his elbows rested on his knees. "Did you like the fiesta, Elizabeth?" he asked.

"Yes."

"Did you ever see one before?"

"I've seen fiestas before," she said, "but never one quite like this. Do you think all the electricity in the air might have made the people wild?"

He turned about and looked into her face. "More likely the wine in their stomachs, dear." His eyes narrowed seriously. "You don't look well, Elizabeth. Are you feeling well?" He stood up and leaned over her anxiously. "Come inside, Elizabeth, it's getting too cold to sit out here."

He went in ahead of her and lighted the lamp hung from a chain in the center of the room, and then he built up a fire in the stove and opened the draft until it roared softly up the chimney. The rain swished gustily on the roof, like a rough broom sweeping. In the kitchen Alice was humming softly in memory of the dance. Elizabeth sat down heavily in a rocking-chair by the stove. "We'll have a little, late supper, dear."

Joseph knelt on the floor beside her. "You look so tired," he said.

"It was the excitement; all the people. And the music was—well, it was strenuous." She paused, trying to think what the music and the dancing meant. "It was such an odd day," she said. "There was the outwardness, the people coming and the mass and the feasting and then the dance, and last of all the storm. Am I being silly, Joseph, or was there a meaning, right under the surface? It seemed like those pictures of simple landscapes they sell in the cities. When you look closely, you see all kinds of figures hidden in the lines. Do you know the kind of pictures I mean? A rock becomes a sleeping wolf, a little cloud is a skull, and the line of trees marching soldiers when you look closely. Did the day seem like that to you, Joseph, full of hidden meanings, not quite understandable?"

He was still kneeling, bending close to her in the low light of the lamp. He watched her lips intently, as though he could not hear. His hands stroked his beard roughly, and he nodded again and again. "You see closely, Elizabeth," he said sharply. "You look too deeply into things."

"And Joseph, you did feel it, didn't you? The meanings seemed to me to be a warning. Oh—I don't know how to say it."

He dropped back and sat on his heels and stared at the specks of light that came from the cracks in the stove. His left hand still caressed his beard, but his right moved up and rested on her knee. The wind cried shrilly in the oak tree over the house, and the stove ticked evenly as the fire died down a little.

Alice sang, "*Corono ale de flores que es cosa mia—*"

Joseph said softly, "You see, Elizabeth; it should make me less lonely that you can see under the covering, but it doesn't. I want to tell you, and I can't. I don't think these are warnings to us, but only indications how the world fares. A cloud is not a sign set up for men to see and to know that it will rain. Today was no warning, but you are right. I think there were things hidden in today." He licked his lips carefully. Elizabeth put out her hand to stroke his head. "The dance was timeless," Joseph said, "do you know?—a thing eternal, breaking through to vision for a day." He fell silent again, and tried to back his mind out of the heavy and vague meanings that rolled about it like grey coils of fog. "The people enjoyed it," he said, "everyone but Burton. Burton was miserable and afraid. I can never tell when Burton will be afraid."

She watched how his lips curved up for a moment in faint amusement. "Will you be hungry soon, dear? You can have your supper any time—just cold things, tonight." These were words to keep a secret in, she knew, but the secret came sneaking out before she could stop it.

"Joseph—I was sick this morning."

He looked at her compassionately. "You worked too hard at the preparation."

"Yes—maybe," she said. "No, Joseph, it isn't that. I didn't mean to tell you yet, but Rama says—do you think Rama knows? Rama says she is never wrong, and Rama should know. She's seen enough, and she says she can tell."

Joseph chuckled, "What does Rama know? You'll choke yourself on words in a moment."

"Well, Rama says I'm going to have a baby."

Her words fell into a curious silence. Joseph had settled back and he was staring at the stove again. The rain had stopped for a moment, and Alice was not singing.

Elizabeth gently, timorously broke into the silence. "Are you glad, dear?"

Joseph's breath broke heavily out. "More glad than I ever have been."—then, in a whisper, "and more afraid."

"What did you say dear? What was that last? I didn't hear."

He stood up and bent down over her. "You must take care," he said sharply. "I'll get a robe to go about your knees. Take care against cold, care against falling." He tucked a blanket about her waist.

She was smiling, proud and glad of his sudden worry. "I'll know what to do, dear, don't fear for me. I'll know. Why," she said confidently, "a whole plane of knowledge opens when a woman is carrying a child. Rama told me."

"See you take care then," he repeated.

She laughed happily. "Is the child so precious to you already?"

He studied the floor and frowned. "Yes—the child is precious, but not so precious as the bearing of it. That is as real as a mountain. That is a tie to the earth." He stopped, thinking of words for the feeling. "It is a proof that we belong here, dear, my dear. The only proof that we are not strangers." He looked suddenly at the ceiling. "The rain has stopped. I'll go to see how the horses are."

Elizabeth laughed at him. "Some place I've read or heard of a strange custom, maybe it's in Norway or Russia, I don't know, but wherever it is, they say the cattle must be told. When anything happens in a family, a birth or a death, the father goes to the barn and tells the horses and cows about it. Is that why you are going, Joseph?"

"No," he said. "I want to see that all the halter ropes are short."

"Don't go," she begged. "Thomas will look after the stock. He always does. Stay with me tonight. I'll be lonely if you go out tonight. Alice," she called, "will you set the supper now? I want you to sit beside me, Joseph."

She hugged his whole forearm against her breast. "When I was little a doll was given me, and when I saw it on the Christmas-tree an indescribable heat came into my heart. Before I ever took up the doll I was afraid for it, and filled with sorrow. I remember it so well! I was sorry the doll was mine, I don't know why. It seemed too precious, too agonizingly precious to be mine. It had real hair for eyebrows and real hair for lashes. Christmas has been like that every time since then, and this is a time like that. If this thing I have told you is true, it is too precious, and I am afraid. Sit with me, dear. Don't go walking in the hills tonight."

He saw that there were tears in her eyes. "Surely I'll stay," he comforted her. "You are too tired; and you must go to bed early from now on."

He sat with her all evening, and went to bed with her, but when her breathing was even he crept out and slipped on his clothes. She heard him going and lay still, pretending to be asleep. "He has some business with the night," she thought, and her mind reverted to what Rama had said. 'If he dreams you'll never know his dreams.' She went cold with loneliness, and shivered, and began to cry softly.

Joseph stepped quietly down from the porch. The sky had cleared, and the night sharpened with frost, but the trees still dripped water, and from the roof a tiny stream fell to the ground. Joseph walked straight to the great oak and stood beneath it. He spoke very softly, so no one could hear.

"There is to be a baby, sir. I promise that I will put it in your arms when it is born." He felt the cold wet bark, drew his fingertips slowly downward. "The priest knows," he thought. "He knows part of it, and he doesn't believe. Or maybe he believes and is fearful."

"There's a storm coming," he said to the tree. "I know I can't escape it. But you, sir, you might know how to protect us from the storm."

For a long time he stood, moving his fingers nervously on the black bark. "This thing is growing strong," he thought. "I began it because it comforted me when my father was dead, and now it is grown so strong that it overtops nearly everything. And still it comforts me."

He walked to the barbecue pit and brought back a piece of meat that remained on the grate. "There," he said, and reaching high up, laid the meat in the crotch of the tree. "Protect us if you can," he begged. "The thing that's coming may destroy us all." He was startled by footsteps near to him.

Burton's voice said, "Joseph, is it you?"

"Yes. It's late. What do you want?"

Burton advanced and stood close. "I want to talk to you, Joseph. I want to warn you."

"This is no time," Joseph said sullenly. "Talk to me tomorrow. I've been out to look at the horses."

Burton did not move. "You are lying, Joseph. You think you have been secret, but I have watched you. I've seen you make offerings to the tree. I've seen the pagan growth in you, and I come to warn you." Burton was excited and his breath came quick. "You saw the wrath of God this afternoon warning the idolators. It was only a warning, Joseph. The lightning will strike next time. I've seen you creeping out to the tree, Joseph, and I've remembered Isaiah's words. You have left God, and his wrath will strike you down." He paused, breathless from the torrent of emotion, and the anger died out of him. "Joseph," he begged, "come to the barn and pray with me. Christ will receive you back. Let us cut down the tree."

But Joseph swung away from him and shook off the hand that was put out to restrain him. "Save yourself, Burton," He laughed shortly. "You're too serious, Burton. Now go to bed. Don't interfere with my games. Keep to your own." He left his brother standing there, and crept back into the house.

17

The spring came richly, and the hills lay deep in grass—emerald green, the rank thick grass; the slopes were sleek and fat with it. Under the constant rains the river ran sturdily on, and its sheltering trees bowed under the weight of leaves and joined their branches over the river so that it ran for miles in a dim cavern. The farm buildings took a deep weathering in the wet winter; the pale moss started on the northerly roofs; the manure piles were crowned with forced grass.

The stock, sensing a great quantity of food shooting up on the sidehills, increased the bearing of young. Rarely did so many cows have two calves as during that spring. The pigs littered and there were no runts. In the barn only a few horses were tied, for the grass was too sweet to waste.

When April came, and warm grass-scented days, the flowers burdened the hills with color, the poppies gold and the lupins blue, in spreads and comforters. Each variety kept to itself and splashed the land with its color. And still the rain fell often, until the earth was spongy with moisture. Every depression in the ground became a spring, and every hole a well. The sleek little calves grew fat and were hardly weaned before their mothers received the bulls again.

Alice went home to Nuestra Señora and bore her son and brought it back to the ranch with her.

In May the steady summer breeze blew in from the sea, with salt and the faint smell of kelp. It was a springtime of work for the men. All the flat lands about the houses grew black under the plows, and the orderly, domestic seed sprouted the barley and the wheat. The vegetable-flat bore so copiously that only the finest fattest vegetables were taken for the kitchens; the pigs received every turnip of questionable shape and every imperfect carrot. The ground squirrels came out to squeak in their doorways, and they were fatter in the spring than fall usually found them. Out on the hills the foals tried practice leaps and fought among themselves while their dams looked on amusedly. When the warm rains fell, the horses and cows no longer sought the protection of the trees, but continued eating while the water streamed down their sides and made them as glossy as lacquer.

In Joseph's house there was a quiet preparation for the birth. Elizabeth worked on the layette for her baby, and the other women, well-knowing that this would be the chief child of the ranch and the inheritor of power, came to sit with her and to help. They lined a wash basket with quilted satin, and Joseph set it on rockers. They hemmed more rough diapers than one child could ever use. They made long baby-dresses and embroidered them. They told Elizabeth that she was having an easy time, for she was rarely ill; in fact, she grew more robust and happy as the time went by. Rama taught her how to quilt the cover for the lying-in bed, and Elizabeth made it as carefully as though it were to last her life, instead of being burned immediately after the child was born. Because this was Joseph's child, Rama added an unheard-of elegance. She made a thick velvet rope, with a loop on either end, to slip over the bed-posts. No other woman had pulled on anything but a twisted sheet during the bearing pains.

When warm weather came the women sat on the porch in the warm sun and went on with the sewing. They prepared everything months too soon. The heavy piece of unbleached muslin that was to bind Elizabeth's hips was made, and fringed and laid away. The small pillows stuffed with duck feathers and all the quilted coverlets were ready by the first of June.

And there was endless talk of babies—how they were born, and all the accidents that might occur, and how the memory of the pain fades from a woman's mind, and how boys differ from girls in their earliest habits. There was endless anecdote. Rama could recount stories of children born with tails, with extra limbs, with mouths in the middle of their backs; but these were not frightening because Rama knew why such things were. Some were the results of drink, and some of disease, but the worst, the very worst monstrosities came of conception during a menstrual period.

Joseph walked in sometimes with grass-blades in the laces of his shoes and green grass stains on the knees of his jeans and sweat still shining on his forehead. He stood stroking his beard and listening to the talk. Rama appealed to him occasionally for corroboration. Joseph was working tremendously in the prodigal spring. He cut the bull calves, moved rocks out of the flowers' way, and went out with his new branding-iron to burn his "JW" into the skins of the stock. Thomas and Joseph worked silently together, stringing the barbed-wire fences out around the land, for it was easy to dig post-holes in a wet spring. Two more vaqueros were hired to take care of the increasing stock.

In June the first heat struck heavily and the grass responded and added a foot to its growth. But with the breathless days, Elizabeth grew sick and irritable. She made a list of things needed for the birth and gave it to Joseph. One morning before the sun was up he drove away in the buckboard to buy the things for her in San Luis Obispo. The trip and return required three days of traveling.

The moment he was gone, fears began to fall upon Elizabeth: Maybe he would be killed. The most unreasonable things seemed to possess verity. He might meet another woman and run off with her. The wagon might overturn in the white pass and throw him into the river.

She had not got up to see him off, but when the sun was up she dressed and went to sit on the porch. Everything irritated her, the noise of grasshoppers ticking as they flew, the pieces of rusty baling wire lying on the ground. The smell of ammonia from the barns nearly nauseated her. When she had seen and hated all the things close to her, she raised her eyes to the hills for more prey, and the first thing she saw was the pine grove on the ridge. Immediately a sharp nostalgia for Monterey assailed her, a homesickness for the dark trees of the peninsula, and for the little sunny streets and for the white houses and for the blue bay with colored fishing boats; but more than anything for the pines. The resinous odor of the needles seemed the most delicious thing in the world. She longed to smell it until her body ached with desire. And all the time she looked at the black pine grove on the ridge.

Gradually the desire changed until she wanted only the trees. They called down to her from their ridge, called for her to come in among the trunks, out of the sun, and to know the peace that lay in a pine forest. She could see herself, and even feel herself lying on a pine needle bed, looking up at the sky between the boughs, and she could hear how the wind would swish softly in the tops of the trees, and go flying away, laden with the pine scent.

Elizabeth stood up from the steps and walked slowly toward the barn. Someone was in there, for she could see forkfuls of manure come bursting through the windows. She walked into the dark sweet barn and approached Thomas. "I want to go for a little ride," she said. "Would you mind hitching up a buggy for me?"

He leaned on the manure-fork. "Will you wait half an hour? When I finish this I will drive you."

She was angry at his interference. "I want to drive myself, I want to be alone," she said shortly.

He regarded her quietly. "I don't know whether Joseph would like you to go out alone."

"But Joseph isn't here. I want to go."

He leaned his fork against the wall then. "All right, I'll hitch up old Moonlight. She's gentle. Don't go off the road, though, you might get stuck in the mud. It's still pretty deep in some of the hollows."

He helped her into the buggy and stood apprehensively watching her as she drove away.

Instinctively Elizabeth knew he didn't want her to go to the pines. She drove a good distance from the house before she turned the old white mare's head up the hill and went bumping over the uneven ground. The sun was very hot and the valley windless. She had driven a long way up the hill before a deep water-cut stopped her progress. In both directions the crevass extended, too far to go around, and the pines were only a short distance away. Elizabeth climbed from the buggy, snapped the tie-strap around a root and unhooked the check-rein. Then she clambered down into the cut and up the other side, and walked slowly toward the pine grove. In a moment she came upon a little twinkling stream that ran from the forest and flowed quietly because there were no stones to bar its way. She stooped and pulled a sprig of cress out of the water and nibbled it as she sauntered upward beside the stream.

All of her irritation was gone now; she went happily forward and entered the forest. The deep needle beds muffled her footsteps and the forest swallowed every other sound except the whispering of the needles in the tree-tops. For a few moments she walked on, unimpeded, and then the screen of vines and brambles barred her way. She turned her shoulder to them and forced a passage through, and sometimes she crawled through an opening on her hands and knees. There was a demand upon her that she penetrate deep into the forest.

Her hands were scratched and her hair pulled down when she came at last through the bramble wall and straightened up. Her eyes grew wide with wonder at the circle of trees and the clear flat place. And then her eyes swept to the huge, misshapen green rock.

She whispered to herself, "I think I knew it was here. Something in my breast told me it was here, this dear good thing." There was no sound at all in the place except the high whispering of the trees, and it was shut out, which only made the silence deeper, more impenetrable. The green moss covering of the rock was as thick as fur, and the long ferns hung down over the little cavern in its side like a green curtain. Elizabeth seated herself beside the tiny stream, slipping secretly away across the glade, and disappearing into the underbrush. Her eyes centered upon the rock and her mind wrestled with its suggestive shape. "Some place I've seen this thing," she thought. "I must have known it was here, else why did I come straight to it?" Her eyes widened as she watched the rock, and her mind lost all sharp thought and became thronged with slowly turning memories, untroubled, meaningless and vague. She saw herself starting out for Sunday School in Monterey, and then she saw a slow procession of white-dressed Portuguese children marching in honor of the Holy Ghost, with a crowned queen leading them. Vaguely she saw the waves driving in from seven different directions to meet and to convulse at Point Joe near Monterey. And then as she gazed at the rock she saw her own child curled head-downward in her womb, and she saw it stir slightly, and felt its movement at the same time.

Always the whispering went on over her head and she could see out of the corners of her eyes how the black trees crowded in and in on her. It came upon her as she sat there that she was alone in all the world; every other person had gone away and left her and she didn't care. And then it came upon her that she could have anything she wished, and in the train of this thought there came the fear that she most wished for death, and after that, for a knowledge of her husband.

Her hand moved slowly from her lap and fell into the cold water of the spring, and instantly the trees rushed back and the low sky flew upward. The sun had leaped forward as she sat there. There was a rustling in the forest now, not soft but sharp and malicious. She looked quickly at the rock and saw that its shape was as evil as a crouched animal and as gross as a shaggy goat. A stealthy cold had crept into the glade. Elizabeth sprang to her feet in panic, and her hands rose up and held her breasts. A vibration of horror was sweeping through the glade. The black trees cut off escape. There was the great rock crouching to spring. She backed away, fearing to take her eyes from it. When she had reached the entrance of the broad trail, she thought she saw a shaggy creature stir within the cave. The whole glade was alive with fear. She turned and ran down the trail, too frightened to scream, and she came, after a great time, to the open, where the warm sun shone.

The forest closed behind her and left her free.

She sat down, exhausted, by the little stream; her heart throbbed painfully and her breath came in gasps. She saw how the stream gently moved the cress that grew in its water, and she saw the mica specks glittering in the sand at the bottom. Then, turning for protection, she looked down on the clustered farm buildings where they were drenched with sun, and on the yellowing grass that bowed in long, flat silver waves before the afternoon wind. These were safe things; she was grateful for having seen them.

Before her fear was gone, she scrambled up to her knees to pray. She tried to think what had happened in the glade, but the memory of it was fading. "It was an old thing, so old that I have nearly forgotten it." She recollected her posture, "It was an unlawful thing." And she prayed, "Our Father which art in Heaven, hallowed be Thy name—" And she prayed, "Lord Jesus protect me from these forbidden things, and keep me in the way of light and tenderness. Do not let this thing pass through me into my child, Lord Jesus. Guard me against the ancient things in my blood." She remembered how her father said his ancestors a thousand years ago followed the Druidic way.

When the prayer was done, she felt better. A clear light entered her mind again and drove out the fear, and with it, a memory of the fear. "It's my condition," she said. "I should have known. Nothing was in that place except my imagination. Rama has told me often enough what kind of things to expect."

She stood up then, reassured and comforted. And as she strolled down the hill she picked an armful of the late flowers to decorate the house against Joseph's return.

18

The summer heat was very great. Every day the sun beat down on the valley, sucking the moisture from the earth, drying the grass and causing every living thing to seek the deep shade of the sage thickets on the hills. All day the horses and cattle lay there, waiting for the night so they might come out for their feeding. The ranch dogs sprawled on the ground, with their quivering dripping tongues falling out of the sides of their mouths and their chests pumping like bellows. Even the noisy insects let the middle of the day be silent. At the meridian there was only a faint whine of rocks and earth, too fiercely scorched. The river receded until it was only a little stream, and when August came, even that disappeared.

Thomas was cutting the hay and shocking it to cure, while Joseph picked out the cattle for sale and drove them into the new corral. Burton prepared for his trip to Pacific Grove to attend the camp-meetings. He piled a tent, utensils, bedding and food in the buckboard, and one morning he and his wife set out behind two good horses to drive the ninety miles to the camp-ground. Rama had agreed to take care of his children for the three weeks of his absence.

Elizabeth came out to wave him off, and she was glowing with health again. After her little spell of illness, she had grown beautiful and well. Her cheeks were red with coursing blood and her eyes shone with a mysterious happiness. Often Joseph, watching her, wondered what she knew or what she thought to make her seem always on the verge of laughter. "She knows something," he said to himself. "Women in this condition have a strong warmth of God in them. They must know things no one else knows. And they must feel a joy beyond any other joy. In some way they take up the nerve-ends of the earth in their hands." Joseph regarded her narrowly, and stroked his beard as slowly as an old man would.

With her coming time, Elizabeth grew increasingly possessive of her husband. She wanted him to sit with her all day and all evening, and she complained a little when he told her of the work to be done. "I'm idle here," she said. "Idleness loves company."

And he replied, "No, you're working." He could see in his mind how she was doing it. Her helpless hands lay crossed in her lap, but her bones were casting bones and her blood was distilling blood and her flesh was moulding flesh. He laughed shortly at the thought that she was idle.

In the evenings when she demanded that he sit with her, she put out her arm to be stroked. "I'm afraid you'll go away," she said. "You might go out by that door and never come back, and then there'd be no father for the baby."

One day when they were sitting on the porch she asked abruptly, "Why do you love the tree so much, Joseph? Remember how you made me sit in it the first time I ever came out here?" She looked up to the high crotch where she had sat.

"Why, it's a fine big tree," he explained slowly. "I like it because it's a perfect tree, I guess."

She caught him up, then. "Joseph, there's more than that. One night I heard you speak to it as though it were a person. You called it 'sir', I heard you."

He looked fixedly at the tree before he answered, and then after a while he told her how his father had died wanting to come West, and he told her about the morning when the letter came. "It's a kind of a game, you see," he said. "It gives me a feeling that I have my father yet."

She turned her wide-set eyes on him, eyes full of wisdom of child bearing. "It isn't a game, Joseph," she said gently. "You couldn't play a game if you wanted to. No, it isn't a game, but it's a good practice." And for the first time she saw into her husband's mind; all in a second she saw the shapes of his thoughts, and he knew that she saw them. The emotion rushed to his throat. He leaned to kiss her, but instead, his forehead fell upon her knees, and his chest filled to breaking.

She stroked his hair and smiled her wise smile. "You should have let me see before." And then she said, "But likely I hadn't proper eyes before."

When he lay with her at night and she rested her head on his arm for a little time before they went to sleep, she begged night after night to be reassured. "When my time comes, Joseph, you'll stay with me? I'm afraid I'll be afraid. I'm afraid I'll call and you won't be near. You won't be far away, will you? And if I call, you'll come?"

And he assured her, a little grimly, "I'll be with you, Elizabeth. Don't be worried about that."

"But not in the same room, Joseph. I wouldn't like you to see it. I don't know why. If you could be sitting in the other room and listening in case I should call, then I don't think I'd be afraid at all."

Sometimes in these nights in bed she told him of the things she knew, how the Persians invaded Greece and were beaten, and how Orestes came to the tripod for protection, and the Furies sat waiting for him to get hungry and let go his hold. She told them laughingly, all her little bits of knowledge that were designed to make her superior. All of her knowledge seemed very silly to her now.

She began to count the weeks until her time—three weeks from Thursday; and then two weeks and one day; and then, just ten days off. "This is Friday. Why, Joseph, it will be on a Sunday. I hope it will. Rama has listened. She says she can even hear the heartbeats. Would you believe that?"

One night she said, "It'll be just about a week now. I get little shivers when I think about it."

Joseph slept very lightly. When Elizabeth sighed in her sleep, his eyes opened and he listened uneasily.

One morning he awakened when the chorus of young roosters crowed on their perches. It was still dark, but the air was alive with the coming dawn and with the freshness of the morning. He heard the older cocks crowing with full rounded notes as though reproving the younger ones for their cracked thin voices. Joseph lay with his eyes open and saw the myriad points of light come in and make the air dark grey. Gradually the furniture began to appear. Elizabeth was breathing shortly in her sleep. A slight catch was in her breath. Joseph prepared to slip out of the bed, to dress and to go out to the horses, when suddenly Elizabeth sprang upright beside him. Her breath stopped and then her legs stiffened and she screamed with pain.

"What is it?" he cried. "What's the matter, dear?"

When she didn't answer he jumped up and lighted the lamp and bent over her. Her eyes were bulging and her mouth had dropped open and her whole body quivered tensely. Then she screamed hoarsely again. He fell to rubbing her hands, until, after a moment, she dropped back on the pillow.

"There's a pain in my back, Joseph," she moaned. "Something's wrong. I'm going to die."

He said, "Just a moment, dear. I'm going for Rama," and he ran out of the room.

Rama, aroused from sleep, smiled gravely. "Go back to her," she commanded. "I'll be right over. It's a little sooner than I thought. She'll be all right for a while now."

"But hurry," he demanded.

"There's no hurry. You'll start walking her right away. I'll get Alice to help now."

The dawn was flushing when the two women came across the yard, their arms full of clean rags. Rama took charge immediately. Elizabeth, still shocked by the sharpness of the pain, looked helplessly at her.

"It's all right," Rama reassured her. "It's just as it should be." She sent Alice to the kitchen to build a fire and to heat a wash-boiler of water. "Now Joseph, help her to her feet, help her to walk." And while he walked her back and forth across the room, Rama slipped the covers from the bed and put the quilted birth pad down and hooked the loops of the velvet rope over the foot posts. When the blighting pain struck again, they let her sit in a straight chair until it was over. Elizabeth tried not to scream, until Rama leaned over her and said, "Don't hold it in. There's no need. Everything you feel like doing is needful now."

Joseph, with his arm around her waist, walked her back and forth across the room, supporting her when she stumbled. He had lost his fear. There was a fierce glad light in his eyes. The pains came closer and closer together. Rama brought the big Seth Thomas clock in from the sitting-room and hung it on the wall, and she looked at it every time the pains came. And the pains grew closer and closer together. The hours passed.

It was nearly noon when Rama nodded her head sharply. "Now let her lie down. You can go out now, Joseph. I'll be getting my hands ready."

He looked at her with half-closed eyes. He seemed entranced. "What do you mean, 'getting your hands ready'?" he demanded.

"Why washing and washing in hot water and soap, and cutting the nails close."

"I'll do it," he said.

"It's time for you to go, Joseph. The time is short."

"No," he said sullenly. "I'll take my own child. You tell me what to do."

"You can't, Joseph. It's not a thing for a man to do."

He looked gravely at her, and her will gave away before his calm. "It's a thing for me to do," he said.

As soon as the sun had risen the children congregated outside the bedroom window, where they stood listening to Elizabeth's weak screaming, and shivering with interest. Martha took charge from the first. "Sometimes they die," she said.

Although the morning sun beat fiercely upon them, they did not leave their post. Martha laid down the rules. "First one that hears the baby cry says, 'I hear it!' and that one gets a present, and that one gets the first baby. Mother told me." The others were very much excited. They cried in unison, "I hear it," every time a new series of screams began. Martha made them help her to climb up where she could peek quickly into the window. "Uncle Joseph is walking with her," she reported. And later, "Now she's lying on the bed and she's holding the red rope that mother made."

The screams grew ever closer together. The other children helped Martha to look again, and she came down a little pale and choking at what she had seen. They gathered close about her for the report. "I saw—Uncle Joseph—and he was leaning over—" She paused to get her breath. "And—and his hands were *red.*" She fell silent and all the children stared at her in amazement. There wasn't any more talking or whispering. They simply stood and listened. The screams were so weak by now that they could barely hear them.

Martha wore a secret look. She cautioned the others to silence in a whisper. They heard three faint smacks, and instantly Martha cried, "I hear it." And even a little after, they all heard the baby cry. They stood in awe, looking at Martha.

"How did you know when to say it?"

Martha was tantalizing. "I'm the oldest, and I've been good for a long time. And mother told me how to listen."

"How?" they demanded. "How did you listen?"

"For the spank!" she said in triumph. "They always spank the baby to make it cry. I won, and I want a hair-doll for a present."

A little later Joseph came out on the porch and leaned over the porch-rail. The children moved over and stood in front of him and looked up. They were disappointed that his hands were not still red. His face was so drawn and haggard and his eyes so listless that they hated to speak to him.

Martha began, lamely, "I heard the first cry," she said. "I want a hair-doll for a present."

He looked down on them and smiled slightly. "I'll get it for you," he said. "I'll have presents for all of you when I go to town."

Martha asked politely, "Is it a boy-baby, or a girl-baby?"

"A boy," Joseph said. "Maybe you can see it after a while." His hands were clenched tightly over the porch-rail, and his stomach still racked with the pains he had received from Elizabeth. He took a deep breath of the hot midday air and went back into the house.

Rama was washing out the baby's toothless mouth with warm water while Alice set the safety pins in the strip of muslin that would bind Elizabeth's hips after the placenta came. "Only a little while yet," Rama said. "It will be over in an hour."

Joseph sat heavily in a chair and watched the women, and he watched the dull, pained eyes of Elizabeth, filled with suffering. The baby lay in its basket-crib, dressed in a gown twice as long as itself.

When the birth was all over, Joseph lifted Elizabeth and held her in his lap while the women took up the foul birth pad and made the bed again. Alice took out all the rags and burned them in the kitchen stove, and Rama pinned the bandage around Elizabeth's hips as tightly as she could pull it.

Elizabeth lay wanly in the clean bed after the women had gone. She put out her hand for Joseph to take. "I've been dreaming," she said weakly. "Here's a whole day gone and I've been dreaming."

He caressed her fingers, one at a time. "Would you like me to bring the baby to you?"

Her forehead wrinkled in a tired frown. "Not yet," she said. "I still hate it for making so much pain. Wait until I've rested a while." Soon after that she fell asleep.

Late in the afternoon Joseph walked out to the barn. He barely looked at the tree as he passed it. "You are the cycle," he said to himself, "and the cycle is too cruel." He found the barn carefully cleaned, and every stall deep with new straw. Thomas was sitting in his usual place, on the manger of Blue's stall. He nodded shortly to Joseph.

"My coyote bitch has a tick in her ear," he observed. "Devil of a place to get it out."

Joseph walked into the stall and sat down beside his brother. He rested his chin heavily in his cupped hands.

"What luck?" Thomas asked gently.

Joseph stared at a sun-sheet cutting the air from a crack in the barn wall. The flies blazed through it like meteors plunging into the earth's air. "It is a boy," he said absently. "I cut the cord myself. Rama told me how. I cut it with a pair of scissors and I tied a knot, and I bound it up against his chest with a bandage."

"Was it a hard birth?" Thomas asked. "I came out here to keep from going in to help."

"Yes, it was hard, and Rama said it was easy. God, how the little things fight against life!"

Thomas plucked a straw from the rack behind him and stripped it with his bared teeth. "I never saw a human baby born. Rama would never let me. I've helped many a cow when she couldn't help herself."

Joseph moved restlessly down from the manger and walked to one of the little windows. He said over his shoulder, "It's been a hot day. The air's dancing over the hills yet." The sun, sinking behind the hills, was melting out of shape. "Thomas, we've never been over the ridge to the coast. Let's go when we have time. I'd like to see the ocean over there."

"I've been to the ridge and looked down," Thomas said. "It's wild over there, redwoods taller than anything you ever saw, and thick undergrowth, and you can see a thousand miles out on the ocean. I saw a little ship going by, half-way up the ocean."

The evening was setting quickly toward night. Rama called, "Joseph, where are you?"

He walked quickly to the barn door. "I'm here. What is it?"

"Elizabeth is awake again. She wants you to sit with her a while. Thomas, your dinner will be ready in a little."

Joseph sat beside Elizabeth's bed in the half-dark, and again she put out her hand to him. "You wanted me?" he asked.

"Yes, dear. I haven't slept enough, but I want to talk to you before I go to sleep again. I might forget what it is I want to say. You must remember for me."

It was getting dark in the room. Joseph lifted her hand to his lips and she wriggled her fingers slightly against his mouth.

"What is it, Elizabeth?"

"Well, when you were away, I drove up to the pine grove on the ridge. And I found a clear place inside, and a green rock in the place." He sat forward tensely. "Why did you go?" he demanded.

"I don't know. I wanted to. The green rock frightened me, and later I dreamed of it. And Joseph, when I am well, I want to go back and look at the rock again. When I am well it won't frighten me any more, and I won't dream about it any more. Will you remember, dear? You're hurting my fingers, Joseph."

"I know the place," he said. "It's a strange place."

"And you won't forget to take me there?"

"No," he said after a pause. "I won't forget. I'll have to think whether you should go."

"Then sit for a while, I'll go to sleep in a few moments," she said.

19

The summer dragged wearily on, and even when the autumn months came the heat did not grow less. Burton came back exalted from the camp-meeting town of Pacific Grove. He described with enthusiasm the lovely peninsula and the blue bay, and he told how the preachers had given the word to the people. "Some time," he said to Joseph, "I'll go up there and build a little house, and I'll live there all the year around. A number of people are settling there. It will be a fine town some day."

He was pleased with the baby. "It's our stock," he said, "just a little changed." And he boasted to Elizabeth, "Ours is a strong stock. It comes out every time. For nearly two hundred years now the boys have had those eyes."

"They aren't far from the color of my eyes," Elizabeth protested. "And besides, babies' eyes change color as they get older."

"It's the expression," Burton explained. "There's always the Wayne expression in the eyes. When will you have him baptized?"

"Oh, I don't know. Maybe we'll be going to San Luis Obispo before very long, and of course I'd like to go home to Monterey for a visit some time."

The day's heat came early over the mountains and drove the chickens from their morning talking on manure piles. By eleven it was unpleasant to be out in the sun, but before eleven, Joseph and Elizabeth often took chairs out of the house and sat under the shading limbs of the great oak. Elizabeth engaged in the morning nursing then, for Joseph liked to watch the baby sucking at the breast.

"It doesn't grow as fast as I thought it would," he complained.

"You're too used to the cattle," she reminded him. "They grow so much more quickly, and they don't live very long."

Joseph silently contemplated his wife. "She's grown so wise," he thought. "Without any study she has learned so many things." It puzzled him. "Do you feel very much different from the girl who came to teach school in Nuestra Señora?" he asked.

She laughed. "Do I seem different, Joseph?"

"Why, of course."

"Then I suppose I am." She changed the breast and shifted the baby to the other knee, and he struck hungrily at the nipple, like a trout at a bait. "I'm split up," Elizabeth went on. "I hadn't really thought of it. I used to think in terms of things I had read. I never do now. I don't think at all. I just do things that occur to me. What will his name be, Joseph?"

"Why," he said, "I guess it will be John. There has always been either a Joseph or a John. John has always been the son of Joseph, and Joseph the son of John. It has always been that way."

She nodded, and her eyes looked far away. "Yes, it's a good name. It won't ever give him any trouble or make him embarrassed. It hasn't even much meaning. There have been so many Johns—all kinds of men, good and bad." She took the breast away and buttoned her dress, and then turned the baby to pat the air bubbles out of him. "Have you noticed, Joseph, Johns are either good or bad, never neutral? If a neutral boy has that name, he doesn't keep it. He becomes Jack." She turned the baby around, to look in its face, and it squinted its eyes like a little pig. "Your name is John, do you hear?" she said playfully. "Do you hear that? I hope it never gets to be Jack. I'd rather you were very bad than Jack."

Joseph smiled amusedly at her. "He has never sat in the tree, dear. Don't you think it's about time?"

"Always your tree!" she said. "You think everything moves by order of your tree."

He leaned back to look up into the great tender branches. "I know it now, you see," he said softly. "I know it now so well that I can look at the leaves and tell what kind of a day it will be. I'll make a seat for the baby up in the crotch. When he's a little older I may cut steps in the bark for him to climb on."

"But he might fall and hurt himself."

"Not from that tree. It wouldn't let him fall."

She looked penetratingly at him. "Still playing the game that isn't a game, Joseph?"

"Yes," he said, "still playing. Give the baby to me now. I'll put him in the arms." The leaves had lost their shine under a coat of summer dust. The bark was pale gray and dry.

"He might fall, Joseph," she warned him. "You forget he can't sit up by himself."

Burton strolled up from the vegetable-patch and stood with them, wiping his wet forehead with a bandana. "The melons are ripe," he said. "The 'coons are getting at them, too. We'd better set some traps."

Joseph leaned toward Elizabeth with his hands outstretched.

"But he might fall," she protested.

"I'll hold him. I won't let him fall."

"What are you going to do with him?" Burton asked.

"Joseph wants to sit him in the tree."

Instantly Burton's face grew hard, and his eyes sullen. "Don't do it, Joseph," he said harshly. "You must not do it."

"I won't let him fall. I'll hold him all the time."

The perspiration stood in large drops on Burton's forehead. Into his eyes there came a look of horror and of pleading. He stepped forward and put a restraining hand on Joseph's shoulder. "Please don't do it," he begged.

"But I won't let him fall, I tell you."

"It isn't that. You know what I mean. Swear to me that you won't ever do it."

Joseph turned on him irritably. "I'll swear nothing," he said. "Why should I swear? I see nothing wrong in what I do."

Burton said quietly, "Joseph, you have never heard me beg for anything. It isn't the manner of our family to beg. But now I am begging you to give up this thing. If I am willing to do that, you must see how important it is." His eyes were wet with emotion.

Joseph's face softened. "If it bothers you so much, I won't do it," he said.

"And will you swear never to do it?"

"No, I won't swear. I won't give up my thing to your thing. Why should I?"

"Because you're letting evil in," Burton cried passionately. "Because you are opening the door to evil. A thing like this will not go unpunished."

Joseph laughed. "Then let me take the punishment," he said.

"But don't you see, Joseph, it isn't only you! All of us will be in the ruin."

"You're protecting yourself, then, Burton?"

"No I'm trying to protect all of us. I'm thinking of the baby, and of Elizabeth here."

Elizabeth had been staring from one to the other of them. She stood up and held the baby against her breast. "What are you two arguing about?" she demanded. "There's something in this I don't know about."

"I'll tell her," Burton threatened.

"Tell her what? What is there to tell?"

Burton sighed deeply. "On your head, then. Elizabeth, my brother is denying Christ. He is worshipping as the old pagans did. He is losing his soul and letting in the evil."

"I'm denying no Christ," Joseph said sharply. "I'm doing a simple thing that pleases me."

"Then the hanging of sacrifices, the pouring of blood, the offering of every good thing to this tree is a simple thing? I've seen you sneak out of the house at night, and I've heard you talk to this tree. Is that a simple thing?"

"Yes, a simple thing," Joseph said. "There's no hurt in it."

"And the offering of your own first-born child to the tree—is that a simple thing, too?"

"Yes, a little game."

Burton turned away and looked out over the land, where the heat waves were so intense that they were blue in color and their twisting made the hills seem to writhe and shudder. "I've tried to help you," he said sadly. "I've tried harder than Scripture tells us to." He swung back fiercely. "You won't swear, then?"

"No," Joseph replied. "I won't swear to anything that limits me, that cuts down my activity. Surely I won't swear."

"Then I cast you out." Burton's hands hid in his pockets. "Then I won't stay to be involved."

"Is what he says true?" Elizabeth asked. "Have you been doing what he says?"

Joseph gazed moodily at the ground. "I don't know." His hand arose to caress his beard. "I don't think so. It doesn't sound like the thing I have been doing."

"I've seen him," Burton cut in. "Night after night I've seen him come out into the dark under the tree. I've done what I can. Now I am going away from this wrong."

"Where will you go, Burton?" Joseph asked.

"Harriet has three thousand dollars. We'll go to Pacific Grove and build a house there. I'll sell my part of the ranch. Maybe I'll open a little store. That town will grow, I tell you."

Joseph stepped forward, as though to intercept his resolve. "I'll be sorry to think I've driven you away," he said.

Burton stood over Elizabeth and looked down at the child. "It isn't only you, Joseph. The rot was in our father, and it was not dug out. It grew until it possessed him. His dying words showed how far he had gone. I saw the thing even before you ever started for the West. If you had gone among people who knew the Word and were strong in the Word, the thing might have died—but you came here." His hands swept out to indicate the country. "The mountains are too high," he cried. "The place is too savage. And all the people carry the seed of this evil thing in them. I've seen them, and I know. I saw the fiesta, and I know. I can only pray that your son will not inherit the rot."

Joseph resolved quickly. "I will swear if you will stay. I don't know how I'll keep it, but I'll swear. Sometimes, you see, I might forget and think in the old way."

"No, Joseph, you love the earth too much. You give no thought to the hereafter. The force of an oath is not strong in you." He moved away toward his house.

"Don't go at least until we talk this over," Joseph called, but Burton did not turn nor answer him.

Joseph looked after him for a minute before he turned back to Elizabeth. She was smiling with a kind of contemptuous amusement. "I think he wants to go," she said.

"Yes, that's partly it. And he really is afraid of my sins, too."

"Are you sinning, Joseph?" she asked.

He scowled in thought. "No," he said at last. "I'm not sinning. If Burton were doing what I am, it would be sin. I only want my son to love the tree." He stretched out his hands for the baby, and Elizabeth put the swathed little body in his hands. Burton looked back as he was entering his house, and he saw that Joseph was holding the baby within the crotch of the tree, and he saw how the gnarled limbs curved up protectingly about it.

20

Burton did not stay long on the ranch after his mind was made up. Within a week he had his things packed and ready. On the night before his departure he worked late, nailing the last of the boxes. Joseph heard him walking about in the night, chopping and hammering, and before daylight he was up again. Joseph found him in the barn, currying the horses he was to take, while Thomas sat nearby on a pile of hay and offered some short advice.

"That Bill will tire soon. Let him rest every little while until he gets well warm. This team has never been through the pass. You may have to lead them through—but maybe not, now that the water is so low."

Joseph strolled in and leaned against the wall, under the lantern. "I'm sorry you're going, Burton," he said.

Burton arrested his curry-comb on the horse's broad rump. "There are a good many reasons for going. Harriet will be happier in a little town where she can have friends to drop in on. We were too cut off out here. Harriet has been lonely."

"I know," Joseph said gently, "but we'll miss you, Burton. It will cut the strength of the family."

Burton dropped his eyes uneasily and went back to currying. "I've never wanted to be a farmer," he said lamely. "Even at home I thought of opening a little store in town." His hands stopped working. He said passionately. "I've tried to lead an acceptable life. What I have done I have done because it seemed to me to be right. There is only one law. I have tried to live in that law. What I have done seems right to me, Joseph. Remember that. I want you to remember that."

Joseph smiled affectionately at him. "I'm not trying to keep you here if you want to go, Burton. This is a wild country. If you do not love it, there's only hatred left. You've had no church to go to. I don't blame you for wanting to be among people who carry your own thoughts."

Burton moved to the next stall. "It's turning light," he said nervously. "Harriet is getting breakfast. I want to start as soon after daylight as I can."

The families and the riders came out into the dawn to watch Burton start away.

"You'll come to see us," Harriet called sadly. "It's nice up there. You must come to visit us."

Burton took up the lines, but before he clucked to the horses, he turned to Joseph. "Good-bye. I've done right. When you come to see it, you'll know it was right. It was the only way. Remember that, Joseph. When you come to see it, you'll thank me."

Joseph moved close to the wagon and patted his brother's shoulder. "I offered to swear, and I would have tried to keep the oath."

Burton raised the lines and clucked. The horses strained into the collars. The children, sitting on the load, waved their hands, and those who were to stay ran behind and hung to the tail-board and dragged their feet.

Rama stood waving a handkerchief, but she said aside to Elizabeth, "They wear out more shoes that way then by all the walking in the world."

Still the family stood in the morning sunlight and watched the departing wagon. It disappeared into the river wood, and after a while it came in sight again, and they saw it mount a little hill and finally drop from sight over the ridge.

When it was gone a listlessness came over the families. They stood silently, wondering what they should do now. They were conscious that a period was over, that a phase was past. At length the children moved slowly away.

Martha said, "Our dog had puppies last night," and they all ran to see the dog, which hadn't had puppies at all.

Joseph turned away at last, and Thomas walked with him. "I'm going to bring in some horses, Joe," he said. "I'm going to level part of the vegetable-flat so the water won't all run off."

Joseph walked slowly, with his head down. "You know I'm responsible for Burton's going."

"No you aren't. He wanted to go."

"It was because of the tree," Joseph went on. "He said I worshipped it." Joseph's eyes raised to the tree, and suddenly he stood still, startled. "Thomas, look at the tree!"

"I see it. What's the matter?"

Joseph walked hurriedly to the trunk and looked up at the branches. "Why, it seems all right." He paused and ran his hand over the bark. "That was funny. When I looked at it, I thought something was wrong with it. It was just a feeling, I guess." And he continued, "I didn't want Burton to go away. It splits the family."

Elizabeth passed behind them, toward the house. "Still at the game, Joseph?" she called mockingly.

He jerked his hand from the bark and turned to follow her. "We'll try to get along without another hand," he told Thomas. "If the work gets too much for us, I'll hire another Mexican." He went into the house and stood idly in the sitting-room.

Elizabeth came out of the bedroom, brushing her hair back with her fingertips. "I hardly had time to dress," she explained. She looked quickly at Joseph. "Are you feeling badly about having Burton go?"

"I think I am," he said uncertainly. "I'm worried about something, and I don't know what it is."

"Why don't you ride? Haven't you anything to do?"

He shook his head impatiently. "I have fruit trees coming to Nuestra Señora. I should go in for them."

"Why don't you go, then?"

He walked to the front door and looked out at the tree. "I don't know," he said. "I'm afraid to go. There's something wrong."

Elizabeth stood beside him. "Don't play your game too hard, Joseph. Don't let the game take you in."

He shrugged his shoulders. "That's what I'm doing, I guess. I told you once I could tell weather by the tree. It's a kind of ambassador between the land and me. Look at the tree, Elizabeth! Does it seem all right to you?"

"You're overwrought," she said. "The tree is all right. Go in and get the fruit trees. It won't do them any good to be standing out of ground."

But it was with a powerful reluctance to leave the ranch that he hitched up the buckboard and drove to town.

It was the time of flies, when they became active before the winter death. They cut dazzling slashes in the sunlight, landed on the horses' ears and sat in circles around their eyes. Although the morning had been cool with the sharpness of autumn, the Indian-summer sun still burned the land. The river had disappeared underground, while in the few deep pools that remained, the black eels swam sluggishly and big trout mouthed the surface without fear.

Joseph drove his team at a trot over the crisp sycamore leaves. A foreboding followed him and enveloped him. "Maybe Burton was right," he thought. "Maybe I've been doing wrong without knowing it. There's an evil hanging over the land." And he thought, "I hope the rain comes early and starts the river again."

The dry river was a sad thing to him. To defeat the sadness he thought of the barn, piled to the rooftrees with hay, and of the haystacks by the corral, all thatched against the winter. And then he wondered whether the little stream in the pine grove still ran from its cave. "I'll go up and see pretty soon," he thought. He drove quickly, and hurried back to the ranch, but it was late at night when he arrived. The tired horses hung down their heads when the checkreins were loosened.

Thomas was waiting at the stable entrance. "You drove too fast," he said. "I didn't expect you back for a couple of hours."

"Put up the horses, will you?" Joseph asked. "I'll pump some water on these little trees." He carried an armload of the switches to the tank and saturated their burlap root-coverings with water. And then he went quickly toward the oak tree. "There *is* something wrong with it," he thought fearfully. "There's no life in it." He felt the bark again, picked off a leaf, crumpled and smelled it, and nothing appeared wrong.

Elizabeth had his supper ready almost as soon as he went into the house. "You look tired, dear. Go to bed early."

But he looked over his shoulder with worried eyes. "I want to talk to Thomas after supper," he said.

And when he had done eating, he walked out past the barn and up on the hillside. He felt with his palms the dry earth, still warm from the day's sun. And he walked to a copse of little live oaks and rested his hands on the bark and crushed and smelled a leaf of each. Everywhere he went, inquiring with his fingers after the earth's health. The cold was coming in over the mountains, chilling the grasses, and on this night Joseph heard the first flight of wild geese.

The earth told him nothing. It was dry but alive, needing only the rain to make it shoot its spears of green. At last, satisfied, he walked back to the house and stood under his own tree. "I was afraid, sir," he said. "Something in the air made me afraid." And as he stroked the bark, suddenly he felt cold and lonely. "This tree is dead," his mind cried. "There's no life in my tree." The sense of loss staggered him, and all the sorrow he should have felt when his father died rolled in on him. The black mountains surrounded him, and the cold grey sky and the unfriendly stars shut him down, and the land stretched out from the center where he stood. It was all hostile, not ready to attack but aloof and silent and cold. Joseph sat at the foot of the tree, and not even the hard bark held any comfort for him. It was as hostile as the rest of the earth, as frigid and contemptuous as the corpse of a friend.

"Now what will I do?" he thought. "Where will I go now?" A white meteor flared into the air and burned up. "Perhaps I'm wrong," Joseph thought. "The tree may be all right after all." He stood up and went into the house; and that night, because of his loneliness, he held Elizabeth so fiercely in his arms that she cried out in pain and was very glad.

"Why are you so lonely, dear?" she asked. "Why do you hurt me tonight?"

"I didn't know I was hurting you, I am sorry," he said. "I think my tree is dead."

"How could it be dead? Trees don't die so quickly, Joseph."

"I don't know how. I think it is dead."

She lay quietly after a while, pretending to be asleep. And she knew he was not sleeping.

When the dawn came he slipped out of bed and went outside. The oak leaves were a little shriveled and some of their glossiness was gone.

Thomas, on his way to the stable, saw Joseph and walked over. "By George, there is something wrong with that tree," he said. Joseph watched anxiously while he inspected the bark and the limbs. "Nothing to kill it here," Thomas said. He picked up a hoe and dug into the soft earth at the base of the trunk. Only two strokes he made, and then stepped back. "There it is, Joseph."

Joseph knelt down beside the hole and saw a chopped path on the trunk. "What did it?" he demanded angrily.

Thomas laughed brutally. "Why, Burton girdled your tree! He's keeping the devil out."

Joseph frantically dug around with his fingers until the whole path of the girdle was exposed. "Can't we do something, Thomas? Wouldn't tar help it?"

Thomas shook his head. "The veins are cut. There's nothing to do," he paused,—"except beat Hell out of Burton."

Joseph sat back on his heels. Now that it was done, the muffling calm settled over him, the blind inability to judge. "That was what he was talking about, then, about being right?"

"I guess it was. I'd like to beat Hell out of him. That was a fine tree."

Joseph spoke very slowly, as though he pulled each word out of a swirling mist. "He wasn't sure he was right. No, he wasn't sure. It wasn't quite his nature to do this thing. And so he will suffer for it."

"Won't you do anything at all to him?" Thomas demanded.

"No." The calm and the sorrow were so great that they bore down on his chest, and the loneliness was complete, a circle impenetrable. "He will punish himself. I have no punishments." His eyes went to the tree, still green, but dead. After a long time he turned his head and looked up to the pine grove on the ridge, and he thought, "I must go there soon. I'll be needing the sweetness and the strength of that place."

21

The cold of late autumn came into the valley, and the high brindled clouds hung in the air for days at a time. Elizabeth felt the golden sadness of the approaching winter, but there was missing the excitement of the storms. She went often to the porch to look at the oak tree. The leaves were all pale tan by now, waiting only the buffeting of rain to fall to the ground. Joseph did not look at the tree any more. When its life was gone, no remnant of his feeling for it remained. He walked often in the brittle grass of the side-hills. He went bareheaded, wearing jeans and a shirt and a black vest. Often he looked up at the grey clouds and sniffed at the air and found nothing in the air to reassure him. "There's no rain in these clouds," he told Thomas. "This is a high fog from the ocean."

Thomas had caught two baby hawks in the spring and he was making hoods for them and preparing to fly them against the wild ducks that whistled down the sky. "It isn't time, Joseph," he said. "Last year the rains came early, I know, but I've heard it isn't usual in this country to get much rain before Christmas."

Joseph stooped and picked up a handful of ash-dry dust and let it trickle through his fingers. "It'll take a lot of rain to do any good," he complained. "The summer drank the water out deep down. Have you noticed how low the water is in the well? Even the potholes in the river are dry now."

"I've smelled the dead eels," Thomas said. "Look! This little leather cap goes on the hawk's head to keep him blind until I'm ready to start him. It's better than shooting ducks." The hawk gashed at his thick gloves while he fitted the leather hood on its head.

When November came and went without rain, Joseph grew quiet with worry. He rode to the springs and found them dried up, and he drove his post-hole digger deep into the ground without finding damp soil. The hills were turning grey as the covering of grass wore off, and the white flints stuck out and caught the light. When December was half gone, the clouds broke and scattered. The sun grew warm and an apparition of summer came to the valley.

Elizabeth saw how the worry was making Joseph thin, how his

eyes were strained and almost white. She tried to find tasks to keep him busy. She needed new cupboard space, new clothes lines; it was time a high-chair was made ready for the baby. Joseph went about the tasks and finished them before Elizabeth could think of new ones. She sent him to town for supplies, and he returned on a wet and panting horse.

"Why do you rush back?" she demanded.

"I don't know. I'm afraid to go away. Something might happen." Slowly in his mind there was arising the fear that the dry years had come. The dusty air and the high barometer did not reassure him. Head colds broke out among the people on the ranch. The children sniffled all day long. Elizabeth developed a hard cough, and even Thomas, who was never sick, wore a cold compress made of a black stocking on his throat at night. But Joseph grew leaner and harder. The muscles of his neck and jaws stood out under a thin covering of brown skin. His hands grew restless, went to playing with pieces of stick, or with a pocket-knife, or worked interminably at his beard, smoothing it down and turning the ends under.

He looked about his land and it seemed to be dying. The pale hills and fields, the dust-grey sage, the naked stones frightened him. On the hills only the black pine grove did not change. It brooded darkly, as always, on the ridge top.

Elizabeth was very busy in the house. Alice had gone home to Nuestra Señora to take up her rightful position as a sad woman whose husband would return some day. She carried the affair with dignity, and her mother received compliments upon Alice's fine restraint and decent mourning. Alice began every day as though Juanito would return by evening.

The loss of her helper made more work for Elizabeth. Caring for her child, washing and cooking filled her days. She remembered the time before her marriage only hazily, and with a good deal of contempt. In the evenings, when she sat with Joseph, she tried to reestablish the fine contact she had made before the baby was born. She liked to tell him things that had happened when she was a little girl in Monterey, although the things didn't seem real to her any more. While Joseph stared moodily at the spots of fire that showed through the little windows of the stove, she talked to him.

"I had a dog," she said. "His name was Camille. I used to think that was the loveliest name in the world. I knew a little girl who was named Camille, and the name fitted her. She had a skin with the softness of camellias, so I named my dog after her, and she was very angry." Elizabeth told how Tarpey shot a squatter and was hanged to the limb of a tree on the fish flats; and she told of the lean stern woman who kept the lighthouse at Point Joe. Joseph liked to hear her soft voice, and he didn't usually listen to her words, but he took her hand and explored it all over with his fingertips.

Sometimes she tried to argue him out of his fear. "Don't worry about the rain. It will come. Even if there isn't much water this year, there will be in another year. I know this country, dear."

"But it would take so much rain. There won't be time if it doesn't start pretty soon. The rain will get behind in the year."

One evening she said, "I think I'd like to ride again. Rama says it won't hurt me now. Will you ride with me, dear?"

"Of course," he said. "Begin a little at a time. Then it won't hurt you."

"I'd like to have you ride up to the pines with me. The smell of pines would be good."

He looked slowly over at her. "I've thought of going there, too. There's a spring in the grove, and I want to see if it is dried up like all the rest." His eyes grew more animated as he thought of the circle in the pines. The rock had been so green when he saw it last. "That must be a deep spring, I don't see how it could dry up," he said.

"Oh I have more reasons than that for wanting to go," she said laughing. "I think I told you something about it. When I was carrying the baby I deceived Thomas one day and drove up to the pines. And I went into that central place where the big rock is, and where the spring is." She frowned, trying to remember the thing exactly. "Of course," she said, "my condition was responsible for what happened. I was oversensitive."

She glanced up to find Joseph eagerly looking at her. "Yes?" he said. "Tell me."

"Well, as I say, it was my condition. When I was carrying the child, little things grew huge. I didn't find the path, going in. I broke my way through the underbrush, and then I came into the circle. It was quiet, Joseph, more quiet than anything I've ever known. I sat in front of the rock because that place seemed saturated with peace. It seemed to be giving me something I needed." In speaking of it, the feeling came back to her. She brushed her hair over her ears, and the wide-set eyes looked far off. "And I loved the rock. It's hard to describe. I loved the rock more than you or the baby or myself. And this is harder to say: While I sat there I went into the rock. The little stream was flowing out of me and I was the rock, and the rock was—I don't know—the rock was the strongest dearest thing in the world." She looked nervously about the room. Her fingers picked at her skirt. The thing she had intended to tell as a joke was forcing itself back upon her.

Joseph took up her nervous hand and held the fingers still. "Tell me," he insisted gently.

"Well, I must have stayed there quite a while, because the sun moved, but it seemed only a moment to me. And then the feeling of the place changed. Something evil came into it." Her voice grew husky with the memory. "Something malicious was in the glade, something that wanted to destroy me. I ran away. I thought it was after me, that great crouched rock, and when I got outside, I prayed. Oh, I prayed a long time."

Joseph's light eyes were piercing. "Why do you want to go back there?" he demanded.

"Why don't you see?" she replied eagerly. "The whole thing was my condition. But I've dreamed about it several times and it comes often to my mind. Now that I'm all well again, I want to go back, and see that it is just an old moss-covered rock in a clearing. Then I won't dream about it any more. Then it won't threaten me any more. I want to touch it. I want to insult it because it frightened me." She released her fingers from Joseph's grip and rubbed them to ease the pain in them. "You've hurt my hand, dear. Are you afraid of the place, too?"

"No," he said. "I'm not afraid. I'll take you up there." He fell silent, wondering whether he should tell her what Juanito had said about the pregnant Indian women who went to sit in front of the rock, and about the old ones who lived in the forest. "It might frighten her," he thought. "It is better that she should lose her fear of the place." He opened the stove and threw in an armful of wood and turned the damper straight, to set the flame roaring. "When would you like to go?" he asked.

"Why, any time. If the day is warm tomorrow, I'll pack a lunch into a saddle bag. Rama will take care of the baby. We'll have a picnic." She spoke eagerly. "We haven't had a picnic since I've been here. I don't know anything I love more. At home," she said, "we took our lunches to Huckleberry Hill, and after we'd eaten, mother and I picked buckets of berries."

"We'll go there tomorrow," he agreed. "I'm going to look in at the barn now, dear."

As she watched him leave the room, she knew that he was concealing something from her. "Probably it's only his worry about the rain," she thought, and from habit she turned her eyes to the barometer and saw that the needle was high.

Joseph stepped down from the porch. He moved close to the oak tree before he realized that it was dead. "If only it were alive," he thought, "I would know what to do. I have no counsel any more." He walked on into the barn, expecting to find Thomas there, but the barn was dark and the horses snorted at him as he walked behind them. "There's plenty of hay for the stock this year," he thought. The knowledge comforted him.

The sky was misty clear when he went back across the yard. He thought he could see a pale ring around the moon, but it was so faint that he could not be sure.

Before sunup the next morning Joseph went to the barn, curried two horses and brushed them, and, as a last elegance, painted their hoofs black and rubbed their coats with oil.

Thomas came in while he was at work. "You're making considerable fuss," he said. "Going to town?"

Joseph rubbed the oil in until the skins shone like dull metal. "I'm taking Elizabeth to ride," he announced. "She hasn't been on a horse for a long time."

Thomas rubbed his hand down one of the shining rumps. "I wish I could go with you, but I've work to do. I'm taking the men down to the river-bed to dig a hole. We may have trouble finding water for the cattle pretty soon."

Joseph stopped his work and looked worriedly at Thomas. "I know it. But there must be water under the river-bed. You should strike it a few feet down."

"It'll rain pretty soon, Joseph. I hope it will. I'm getting sick of a dusty throat."

The sun came up behind a high thin film of cloud that sucked the warmth and paled the light. Over the hills there came a cold steady wind that blew the dust to ripples and made little drifts of yellow

fallen leaves. It was a lonely wind, scudding along the ground, flowing evenly, with very little sound.

After breakfast Joseph led out the saddle-horses, and Elizabeth,
in her divided skirt and high-heeled boots, came out of the house
carrying a bag of lunch.

"Take a warm coat," Joseph warned her.

She lifted her face to the sky. "It's winter at last, isn't it, Joseph?
The sun has lost its heat."

He helped her on her horse and she laughed because of the good
feeling of the saddle, and she patted the flat horn-top affectionately.
"It's good to be able to ride again," she said. "Where shall we go
first?"

Joseph pointed to a little peak on the eastern ridge above the
pines. "If we go to the top of that we can look through the pass of
the Puerto Suelo and see the ocean," he said. "And we can see the
tops of the redwoods."

"It's good to feel the horse moving," she repeated. "I've been
missing it, and I didn't know."

The flashing hoofs kicked up a fine white dust which stayed in
the air after they had passed, and made a path behind them like the
smoke of a train. They rode up the gentle slope through the thin
spare grass, and at the water cuts they went down and up again with
a quick jerk.

"Remember how the cuts raced with water last year?" she reminded him. "Pretty soon it'll be that way again."

Far off on a hillside they saw a dead cow, almost covered by slow
gluttonous buzzards. "I hope we don't get to windward of that,
Joseph."

He looked away from the feast. "They don't give meat a chance
to spoil," he said. "I've seen them standing in a circle around a dying
animal, waiting for the moment of death. They know that moment."

The hill grew steeper, and they entered the crackling sage, dark
and dry and leafless now. The twigs were so brittle that they seemed
dead. In an hour they came to the peak, and from there, sure enough,
they saw the triangle of ocean through the pass. The ocean was not
blue, it was steel-grey, and on the horizon the dark fog banks rose
in heavy ramparts.

"Tie up the horses, Joseph," she said. "Let's sit a while. I haven't
seen the ocean for so long. Sometimes I wake up in the night and

listen for the waves and for the foghorn of the lighthouse, and the bell buoy off China Point. And sometimes I can hear them, Joseph. They must be very deeply fixed in me. Sometimes I can hear them. In the mornings, early, when the air was still, I remember how I could hear the fishing boats pounding out and the voices of the men calling back and forth from boat to boat."

He turned away from her. "I haven't that to miss," he said. These things of hers seemed like a little heresy to him.

She sighed deeply. "When I hear those things in my head I get homesick, Joseph. This valley traps me and I have the feeling that I can never escape from it and that I'll never really hear the waves again, nor the bell buoy, nor see the gulls sliding on the wind."

"You can go back to visit any time," he said gently. "I'll take you back."

But she shook her head. "It wouldn't ever be the same. I can remember how excited I was at Christmas, but I couldn't be again."

He lifted his head and sniffed the wind. "I can smell the salt," he said. "I shouldn't have brought you here, Elizabeth, to make you sad."

"But it's a good full sadness, dear. It's a luxurious sadness. I can remember how the pools were in the early morning at low tide, glistening and damp, the crabs scrambling over the rocks, and the little eels under the round stones. Joseph," she asked, "Can't we eat lunch now?"

"It isn't nearly noon yet. Are you hungry already?"

"I'm always hungry at a picnic," she said smiling. "When mother and I went up to Huckleberry Hill we sometimes started to eat lunch before we were out of sight of the house. I'd like to eat while I'm up here."

He walked to the horses and loosened their cinches and brought back the saddle bags, and he and Elizabeth munched the thick sandwiches and stared off at the pass and at the angry ocean beyond.

"The clouds seem to be moving in," she observed. "Maybe there'll be rain tonight."

"It's only fog, Elizabeth. It's always fog this year. The earth is turning white. Do you see? The brown is going out of it."

She chewed her sandwich and gazed always at the little patch of sea. "I remember so many things," she said. "They pop up in my mind suddenly, like ducks in a shooting gallery. I just thought then how the Italians go out on the rocks at low tide with big slabs of bread in their hands. They crack open the sea urchins and spread part of them on the bread. The males are sweet and the females sour—the urchins, not the Italians, of course." She scrunched up the papers from the lunch and wadded them back into the saddle bag. "We'd better ride on now, dear. It won't do to stay out very long."

Although there had been no movement of the clouds, the haze was thickening about the sun and the wind grew colder. Joseph and Elizabeth walked their horses down the slope. "You still want to go to the pine grove?" he asked.

"Why of course. That's the main reason for the trip. I'm going to scotch the rock." As she spoke a hawk shot from the air with doubled fists. They heard the shock of flesh, and in a second the hawk flew up again, bearing a screaming rabbit in its claws. Elizabeth dropped her reins and covered her ears until the sound was out of hearing. Her lip trembled. "It's all right; I know it is. I hate to see it, though."

"He missed his stroke," Joseph said. "He should have broken its neck with the first blow, but he missed." They watched the hawk fly to the cover of the pine grove and disappear among the trees.

They had not far to go, down a long slope and then along the ridge until they came at last to the outpost trees. Joseph pulled up. "We'll tie the horses here and walk in," he said. When they were afoot, he hurried ahead to the little stream. "It isn't dry," he called. "It isn't down a bit."

Elizabeth walked over and stood beside him. "Does that make you feel better, Joseph?"

He glanced quickly at her, feeling a little mockery in her words, but he could see none in her face. "It's the first running water I've seen for a long time," he said. "It's as though the country were not dead while this stream is running. This is like a vein still pumping blood."

"Silly," she said, "you come from a country where it rains often. See how the sky is darkening, Joseph. I wouldn't be surprised if it should rain."

He glanced upward. "Only fog," he said. "But it will be cold soon. Come, let's go in."

The glade was silent, as always, and the rock was still green. Elizabeth spoke loudly to break the silence. "You see, I knew it was only my condition that made me afraid of it."

"It must be a deep spring to be still running," Joseph said. "And the rock must be porous to suck up water for the moss."

Elizabeth leaned down and looked into the dark cave from which the stream flowed. "Nothing in there," she said. "Just a deep hole in the rock, and the smell of wet ground." She stood up again and patted the shaggy sides of the rock. "It's lovely moss, Joseph. See how deep." She pulled out a handful and held up the damp black roots for him to see. "I'll never dream of you any more," she said to the rock. The sky was dark grey by now, and the sun had gone.

Joseph shivered and turned away. "Let's start for home, dear. The cold's coming." He strolled toward the path.

Elizabeth still stood beside the rock. "You think I'm silly, don't you, Joseph," she called. "I'll climb up on its back and tame it." She dug her heel into the steep side of the mossy rock, and made a step and pulled herself up, and then another.

Joseph turned around. "Be careful you don't slip," he called.

Her heel dug for a third step. And then the moss stripped off a little. Her hands gripped the moss and tore it out. Joseph saw her head describe a little arc and strike the ground. As he ran toward her, she turned slowly on her side. Her whole body shuddered violently for a second, and then relaxed. He stood over her for an instant before he ran to the spring and filled his hands with water. But when he came back to her, he let the water fall to the ground, for he saw the position of her neck, and the grey that was stealing into her cheeks. He sat stolidly on the ground beside her, and mechanically picked up her hand and opened the fingers clenched full of pine needles. He felt for her pulse and found none there. Joseph put her hand gently down as though he feared to awaken her. He said aloud, "I don't know what it is." The icy chill was creeping inward upon him. "I should turn her over," he thought. "I should take her home." He looked at the black scars on the rock where her heels had dug a moment before. "It was too simple, too easy, too quick," he said aloud. "It was too quick." He knew that his mind could not grasp what had happened. He tried to make himself realize it. "All the stories, all the incidents that made the life were stopped in a second—opinions stopped, and the ability to feel, all stopped without any meaning." He wanted to make himself know what happened, for he could feel the beginning of the calm settling upon him. He wanted to cry out once in personal pain before he was cut off and unable to feel sorrow or resentment. There were little stinging drops of cold on his head. He looked up and saw that it was raining gently. The drops fell on Elizabeth's cheeks and flashed in her hair. The calm was settling on Joseph. He said, "Good-bye, Elizabeth," and before the words were completely out he was cut off and aloof. He removed his coat and laid it over her head. "It was the one chance to communicate," he said. "Now it is gone."

The pattering rain was kicking up little explosions of dust in the glade. He heard the faint whisper of the stream as it stole across the flat and disappeared into the brush. And still he sat by the body of Elizabeth, loath to move, muffled in the calm. Once he stood up and touched the rock timidly, and looked up at its flat top. In the rain a vibration of life came into the place. Joseph lifted his head as though he were listening, and then he stroked the rock tenderly. "Now you are two, and you are here. Now I will know where I must come."

His face and beard were wet. The rain dripped into his open shirt. He stooped and picked up the body in his arms and supported the sagging head against his shoulder. He marched down the trail and into the open.

There was a dull rainbow in the east, fastened by its ends to the hills. Joseph turned the extra horse loose to follow. He slung his burden to one shoulder while he mounted his horse, and then settled the loose bundle on the saddle in front of him. The sun broke through and flashed on the windows of the farm buildings below him. The rain had stopped now; the clouds withdrew toward the ocean again. Joseph thought of the Italians on the rocks, cracking sea urchins to eat on their bread. And then his mind went back to a thing Elizabeth had said ages before. "Homer is thought to have lived nine hundred years before Christ." He said it over and over, "before Christ, before Christ. Dear earth, dear land! Rama will be sorry. She can't know. The forces gather and center and become one and strong. Even I will join the center." He shifted the bundle to rest his arm. And he knew how he loved the rock, and hated it. The lids drew halfway down over his eyes with fatigue. "Yes, Rama will be sorry. She will have to help me with the baby."

Thomas came into the yard to meet Joseph. He started to ask a question, and then, seeing how tight and grey Joseph's face was, he advanced quietly and held up his arms to take the body. Joseph dismounted wearily, caught the free horse and tied it to the corral fence. Thomas still stood mutely, holding the body in his arms.

"She slipped and fell," Joseph explained woodenly. "It was only a little fall. I guess her neck is broken." He reached out to take the burden again. "She tried to climb the rock in the pines," he went on. "The moss skinned off. Just a little fall. You wouldn't believe it. I thought at first she had only fainted. I brought water before I saw."

"Be still!" Thomas said sharply. "Don't talk about it now." And Thomas withheld the body from him. "Go away, Joseph, I'll take care of this. Take your horse and ride. Go into Nuestra Señora and get drunk."

Joseph received the orders and accepted them. "I'll go to walk along the river," he said. "Did you find any water today?"

"No."

Thomas turned away and walked toward his own house, carrying the body of Elizabeth. For the first time that he could remember, Thomas was crying. Joseph watched him until he climbed the steps, and then he walked away at a quick pace, nearly a run. He came to the dry river and hurried up it, over the round smooth stones. The sun was going down in the mouth of the Puerto Suelo, and the clouds that had rained a little towered in the east like red walls and threw back a red light on the land and made the leafless trees purple. Joseph hurried on up the river. "There was a deep pool," he thought. "It couldn't be all dry, it was too deep." For at least a mile he went up the stream bed, and at last he found the pool, deep and brown and ill-smelling. In the dusk-light he could see the big black eels moving about in slow convolutions. The pool was surrounded on two sides by round, smooth boulders. In better times a little waterfall plunged into it. The third side gave on a sandy beach, cut and trampled with the tracks of animals; the dainty spear-heads of deer and the pads of lions and the little hands of racoons, and over everything the miring spread of wild pigs' hoofs. Joseph climbed to the top of one of the water-worn boulders and sat down, clasping one knee in his arms. He shivered a little with the cold, although he did not feel it. As he stared down into the pool, the whole day passed before him, not as a day, but as an epoch. He remembered little gestures he had not known he saw. Elizabeth's words came back to him, so true in intonation, so complete in emphasis that he thought he really heard them again. The words sounded in his ears.

"This is the storm," he thought. "This is the beginning of the thing I knew. There is some cycle here, steady and quick and unchangeable as a fly-wheel." And the tired thought came to him that if he gazed into the pool and cleaned his mind of every cluttering picture he might come to know the cycle.

There came a sharp grunting from the brush. Joseph lost his thought and looked toward the beach. Five lean wild pigs and one great curved-tusked boar came into the open and approached the water. They drank cautiously, and then wading noisily into the water they began to catch the eels and to eat them while the slimy fish slapped and struggled in their mouths. Two pigs caught one eel and squalling angrily tore it in two, and each chewed up its portion. The night was almost down before they waded back to the beach and drank once more. Suddenly there came a flash of yellow light. One of the pigs fell under the furious ray. There was a crunch of bone and a shrill screaming, and then the ray arched its back as the lean and sleek lion looked around and leaped back from the charging boar. The boar snorted at its dead and then whirled and led the four others into the brush. Joseph stood up and the lion watched him, lashing its tail. "If I could only shoot you," Joseph said aloud, "there would be an end and a new beginning. But I have no gun. Go on with your dinner." He climbed down from the rock and walked away, through the trees. "When that pool is gone the beasts will die," he thought, "or maybe they'll move over the ridge." He walked slowly back to the ranch, reluctant to go, and yet fearing a little to be out in the night. He thought how a new bond tied him to the earth, and how this land of his was closer now.

A lantern shone in the shed behind the barn, and there came a sound of hammering. Joseph went to the door and saw Thomas working on the box, and entered. "It hardly looks large enough," he said.

Thomas did not look up. "I measured. It will be right."

"I saw a lion, Thomas; saw it kill a wild pig. Some time soon you'd better take some dogs and kill it. The calves will suffer, else." He hurried on, "Tom, we talked when Benjy died. We said it takes

graves to make a place one's own. That is a true thing. That makes
us a part of the place. There's some enormous truth in this."

Thomas nodded over his work. "I know. Jose and Manuel will
dig in the morning. I don't want to dig for our own dead."

Joseph turned away, trying to leave the shed. "You are sure it's
big enough?"

"Sure, I measured."

"And, Tom, don't put a little fence around. I want it to sink and
be lost as soon as it can." He went, then, quickly. In the yard he
heard the warned children whispering.

"There he goes," and Martha, "You're not to say anything
to him."

He went to his own dark house and lighted the lamps and set fire
in the stove. The clock wound by Elizabeth still ticked, storing in
its spring the pressure of her hand, and the wool socks she had hung
to dry over the stove screen were still damp. These were vital parts
of Elizabeth that were not dead yet. Joseph pondered slowly over
it—Life cannot be cut off quickly. One cannot be dead until the
things he changed are dead. His effect is the only evidence of his life.
While there remains even a plaintive memory, a person cannot be
cut off, dead. And he thought, "It's a long slow process for a human
to die. We kill a cow, and it is dead as soon as the meat is eaten, but
a man's life dies as a commotion in a still pool dies, in little waves,
spreading and growing back toward stillness." He leaned back in his
chair and turned the lamp wick down until only a little blue light
came from it. And then he sat relaxed and tried to shepherd his
thoughts again, but they had spread out, feeding in a hundred different places, so that his attention was lost. And he thought in tones,
in currents of movement, in color, and in a slow plodding rhythm.
He looked down at his slouched body, at his curved arms and hands
resting in his lap.

Size changed.

A mountain range extended in a long curve and on its end were
five little ranges, stretching out with narrow valleys between them.
If one looked carefully, there seemed to be towns in the valleys. The
long curved range was clad in black sage, and the valleys ended on
a flat of dark tillable earth, miles in length, which dropped off at last
to an abyss. Good fields were there, and the houses and the people

were so small they could be seen only a little. High up on a tremendous peak, towering over the ranges and the valleys, the brain of the world was set, and the eyes that looked down on the earth's body. The brain could not understand the life on its body. It lay inert, knowing vaguely that it could shake off the life, the towns, the little houses of the fields with earthquake fury. But the brain was drowsed and the mountains lay still, and the fields were peaceful on their rounded cliff that went down to the abyss. And thus it stood a million years, unchanging and quiet, and the world-brain in its peak lay close to sleep. The world-brain sorrowed a little, for it knew that some time it would have to move, and then the life would be shaken and destroyed and the long work of tillage would be gone, and the houses in the valleys would crumble. The brain was sorry, but it could change nothing. It thought, "I will endure even a little discomfort to preserve this order which has come to exist by accident. It will be a shame to destroy this order." But the towering earth was tired of sitting in one position. It moved, suddenly, and the houses crumbled, the mountains heaved horribly, and all the work of a million years was lost.

And size changed, and time changed.

There were light footsteps on the porch. The door opened and Rama came in, her dark eyes wide and glittering with sorrow. "You are sitting in the dark, almost, Joseph," she said.

His hands rose to stroke his black beard. "I turned down the lamp."

She stepped over and turned up the wick a little. "It is a hard time, Joseph. I want to see how you look at this time. Yes," she said. "There is no change. That makes me strong again. I was afraid there might have been a break. Are you thinking about Elizabeth?"

He wondered how to answer. There was an impulse in him to tell the thing as truly as he could. "Yes, somewhat," he said slowly and uncertainly, "of Elizabeth and of all the things that die. Everything seems to work with a recurring rhythm except life. There is only one birth and only one death. Nothing else is like that."

Rama moved close and sat down beside him. "You loved Elizabeth."

"Yes," he said, "I did."

"But you didn't know her as a person. You never have known a person. You aren't aware of persons, Joseph; only people. You can't see units, Joseph, only the whole." She shrugged her shoulders and sat up straight. "You aren't even listening to me. I came over to see if you had had anything to eat."

"I don't want to eat," he said.

"Well, I can understand that. I have the baby, you know. Do you want me to keep it over at my house?"

"I'll get someone to take care of it as soon as I can," he said.

She stood up, preparing to go. "You are tired, Joseph. Go to bed and get some sleep if you can. And if you can't, at least lie down. In the morning you'll be hungry, and then you can come to breakfast."

"Yes," he said absently, "in the morning I'll be hungry."

"And you'll go to bed now?"

He agreed, hardly knowing what she had said. "Yes, I'll go to bed." And when she went out he obeyed her automatically. He took off his clothes and stood in front of the stove, looking down at his lean hard stomach and legs. Rama's voice kept repeating in his head, "You must lie down and rest." He took the lamp from its hanging ring and walked into the bedroom and got into bed, leaving the light on the table. Since he had entered the house his senses had been boxed up in his thoughts, but now, as his body stretched and relaxed, sounds of the night became available to his ears, so that he heard the murmuring of the wind and the harsh whisper of the dry leaves in the dead oak tree. And he heard the far-off moaning of a cow. Life flowed back into the land, and the movement that had been deadened by thought started up again. He considered turning off the lamp, but his reluctant body refused the task.

A furtive step sounded on the porch. He heard the front door open quietly. A rustling sound came from the sitting-room. Joseph lay still and listened, and wondered idly who was there, but he did not call out. And then the bedroom door opened, and he turned his head to look. Rama stood naked in the doorway, and the lamplight fell upon her. Joseph saw the full breasts, ending in dark hard nipples, and the broad round belly and the powerful legs, and the triangle of crisp black hair. Rama's breath came panting, as though she had been running.

"This is a need," she whispered hoarsely.

In Joseph's throat and chest a grinding started, like hot gravel, and it moved downward.

Rama blew out the light and flung herself into the bed. Their bodies met furiously, thighs pounding and beating, her thewed legs clenched over him. Their breath sobbed in their throats. Joseph could feel the hard nipples against his breast; then Rama groaned harshly, and her broad hips drummed against him, and her body quivered until the pressure of her straining arms crushed the breath from his chest, and her hungry limbs drew irresistibly the agonizing seed of his body.

She relaxed, breathing heavily. The strong muscles grew soft; they lay together in exhaustion.

"It was a need to you," she whispered. "It was a hunger in me, but a need to you. The long deep river of sorrow is diverted and sucked into me, and the sorrow which is only a warm wan pleasure is drawn out in a moment. Do you think that, Joseph?"

"Yes," he said. "The need was there." He arose from her and turned on his back and lay beside her.

She spoke sleepily: "It's in my memory now. Once in my life— once in my life! My whole life approaching it, and after, my whole life backing away hungrily. It was not for you. It seems enough now, perhaps it is, but I am afraid it will bear litters of desires, and each one will grow larger than its mother." She sat up and kissed his forehead, and for a moment her hair fell about his face. "Is there a candle on the table, Joseph? I'll need a little light."

"Yes, on the table, in a tin candle-stick, and matches in the tray."

She got up and put flame to the candle. She looked down at herself and with her finger explored the dark-red bruises on her breast. "I've thought of this," she said. "Often I've thought of it. And in my thought we lay together after we had joined, and I asked you a great many questions. Always in my thought that was the way it was." As though a modesty crept upon her, she shielded the candle-light from her body with her hand. "I think I've asked my questions and you have answered them."

Joseph supported himself on one elbow. "Rama, what do you want of me?" he demanded.

She turned, then, to the door and opened it slowly. "I want noth-ing now. You are complete again. I wanted to be a part of you, and perhaps I am. But—I do not think so." Her voice changed then. "Go to sleep now. And in the morning come to breakfast." She closed the door after her. He heard the rustling of her dressing, but sleep fell so quickly upon him that he did not hear her leave the house.

22

In January there was a time of shrill cold winds and mornings when the frost lay on the ground like a light snow. The cattle and horses ranged the hillsides, picking up forgotten wisps of grass, reaching up to nibble the live oak leaves, and finally they moved in and stood all day about the fenced haystacks. Morning and night Joseph and Thomas pitched hay over the fence to them and filled the troughs with water. And when the stock had eaten and drunk, they stood about waiting for the next feeding. The hills were picked clean.

The earth grew more grey and lifeless every week and the haystacks dwindled. One was finished and another started, and it melted, too, under the appetites of the hungry cows. In February an inch of rain fell and the grass started up, grew a few inches and turned yellow. Joseph walked moodily about with his hands knotted and thrust into his pockets.

The children played quietly. They played "Aunt Elizabeth's Funeral" for weeks, burying a cartridge box over and over. And later in the year they played at gardening, dug tiny plots of ground and planted wheat and watched the long thin blades shoot up under poured water. Rama still cared for Joseph's baby. She gave more time to it than she had devoted to her own.

But it was Thomas who really grew afraid. When he saw that the cattle could find no more feed in the hills the terror of starvation began to arise in him. When the second haystack was half gone, he came nervously to Joseph.

"What will we do when the other two stacks run out?" he demanded.

"I don't know. I'll think what to do."

"But Joseph, we can't buy hay."

"I don't know. I'll have to think what to do."

There were showers in March, and a little stand of feed started up and wildflowers began to grow. The cattle moved out from the stacks and nibbled hungrily all day long at the short grass to get their stomachs full. April dried out the ground again, and the hope of the country was gone. The cattle were thin and laced with ribs.

Hip-bones stood out. There were few calves born. Two sows died with a mysterious illness before they littered. Some of the cows took a harsh cough from the dusty air. The game was going away from the hills. The quail came no longer to the house to sing in the evenings. And the nights when the coyotes jibbered were rare. It was an odd thing to see a rabbit.

"The wild things are going away," Thomas explained. "Everything that can move is going over the range to the coast. We'll go there soon, Joseph, just to see it."

In May the wind blew for three days from the sea, but it had done that so often that no one believed it. There was a day of massed clouds, and then the rain fell in torrents. Bcth Joseph and Thomas walked about, getting wet, gloating a little in the water, although they knew it was too late. Almost overnight the grass sprang up again and clothed the hills and grew furiously. The cattle spread a little fat on their ribs. And then one morning there was a burn in the sunlight, and at noon the weather was hot. The summer had come early. Within a week the grass withered and drooped, and within two weeks the dust was in the air again.

Joseph saddled a horse one morning in June and rode to Nuestra Señora and found the teamster Romas. Romas came out into his chicken yard and sat on a wagon-tongue, and he played with a bull whip while he talked.

"These are the dry years?" Joseph asked sullenly.

"It looks that way, Mr. Wayne."

"Then these are the years you talked about."

"This is one of the worst I ever saw, Mr. Wayne. Another like this and there will be trouble in the family."

Joseph was scowling. "I have one stack of hay left. When that is gone, what do I feed the cattle?" He took off his hat and wiped the sweat out with a handkerchief.

Romas snapped his bull-whip, and the popper spat up the dirt like an explosion. And then he hung the whip over his knee and took tobacco and papers from his vest and rolled a cigarette. "If you can keep your cows until next winter, you may save them. If you haven't enough hay for that, you'll have to move them or they'll starve. This sun won't leave a straw."

"Can't I buy hay?" Joseph asked.

Romas chuckled. "In three months a bale of hay will be worth a cow."

Joseph sat down on the wagon-tongue beside him and looked at the ground, and picked up a handful of the hot dust. "Where do you people drive the stock?" he asked finally.

Romas smiled. "That's a good time for me. I drive the cattle. I'll tell you, Mr. Wayne, this year has hit not only this valley but the Salinas valley, beyond. We won't find grass this side of the San Joaquin river."

"But that's over a hundred miles away."

Romas picked up the bull-whip from his lap again. "Yes, over a hundred miles," he said. "And if you haven't much hay left, you'd better start the herd pretty soon, while they have the guts to go."

Joseph stood up and walked toward his horse. And Romas walked beside him.

"I remember when you came," Romas said quietly. "I remember when I hauled the lumber to your place. You said the drought would never come again. All of us who live here and were born here know it will come again."

"Suppose I sell all my stock and wait for the good years?"

Romas laughed loudly at that. "Man, you aren't thinking. What does your stock look like?"

"It's pretty poor," Joseph admitted.

"Fat beef is cheap enough, Mr. Wayne. You couldn't sell Nuestra Señora beef this year."

Joseph untied his lead rope and slowly mounted. "I see. Drive the cows then, or lose them—"

"Looks that way, Mr. Wayne."

"And if I drive, how many do I lose?"

Romas scratched his head and pretended to be thinking. "Sometimes half, sometimes two-thirds, and sometimes all of them."

Joseph's mouth tightened as though he had been struck. He lifted his reins and moved his spurred boot in toward the horse's belly.

"Do you remember my boy Willie?" Romas asked. "He drove one of the teams when we brought the lumber."

"Yes, I remember. How is he?"

"He's dead," said Romas. And then, in a shamed voice, "He hung himself."

"Why, I hadn't heard. I'm sorry. Why did he do that?"

Romas shook his head bewilderedly. "I don't know, Mr. Wayne. He never was very strong in the head." He smiled up at Joseph. "That's a Hell of a way for a father to talk." And then, as though he spoke to more than one person, he looked at a spot beside Joseph, "I'm sorry I said a thing like that. Willie was a good boy. He never was very well, Mr. Wayne."

"I'm sorry, Romas," Joseph said, and then he continued, "I may be needing you to drive stock for me." The spur lightly touched the horse and Joseph trotted off toward the ranch.

He rode slowly home along the banks of the dead river. The dusty trees, ragged from the sun's flaying, cast very little shade on the ground. Joseph remembered how he had ridden out in a dark night and flung his hat and quirt away to save a good moment out of a tide of moments. And he remembered how thick and green the brush had been under the trees, and how the grass of the hills bowed under its weight of seed; how the hills were heavy-coated as a fox's back. The hills were gaunt now; here was a colony from the southern desert come to try out the land for a future spreading of the desert's empire.

The horse panted in the heat, and the sweat dripped from the cowlick in the center of its belly. It was a long trip and there was no water on the way. Joseph didn't want to go home, for he was feeling a little guilty at the news he carried. This would break up the ranch and leave it abandoned to the sun and to the desert's outposts. He passed a dead cow with pitifully barred sides, and with a stomach swelled to bursting with the gas of putrefaction. Joseph pulled his hat down and bent his head so that he might not see the picked carcass of the land.

It was late afternoon when he arrived. Thomas had just ridden in from the range. He walked excitedly to Joseph, his red face drawn.

"I found ten dead cows," he said. "I don't know what killed them. The buzzards are working on them." He grasped Joseph's arm and shook it fiercely. "They're over the ridge there. In the morning there will be only a little plot of bones."

Joseph looked away from him in shame. "I'm failing to protect the land," he thought sadly. "The duty of keeping life in my land is beyond my power."

"Thomas," he said. "I rode to town today for news of the country."

"Is it all this way?" Thomas demanded. "The water in the well is low."

"Yes; all this way. We'll have to move the cows—over a hundred miles. There's pasturage along the San Joaquin."

"Christ, let's get moving, then!" Thomas cried. "Let's get out of this bastard valley, this double-crossing son-of-a-bitch. I don't want to come back to it! I can't trust it any more!"

Joseph shook his head slowly. "I keep hoping something may happen. I know there's no chance. A heavy rain wouldn't help now. We'll start the cows next week."

"Why wait for next week? Let's get 'em ready tomorrow!"

Joseph tried to soothe him. "This is a week of heat. It may be a little cooler next week. We'll have to feed them up so they can make the trip. Tell the men to pitch out more hay."

Thomas nodded. "I hadn't thought about the hay." Suddenly his eyes, brightened. "Joseph, we'll go over the range to the coast while the men are feeding up the cows. We'll get a look at some water before we start riding in the dust."

Joseph nodded. "Yes, we can do that. We can go tomorrow."

They started in the night, to get ahead of the sun. They headed their horses toward the dark west, and let the horses find the trail. The earth still radiated heat from the day before, and the hillsides were quiet. The ringing of hoofs on the rocky trail splashed uneasy sounds in the quietness. Once, when the dawn was coming, they stopped to rest their horses, and they thought they heard a little bell tinkling in front of them.

"Did you hear it?" Thomas asked.

"It might be a belled animal," said Joseph. "It isn't a cowbell. It sounds more like a sheep bell. We'll listen for it when the daylight comes."

The day's heat started when the sun appeared. There was no cool dawn. A few grasshoppers rattled and snapped through the air. The cooked bay trees spiced the air and drops of sweet heavy juice boiled out of the greasewood. As the men rode up the steep slope, the trail grew more rocky and the earth more desolate. Everywhere the bones of the earth stuck through and flung the dazzling light away. A snake rattled viciously in the path ahead. Both horses stopped stiffly in their tracks and backed away. Thomas reached down and slipped a carbine from the saddle scabbard under his leg. The gun crashed and the thick snake's body rotated slowly around its crushed head. The horses turned downhill to rest, and closed their eyes against the cutting light. A faint whining came from the earth, as though it protested against the intolerable sun.

"It makes me sad," Joseph said. "I wish I could be less sad about it."

Thomas threw a leg around his saddle horn. "You know what the whole damn country looks like?" he asked. "It looks like a smoking heap of ashes with cinders sticking out." They heard the faint tinkling of the bell again. "Let's see what it is," Thomas said. They turned the horses back uphill. The slope was strewn with great boulders, ruins of perfect mountains that once were, and the trail twisted about among the rocks. "I think I heard that bell go by the house in the night," Thomas said. "I thought it was a dream then, but I remember it now that I hear it again. We're nearly to the top now."

The trail went into a pass of shattered granite, and the next moment the two men looked down on a new fresh world. The downward slope was covered with tremendous redwood trees, and among the great columned trunks there grew a wild tangle of berry vines, of gooseberry, of swordferns as tall as a man. The hill slipped quickly down, and the sea rose up level with the hilltops. The two men stopped their horses and stared hungrily at the green underbrush. The hills stirred with life. Quail skittered and rabbits hopped away from the path. While the men looked, a little deer walked into an open place, caught their scent and bounced away. Thomas wiped his eyes on his sleeve. "All the game from our side is here," he said. "I wish we could bring our cattle over, but there isn't a flat place for a cow to stand." He turned about to face his brother. "Joseph, wouldn't you like to crawl under the brush, into a damp cool hollow there, and curl up and go to sleep?"

Joseph had been staring at the up-ended sea. "I wonder where the moisture comes from." He pointed to the long barren sweeps that dropped to the ocean far below. "No grass is there, but here in the creases it's as green as a jungle." And he said, "I've seen the fog heads looking over into our valley. Every night the cool grey fog must lie in these creases in the mountains and leave some of its moisture. And in the daytime it goes back to the sea, and at night it comes again, so that this forest is never kept waiting, never. Our land is dry, and there's no help for it. But here—I resent this place, Thomas."

"I want to get down to the water," Thomas said. "Come on, let's move." They started down the steep slope on the trail that wound among the columns of the redwoods, and the brambles scratched at their faces. Part of the way down, they came to a clearing, and in it two packed burros stood with drooped heads, and an old, white-bearded man sat on the ground in front of them. His hat was in his lap and his damp white hair lay plastered against his head. He looked up at the two with sharp shiny black eyes. He held one nostril shut and blew out of the other, and then reversed and blew again.

"I heard you coming a long way back," he said. And he laughed without making a sound. "I guess you heard my burro bell. It's a real silver bell my burro wears. Sometimes I let one wear it, and sometimes the other." He put on his hat with dignity and lifted his beaked nose like a sparrow. "Where are you going, down the hill?"

Thomas had to answer, for Joseph was staring at the little man in curious recognition. "We're going to camp on the coast," Thomas explained. "We'll catch some fish, and we'll swim if the sea is calm."

"We heard your bell a long way back," said Joseph. "I've seen you somewhere before." He stopped suddenly in embarrassment, for he knew he had never really seen the old man before at all.

"I live over to the right, on a flat," the old man said. "My house is five hundred feet above the beach." He nodded at them impressively. "You shall come to stay with me. You will see how high it is." He paused, and a secret hesitant mist settled over his eyes. He looked at Thomas, and then looked long at Joseph. "I guess I can tell you," he said. "Do you know why I live out there on the cliff? I've only told the reason to a few. I'll tell you, because you're coming to stay with me." He stood up, the better to deliver his secret. "I am the last man in the western world to see the sun. After it is gone to everyone else, I see it for a little while. I've seen it every night for twenty years. Except when the fog was in or the rain was falling, I've seen the sun set." He looked from one to the other, smiling proudly. "Sometimes," he went on, "I go to town for salt and pepper and thyme and tobacco. I go fast. I start after the sun has set, and I'm back before it sets again. You shall see tonight how it is." He looked anxiously at the sky. "It's time to be going. You follow after me. Why, I'll kill a little pig, and we'll roast it for dinner. Come, follow after me." He started at a half run down the trail, and the burros trotted after him, and the silver bell jingled sharply.

"Come," Joseph said. "Let's go with him."

But Thomas hung back. "The man is crazy. Let him go on."

"I want to go with him, Thomas," Joseph said eagerly. "He isn't crazy, not violently crazy. I want to go with him."

Thomas had the animals' fear of insanity. "I'd rather not. If we do go with him, I'll take my blankets off into the brush."

"Come on, then, or we'll lose him." They clucked up their horses and started down the hill, through the underbrush and in and out among the straight red pillars of the trees. So fast had the old man gone that they were nearly down before they took sight of him. He waved his hand and beckoned to them. The trail left the crease where the redwoods grew and led over a bare ridge to a long narrow flat. The mountains sat with their feet in the sea, and the old man's house was on the knees. All over the flat was tall sagebrush. A man riding the trail could not be seen above the scrub. The brush stopped a hundred feet from the cliff, and on the edge of the abyss was a pole cabin, hairy with stuffed moss and thatched with a great pile of grass. Beside the house there was a tight pigpen of poles, and a little shed, and a vegetable garden, and a patch of growing corn. The old man spread his arms possessively.

"Here is my house." He looked at the lowering sun. "There's over an hour yet. See, that hill is blue," he said, pointing. "That's a mountain of copper." He started to unpack the mules, laying his boxes of supplies on the ground. Joseph slipped his saddle and hobbled his horse, and Thomas reluctantly did the same. The burros trotted away into the brush, and the horses hopped after them.

"We'll find them by the bell," said Joseph. "The horses will never leave the burros."

The old man led them to the pigpen, where a dozen lean wild pigs eyed them suspiciously and tried to force their way through the farther fence. "I trap them." He smiled proudly. "I have my traps all over. Come, I'll show you." He walked to the low, thatched shed and, leaning down, pointed to twenty little cages, woven and plaited with willows. In the cages were grey rabbits and quail and thrushes and squirrels, sitting in the straw behind their wooden bars and peering out. "I catch all of them in my box-traps. I keep them until I need them."

Thomas turned away. "I'm going for a walk," he said sharply. "I'm going down the cliff to the ocean."

The old man stared after him as he strode away. "Why does that man hate me?" he demanded of Joseph. "Why is he afraid of me?"

Joseph looked affectionately after Thomas. "He has his life as you have, and as I have. He doesn't like things caged. He puts himself in the place of the beasts, and can feel how frightened they are. He doesn't like fear. He catches it too easily." Joseph smoothed down his beard. "Let him alone. He'll come back after a while."

The old man was sad. "I should have told him. I am gentle with the little creatures. I don't let them be afraid. When I kill them, they never know. You shall see." They strolled around the house, toward the cliff. Joseph pointed to three little crosses stuck in the ground close to the cliff's edge.

"What are those?" he asked. "It's a strange place for them."

His companion faced him eagerly. "You like them. I can see you like them. We know each other. I know things you don't know. You will learn them. I'll tell you about the crosses. There was a storm. For a week the ocean down there was wild and grey. The wind blew in from the center of the sea. Then it was over. I looked down the cliff to the beach. Three little figures were there. I went down my own trail that I built with my hands. I found three sailors washed up on the beach. Two were dark men, and one was light. The light one wore a saint's medallion on a string around his neck. Then I carried them up here. That was work. And I buried them on the cliff. I put the crosses there because of the medallion. You like the crosses, don't you?" His bright black eyes watched Joseph's face for any new expression.

And Joseph nodded. "Yes, I like the crosses. It was a good thing to do."

"Then come to see the sunset place. You'll like that, too." He half ran around his house in his eagerness. A little platform was built on the cliff's edge, with a wooden railing in front and a bench a few feet back. In front of the bench was a large stone slab, resting on four blocks of wood, and the smooth surface of the stone was scoured and clean. The two men stood at the railing and looked off at the sea, blue and calm, and so far below that the rollers sliding in seemed no larger than ripples, and the pounding of the surf on the beach sounded like soft beating on a wet drum-head. The old man pointed to the horizon, where a rim of black fog hung. "It'll be a good one," he cried. "It'll be a red one in the fog. This is a good night for the pig."

The sun was growing larger as it slipped down the sky. "You sit here every day?" Joseph asked. "You never miss?"

"I never miss except when the clouds cover. I am the last man to see it. Look at a map and you'll see how that is. It is gone to everyone but me." He cried, "I'm talking while I should be getting ready. Sit on the bench there and wait."

He ran around the house. Joseph heard the angry squealing of the pig, and then the old man reappeared, carrying the struggling animal in his arms. He had trussed its legs all together. He laid it on the stone slab and stroked it with his fingers, until it ceased its struggling and settled down, grunting contentedly.

"You see," the old man said, "it must not cry. It doesn't know. The time is nearly here, now." He took a thick short-bladed knife from his pocket and tried its edge on his palm, and then his left hand stroked the pig's side and he turned to face the sun. It was rushing downward toward the far-off rim of fog, and it seemed to roll in a sac of lymph. "I was just in time," the old man said. "I like to be a little early."

"What is this," Joseph demanded. "What are you doing with the pig?"

The old man put his finger to his lips. "Hush! I'll tell you later. Hush now."

"Is it a sacrifice? Are you sacrificing the pig?" Joseph asked. "Do you kill a pig every night?"

"Oh no. I have no use for it. Every night I kill some little thing, a bird, a rabbit or a squirrel. Yes, every night some creature. Now, it's nearly time." The sun's edge touched the fog. The sun changed its shape; it was an arrowhead, an hour glass, a top. The sea turned red, and the wave-tops became long blades of crimson light. The old man turned quickly to the table. "Now!" he said, and cut the pig's throat. The red light bathed the mountains and the house. "Don't cry, little brother." He held down the struggling body. "Don't cry. If I have done it right, you will be dead when the sun is dead." The struggling grew weaker. The sun was a flat cap of red light on the fog wall, and then it disappeared, and the pig was dead.

Joseph had been sitting tensely on his bench, watching the sacrifice. "What has this man found?" he thought. "Out of his experience he has picked out the thing that makes him happy." He saw the old man's joyful eyes, saw how in the moment of the death he became straight and dignified and large. "This man has discovered a secret," Joseph said to himself. "He must tell me if he can."

His companion sat on the bench beside him now, and looked out to the edge of the sea, where the sun had gone. And the sea was dark and the wind was whipping it to white caps. "Why do you do this?" Joseph asked quietly.

The old man jerked his head around. "Why?" he asked excitedly. And then he grew more calm. "No, you aren't trying to trap me. Your brother thinks I'm crazy. I know. That's why he went to walk. But you don't think that. You're too wise to think that." He looked out on the darkening sea again. "You really want to know why I watch the sun—why I kill some little creature as it disappears." He paused and ran his lean fingers through his hair. "I don't know," he said quietly. "I have made up reasons, but they aren't true. I have said to myself, 'The sun is life. I give life to life'—'I make a symbol of the sun's death.' When I made these reasons I knew they weren't true." He looked around for corroboration.

Joseph broke in, "These were words to clothe a naked thing, and the thing is ridiculous in clothes."

"You see it. I gave up reasons. I do this because it makes me glad. I do it because I like to."

Joseph nodded eagerly. "You would be uneasy if it were not done. You would feel that something was left unfinished."

"Yes," the old man cried loudly. "You understand it. I tried to tell it once before. My listener couldn't see it. I do it for myself. I can't tell that it does not help the sun. But it is for me. In the moment, I am the sun. Do you see? I, through the beast, am the sun. I burn in the death." His eyes glittered with excitement. "Now you know."

"Yes," Joseph said. "I know now. I know for you. For me there is a difference that I don't dare think about yet, but I will think about it."

"The thing did not come quickly," the old man said. "Now it is nearly perfect." He leaned over and put his hands on Joseph's knees. "Some time it will be perfect. The sky will be right. The sea will be right. My life will reach a calm level place. The mountains back there will tell me when it is time. Then will be the perfect time, and it will be the last." He nodded gravely at the slab where the dead pig lay. "When it comes, I, myself, will go over the edge of the world with the sun. Now you know. In every man this thing is hidden. It tries to get out, but a man's fears distort it. He chokes it back. What does get out is changed—blood on the hands of a statue, emotion over the story of an ancient torture—the giving or drawing of blood in copulation. Why," he said. "I've told the creatures in the cages how it is. They are not afraid. Do you think I am crazy?" he demanded.

Joseph smiled. "Yes, you're crazy. Thomas says you are. Burton would say you are. It is not thought safe to open a clear path to your soul for the free, undistorted passage of the things that are there. You do well to preach to the beasts in the cage, else you might be in a cage yourself."

The old man stood up and picked up the pig and carried it away. He brought water and scrubbed the blood off the slab and dusted the ground under it with fresh gravel.

It was almost dark when he had finished cleaning the little pig. A great pale moon looked over the mountains, and its light caught the white-caps as they rose and disappeared. The pounding of the waves on the beach grew louder. Joseph sat in the little cave-like hut and the old man turned pieces of the pig on a spit in the fireplace. He talked quietly about the country.

"The tall sage hides my house," he said. "There are little cleared places in the sage. I've found some of them. In autumn the bucks fight there. I can hear the clashing of their horns at night. In the spring the does bring their spotted fawns to those same places to teach them. They must know many things if they are to live at all —what noises to run from; what the odors mean, how to kill snakes with their front hoofs." And he said, "The mountains are made of metal; a little layer of rock and then black iron and red copper. It must be so."

There were footsteps outside the house. Thomas called, "Joseph, where are you?"

Joseph got up from the floor of the hut and went out. "The dinner is waiting. Come in and eat," he said.

But Thomas protested, "I don't like to be with this man. I have abalones here. Come down to the beach. We'll build a fire and eat down there. The moon lights up the trail."

"But the supper is ready," Joseph said. "Come in and eat, at least."

Thomas entered the low house warily, as though he expected some evil beast to pounce upon him out of a dark corner. There was no light except from the fireplace. The old man tore at his meat with his teeth and threw the bones into the fire, and when he was finished, he stared sleepily into the blaze.

Joseph sat beside him. "Where did you come from?" Joseph asked. "What made you come here?"

"What do you say?"

"I say, why did you come here to live alone?"

The sleepy eyes cleared for a moment and then drooped sullenly. "I don't remember," he said. "I don't want to remember. I would have to think back, looking for what you want. If I do that, I'll stumble against other things in the past that I don't want to meddle with. Let it alone."

Thomas stood up. "I'll take my blanket out on the cliff to sleep," he said.

Joseph followed him out of the house, calling "Good-night," over his shoulder. The brothers walked in silence toward the cliff and laid their blankets side by side on the ground.

"Let's ride up the coast tomorrow," Thomas begged. "I don't like it here."

Joseph sat on his blankets and watched the faint far movement of the moonlit sea. "I'm going back tomorrow, Tom," he said. "I can't stay away. I must be there in case anything happens."

"Yes, but we'd planned to stay three days," Thomas objected. "I'll need a rest from the dust if I'm to drive the cows a hundred miles, and so will you."

Joseph sat silent for a long time. "Thomas," he asked. "Are you asleep yet?"

"No."

"I'm not going with you, Thomas. You take the cows. I'll stay with the ranch."

Thomas rolled up on his elbow. "What are you talking about? Nothing will hurt the ranch. It's the cows we have to save."

"You take the cows," Joseph repeated. "I can't go away. I've thought of going, I've put my mind to the act of going, and I can't. Why, it'd be like leaving a sick person."

Thomas grunted, "like leaving a dead body! And there's no harm in that."

"It isn't dead," Joseph protested. "The rain will come next winter, and in the spring the grass will be up and the river will be flowing. You'll see, Tom. There was some kind of accident that made this. Next spring the ground will be full of water again."

Thomas jeered: "And you'll get another wife, and there won't ever be another drought."

"It might be so," Joseph said gently.

"Then come with us to the San Joaquin and help us with the cows."

Joseph saw lights of a ship passing far out on the ocean, and he watched the lights and held up his finger to see how fast they moved. "I can't go away," he said. "This is my land. I don't know why it's mine, what makes it mine, but I cannot leave it. In the spring when the grass is up you'll see. Don't you remember how the grass was green all over the hills, even in the cracks of the rocks, and how the mustard was yellow? The redwing blackbirds built nests in the mustard stems."

"I remember it," Thomas said truculently, "and I remember how it was this morning, burned to a cinder and picked clean. Sure, and I remember the circle of dead cows. I can't get out too quickly. It's a treacherous place." He turned on his side. "We'll go back tomorrow if you say so. I hope you won't stay on the damn place."

"I'll have to stay," Joseph said. "If I went with you, I'd be wanting to start back every moment to see if the rain had fallen yet, or if there was any water in the river. I might as well not go away."

23

They awakened to a world swaddled in grey fog. The house and the sheds were dark shadows in the mist, and from below the cliff the surf sounded muffled and hollow. Their blankets were damp. The moisture clung in fine drops to their faces and hair. Joseph found the old man sitting beside a smouldering fire in his hut, and he said, "We must start back as soon as we can find our horses."

The old man seemed sad at their going. "I hoped you would stay a little while. I've told you my knowledge. I thought you might give me yours."

Joseph laughed bitterly. "I have none to give. My knowledge has failed. How can we find our horses in the mist?"

"Oh, I'll get them for you." He went to the door and whistled shrilly, and in a moment the silver bell began to ring. The burros came trotting in, and the two horses after them.

Joseph and Thomas saddled their horses and tied the blankets on them, and then Joseph turned to say good-bye to the old man, but he had disappeared into the mist, and he didn't answer when Joseph called.

"He's crazy," Thomas said. "Come on, let's go." They turned the horses into the trail and let them have their heads, for the fog was too thick for a man to find his way. They came to the crease where the violent growth and the redwoods were. Every leaf dripped moisture, and the shreds of the mist clung to the tree trunks like tattered flags. The men were half way to the pass before the fog began to thin and break and whirl about like a legion of ghosts caught by the daylight. At last the trail climbed above the mist level and, looking back, Joseph and Thomas saw the tumbling sea of fog extending to the horizon, covering from sight the sea and the mountain slopes. And in a little they reached the pass and looked over at their own dry dead valley, burning under the vicious sun, smoking with heat waves. They paused in the pass and looked back at the green growth in the canyon they had come from, and at the grey sea of fog.

"I hate to leave it," Thomas said. "If there were only feed for the cattle I would move over."

Joseph looked back only for a moment, and then he started ahead over the pass. "It isn't ours, Thomas," he said. "It's like a beautiful woman, and she isn't ours." He urged his horse over the hot broken rock. "The old man knew a secret, Tom. He told me some straight clean things."

"He was crazy," Thomas insisted. "In any other place he would be locked up. What did he have all of those caged creatures for?"

Joseph thought of explaining. He tried to think how he would begin. "Oh, he—keeps them to eat," he said. "It isn't easy to shoot game, and so he traps the things and keeps them until he needs them."

"But that's all right," Thomas said more easily. "I thought there was something else. If that's all it is, I don't mind. His craziness hasn't to do with the animals and birds then."

"Not at all," said Joseph.

"If I'd known that, I wouldn't have walked away. I was afraid there was some ceremony."

"You are afraid of every kind of ritual, Thomas. Do you know why?" Joseph slowed his horse so that Thomas could come closer.

"No, I don't know why," Thomas admitted slowly, "it seems a trap, a kind of little trap."

"Perhaps it is," Joseph said. "I hadn't thought of it."

When they had got down the slope to the river source with its dry and brittle moss and its black ferns, they drew up under a bay tree. "Let's go over the ridge and drive in any cattle we can see," Thomas said. They left the river and followed the shoulder of the ridge, and the dust clouded up and clung about them. Suddenly Thomas pulled up his horse and pointed down the slope. "There, look there." Fifteen or twenty little piles of picked bones lay on the side-hill, and grey coyotes were slinking away toward the brush, and vultures roosted on the ribs and pulled off the last strips of flesh.

Thomas' face was pinched. "That's what I saw before. That's why I hate the country. I'll never come back," he cried. "Come on, I want to get to the ranch. I want to start away tomorrow if I can." He swung his horse down the hill and spurred it to a trot, and he fled from the acre of bones.

Joseph kept him in sight, but he did not try to follow him. Joseph's heart was filled with sorrow and with defeat. "Something has failed," he thought. "I was appointed to care for the land, and I have

failed." He was disappointed in himself and in the land. But he said,
"I won't leave it. I'll stay here with it. Maybe it isn't dead." He
thought of the rock in the pines, and excitement arose in him. "I
wonder if the little stream is gone. If that still flows, the land is not
dead. I'll go to see, pretty soon." He rode over the ridge top in time
to see Thomas gallop up to the houses. The fences were down around
the last stacks of hay, and the voracious cattle were eating holes in
it. As Joseph came close, he saw how lean they were, and poor, and
how their hips stuck out. He rode to where Thomas talked with the
rider Manuel.

"How many?" he demanded.

"Four hundred and sixteen," Manuel said. "Over a hundred
gone."

"Over a hundred!" Thomas walked quickly away. Joseph, looking
after him, saw him go into the barn. He turned back to the rider.

"Will these others make it to the San Joaquin, Manuel?"

Manuel shrugged slightly. "We go slow. Maybe we find a little
grass. Maybe we get some over there. But we lose some cows, too.
Your brother hates to lose the cows. He likes the cows."

"Let them eat all the hay," Joseph ordered. "When the hay is
gone, we will start."

"The hay will be gone tomorrow," Manuel said.

They were loading the wagons in the yard, mattresses and chicken
coops and cooking utensils, piled high and carefully. Romas came in
with another rider to help with the herds. Rama would drive a buckboard, Thomas, a Studebaker wagon with grain for the horses and
two barrels of water. There were folded tents on the wagons, supplies
of food, three live pigs and a couple of geese. They were taking
everything to last until winter.

In the evening Joseph sat on his porch, watching the last of the
preparation, and Rama left her work and came to him and sat on the
step. "Why do you stay?" she asked.

"Someone must take care of the ranch, Rama."

"But what remains to be taken care of? Thomas is right, Joseph;
there's nothing left."

His eyes sought the ridge where the dark pines were. "There's
something left, Rama. I'll stay with the ranch."

She sighed deeply. "I suppose you want me to take the baby."

"Yes. I wouldn't know how to care for it."

"You know it won't be a very good life for him in a tent."

"Don't you want to take him, Rama?" he asked.

"Yes, I want him. I want him for my own."

Joseph turned away and looked up at the pine forest again. The last of the sun was sinking over the Puerto Suelo. Joseph thought of the old man and of his sacrifice. "Why do you want the child?" he asked softly.

"Because he is part of you."

"Do you love me, Rama? Is that it?"

Her breath caught harshly in her throat. "No," she cried, "I am very near to hating you."

"Then take the child," he said quickly. "This child is yours. I swear it now. He is yours forever. I have no more claim on him." And he looked quickly back to the pine ridge, as though for an answer.

"How can I be sure?" Rama fretted. "When I have made my mind over so the baby is my own, when he has come to think of me as his mother, how can I be sure you will not come and take him away?"

He smiled at her, and the calm he knew came upon him. He pointed to the dead and naked tree beside the porch. "Look, Rama! That was my tree. It was the center of the land, a kind of father of the land. And Burton killed it." He stopped and stroked his beard and turned the ends under, as his father had done. His eyes drooped with pain and tightened with resistance to the pain. "Look on the ridge where the pines are, Rama," he said. "There's a circle in the grove, and a great rock in the circle. The rock killed Elizabeth. And on the hill over there are the graves of Benjy and Elizabeth." She stared at him uncomprehendingly. "The land is struck," he went on. "The land is not dead, but it is sinking under a force too strong for it. And I am staying to protect the land."

"What does all this mean to me?" she asked. "to me or to the child?"

"Why," he said, "I don't know. It might help, to give the child to you. It seems to me a thing that might help the land."

She brushed her hair back nervously, smoothed it beside the part. "Do you mean you're sacrificing the child? Is that it, Joseph?"

"I don't know what name to give it," he said. "I am trying to help the land, and so there's no danger that I shall take the child again."

She stood up then, and backed away from him slowly. "Good-bye to you, Joseph," she said. "I am going in the morning, and I am glad, for I shall always be afraid of you now. I shall always be afraid." Her lips trembled, and her eyes filled with tears. "Poor lonely man!" She hurried away toward her house, but Joseph smiled gravely up at the pine grove.

"Now we are one," he thought, "and now we are alone; we will be working together." A wind blew down from the hills and raised a choking cloud of dust into the air.

The cattle munched at the hay all night.

The wagons set out well before daylight. For two hours the lanterns moved about. Rama got breakfast for the children and saw them to their high secure seat on top of the load. She put the baby in its basket on the floor of the wagon, in front of her. At last they were ready, and the horses hitched in. Rama climbed to her seat, and Thomas stood beside her. Joseph strode up. They stood in the dark, and all three unconsciously sniffed the air. The children were very quiet. Rama put her foot out on the brake. Thomas sighed deeply. "I'll write you how we get through," he said.

"I'll be waiting to hear," Joseph replied.

"Well, we may as well get started."

"You'll stop in the hot part of the day?"

"If we can find a tree to stop under. Well, good-bye," Thomas said. "It's a long trip." One of the horses bowed its neck against the check-rein and stamped.

"Good-bye, Thomas. Good-bye, Rama."

"I'll have Thomas write you how the baby is," Rama said.

Still Thomas stood waiting. But suddenly he turned and walked away without another word. His brake whispered for a moment, and the axles creaked under the load. Rama started her horses and the teams moved off. Martha, on top of the load, cried bitterly because no one could see her waving a handkerchief. The other children had gone to sleep, but Martha awakened them. "We're going to a bad place," she said quietly, "but I'm glad we're going because this place will burn up in a week or two."

Joseph could hear the creaking wheels after the teams disappeared.

He strolled to the house that had been Juanito's, where the drovers were finishing their coffee and fried meat. As the first dawn appeared, they emptied their cups and rose heavily to their feet. Romas walked out to the corral with Joseph.

"Take them slowly," Joseph said.

"Sure, I will. It's a good bunch of riders, Mr. Wayne. I know all of them."

The men were wearily saddling their horses. A pack of six long-haired ranch dogs got up out of the dust and walked tiredly out to go to work, serious dogs. The red dawn broke. The dogs lined out. Then the corral gate swung open and the herd started, three dogs on each side to keep them in the road, and the riders fanned out behind. With the first steps the dust billowed into the air. The riders raised their handkerchiefs and tied them over the bridges of their noses. In a hundred yard the herd had almost disappeared in the dust cloud. Then the sun started up and turned the cloud to red. Joseph stood by the corral and watched the line of dust that crawled like a worm over the land, spreading in the rear like a yellow mist.

The thick cloud moved over the hill at last, but the dust hung in the air for hours.

Joseph felt the weariness of the long journey. The heat of the early sun burned him and the dust stung his nose. For a long time he did not move away from his place, but stood and watched the dust-laden air where the herd had passed. He was filled with sorrow. "The cattle are gone for good," he thought. "Most of them were born here, and now they're gone." He thought how they had been fresh-coated calves, sleek and shiny with the licking of their mothers; how they had flattened little beds in the grass at night. He remembered the mournful bellowing of the cows when the calves got lost; and now there were no cows left. He turned away at last to the dead houses, the dead barn and the great dead tree. It was quieter than anything should be. The barn door swung open on its hinges. Rama's house was open, too. He could see the chairs inside, and the polished stove. He picked up a piece of loose baling wire from the ground, rolled it up and hung it on the fence. He walked into the barn, empty of hay. Hard black clods were on the floor, on the packed straw. Only one horse was left. Joseph walked down the long line of empty stalls, and his mind made history of his memories. "This is the stall where Thomas sat when the loft was full of hay." He looked up and tried to imagine how it had been. The air was laced with flashing yellow streaks of sun. The three barn-owls sat, faces inward, in their dark corners under the eaves. Joseph walked to the feed-room and brought an extra measure of rolled barley and poured it in the horse's barley box, and he carried out another measure and scattered it on the ground outside the door. He sauntered slowly across the yard.

It would be about now that Rama came out with a basket of washed clothes and hung them on the lines, red aprons and jeans, pale blue with so much soaking, and the little blue frocks and red knitted petticoats of the girls. And it would be about now that the horses were turned out of the barn to stretch their necks over the watering trough and to snort bubbles into the water. Joseph had never felt the need for work as he did now. He went through all the houses and locked the doors and the windows and nailed up the doors of the sheds. In Rama's house he picked up a damp drying cloth from the floor and hung it over the back of a chair. Rama was a neat woman; the bureau drawers were closed and the floor was swept, the broom and dustpan stood in their corner, and the turkey wing had been used on the stove that morning. Joseph lifted the stove lid and saw the last coals darkening. When he locked the door of Rama's house he felt a guilt such as one feels when the lid of a coffin is closed for the last time, and the body is deserted and left alone.

He went back to his own house, spread up his bed, and carried in wood for the night's cooking. He swept his house and polished the stove and wound the clock. And everything was done before noon. When he had finished everything, he went to sit on the front porch. The sun beat down on the yard and glittered on bits of broken glass. The air was still and hot, but a few birds hopped about, picking up the grain Joseph had scattered. And, led on by the news that the ranch was deserted, a squirrel trotted fearlessly across the yard, and a brown weasel ran at him and missed, and the two rolled about in the dust. A horned toad came out of the dust and waddled to the bottom step of the porch, and settled to catch flies. Joseph heard his horse stamping the floor, and he felt friendly toward the horse for making a sound. He was rendered stupid by the quiet. Time had slowed down and every thought waddled as slowly through his brain as the horned toad had when he came out of the fine dust. Joseph looked up at the dry, white hills and squinted his eyes against their reflection of the glaring sun. His eyes followed the water scars up the hill to the dry springs and over the unfleshed mountains. And, as always, his eyes came at last to the pine grove on the ridge. For a long time he stared at it, and then he stood up and walked down the steps. And he walked toward the pine grove—walked slowly up on the gentle slope. Once, from the foothills, he looked back on the dry houses, huddled together under the sun. His shirt turned dark with perspiration. His own little dust cloud followed him, and he walked on and on toward the black trees.

At last he came to the gulch where the grove stream flowed. There was a trickle of water in it, and the green grass grew on the edges. A little watercress still floated on the water. Joseph dug a hole in the bed under the tiny stream, and when the water had cleared, he knelt and drank from it, and he felt the cool water on his face. Then he walked on, and the stream grew a little wider and the streak of green grass broadened. Where it ran close under the bank of the gully, a few ferns grew in the black and mossy earth, out of reach of the sun. Some of the desolation left Joseph then. "I knew it would still be here," he said. "It couldn't fail. Not from that place." He took off his hat and walked quickly on. He entered the glade bareheaded and stood looking at the rock.

The thick moss was turning yellow and brittle, and the ferns around the cave had wilted. The stream still stole out of the hole in the rock, but it was not a quarter as large as it had been. Joseph walked to the rock apprehensively and pulled out some of the moss. It was not dead. He dug a hole in the stream bed, a deep hole, and when it was full he took up water in his hat and threw it over the rock and saw it go sucking into the dying moss. The hole filled slowly. It took a great many hatfuls of water to dampen the moss, and the moss drank thirstily, and showed no sign that it had been dampened. He threw water on the scars where Elizabeth's feet had slipped. He said, "Tomorrow I'll bring a bucket and a shovel. Then it will be easier." As he worked, he knew the rock no longer as a thing separated from him. He had no more feeling of affection for it than he had for his own body. He protected it against death as he would have saved his own life.

When he had finished throwing water, he sat down beside the pool and washed his face and neck in the cold water and drank from his hat. After a while he leaned back against the rock and looked across at the protecting ring of black trees. He thought of the country outside the ring, the hard burned hills, the grey and dusty sage. "Here it is safe," he thought. "Here is the seed that will stay alive until the rain comes again. This is the heart of the land, and the heart is still beating." He felt the dampness of the watered moss soaking through his shirt, and his thought went on, "I wonder why the land seems vindictive, now it is dead." He thought of the hills, like blind snakes with frayed and peeling skins, lying in wait about this stronghold where the water still flowed. He remembered how the land sucked down his little stream before it had run a hundred yards. "The land is savage," he thought, "like a dog far gone in hunger." And he smiled at the thought because he nearly believed it. "The land would come in and blot this stream and drink my blood if it could. It is crazy with thirst." He looked down at the little stream stealing across the glade. "Here is the seed of the land's life. We must guard against the land gone crazy. We must use the water to protect the heart, else the little taste of water may drive the land to attack us.

The afternoon was waning now; the shadow of the tree-line crossed the rock and closed on the other side of the circle. It was peaceful in the glade. "I came in time," Joseph said to the rock and to himself. "We will wait here, barricaded against the drought." His head nodded forward after a while, and he slept.

The sun slipped behind the hills and the dust withdrew, and the night came before he awakened. The hunting owls were coasting in front of the stars and the breeze that always follows the night was slipping along the hills. Joseph awakened and looked into the black sky. In a moment his brain reeled up from sleep and he knew the place. "But some strange thing has happened," he thought. "I live here now." The farmhouses down in the valley were not his home any more. He would go creeping down the hill and hurry back to the protection of the glade. He stood up and kicked his sleeping muscles awake, and then he walked quietly away from the rock, and when he reached the outside he walked secretly, as though he feared to awaken the land.

There were no lights in the houses to guide him this time. He walked in the direction of his memory. The houses were close before he saw them. And then he saddled his horse and tied blankets and a sack of grain and bacons and three hams and a great bag of coffee to the saddle. At last he crept away again, leading the packed horse.

The houses were sleeping; the land rustled in the night wind. Once he heard some heavy animal walking in the brush and his hair pricked with fear, and he waited until the steps had died away before he went on.

He arrived back at the glade in the false dawn. This time the horse did not refuse the path. Joseph tied it to a tree and fed it from the bag of rolled barley; then he went back to the rock and spread his blankets beside the little pool he had built. The light was coming when he lay down to sleep in safety beside the rock. A little tattered fragment of cloud, high in the air, caught fire from the hidden sun, and Joseph fell asleep while he watched it.

24

Although the year turned into autumn and the weeks built months, the summer's heat continued on, and at length withdrew so gradually that no change of season was perceptible. The doves, which flocked near water, were gone long ago, and the wild ducks flying over looked for their resting ponds in the evening and flew tiredly on, while the weaklings landed in dry fields and joined some new flock in the morning. It was November before the air cooled and the winter seemed really coming in, and by then the earth was tinder-dry. Even dry lichens had scaled off the rocks.

The hot weeks drew on, and Joseph lived in the circle of the pines and waited for the winter. His new life had built its habits. Each morning he carried water from the deep wide pool he had dug and flooded the mossy rock with it, and in the evening he watered it again. The moss had responded; it was sleek and thick and green. And in the whole land there was no other green thing. Joseph watched it closely to see that there was no sign of dryness. The stream decreased little by little, but winter was coming, and there was still plenty of water to keep the rock dripping with moisture.

Every two weeks Joseph rode through the parched hills to Nuestra Señora for his food supply. Early in the fall he found a letter waiting for him there.

Thomas wrote only information: "There is grass here. We lost three hundred head of stock on the way over. What's left is fat. Rama is well, and the children. The pasture rent is too high because of the dry years. The children swim in the river."

Joseph found Romas in town, and Romas told dully of the trip over the mountains. He told how the cows dropped, one by one, and did not get up under the goad, but only looked tiredly at the sky. Romas could tell their condition to an ounce of strength. He looked at their eyes, and then he shot the tired beasts, and the weary eyes set and glazed, but did not change. Little feed and little water —the moving herds filled the road and the farmers along the road were hostile. They patrolled their fence lines and shot any stock that broke through. The roads were lined with dust covered carcasses and the path of travel stank from end to end with rotting flesh. Rama, afraid the children might sicken with the smell, kept their faces covered with wet handkerchiefs. The miles covered daily grew fewer and fewer, and the tired stock rested all night, and did not search for food. A rider was sent back, and then another, as the herd dwindled, but Romas stayed, and the two home men, until the little band came stiffly to the river and rested on their knees to eat all night. Romas smiled as he told it, and his voice had no inflection. When the account was finished he walked quickly away, calling over his shoulder, "Your brother paid me," and he went into the saloon, out of sight.

While Joseph listened to the report a hollow pain came into his stomach, and he was glad when Romas went away. He bought his supplies and rode back to the barricade. For once he did not see the dry earth, cracked in long lightning lines. He did not feel the feeble tugging of the brittle brush as he rode through. His mind was a dusty road, and the weary cattle died in his brain. He was sorry he had heard, for now this new enemy would crowd up against the protecting pines.

The underbrush of the grove was dead by now, but the straight trunks still guarded the rock. The drought crept along the ground first, and killed all the low vines and the shrubs, but the pine roots pierced to bedrock and still drank a little water, and the needles were still black-green. Joseph rode back to the glade and he felt the rock to be sure it was moist, and he studied the little stream of water. This was the first time he set markers on the water's edge to determine how quickly it diminished.

In December the black frost struck the country. The sun rose and set redly and the north wind surged through the country every day, filling the air with dust, and tattering the dry leaves. Joseph went down to the houses and brought up a tent to sleep in. While he was among the quiet houses, he started the windmill and listened for a moment while it sucked air through the pipes, and then he turned the little crank that stopped the blades. He did not look back on the houses as he rode up the slope. He cut a wide path around the graves on the sidehill.

That afternoon he saw the fog heads on the western range. "I might go back to the old man," he thought. "There may be more things he could tell me." But his thought was play. He knew he couldn't leave the rock, for fear the moss would wilt. He went back into the silent glade and spread his tent. He picked the bucket from his gear and walked over to throw water on the rock. Something had happened. The stream had receded from his marking pegs a good two inches. Somewhere under the earth the drought had attacked the spring. Joseph filled his bucket at the pool and threw water on the rock, and then filled again. And soon the pool was empty—he had to wait half an hour for the dying stream to fill it again. For the first time a panic fell upon him. He crawled into the little cave and looked at the fissure from which the water slowly trickled, and he crawled out again, covered with the moisture of the cave. He sat beside the stream and watched it flow into the pool. And he thought he could see it decrease while he looked. The wind ruffled the pine branches nervously.

"It will win," Joseph said aloud. "The drought will get in at us." He was frightened.

In the evening he walked out the path and watched the sun setting in the Puerto Suelo. The fog came out of the hidden sea and swallowed the sun. In the chill winter evening Joseph gathered an armful of dead pine twigs and a bag of cones for his evening's fire. He built his fire close to the pool this night, so that it's light fell on the tiny stream. When his meager supper was finished, he leaned back against his saddle and watched the water, slipping noiselessly into the pool. The wind had fallen, and the pines were quiet. All around the grove Joseph could hear the drought creeping, slipping on dry scales over the ground, circling and exploring the edges of the grove. And he heard the dry frightened whisper of the earth as the drought passed over it. He stood up now and put his bucket in the pool, under the stream, and each time it filled he poured it over the rock and sat down to wait for the bucket to fill again. It seemed to take a longer time with each bucketful. The owls flew ceaselessly about in the air, for there were few little creatures to catch. Then Joseph heard a faint slow pounding on the earth. He stopped breathing to listen.

"It's coming up the hill now. It will get in tonight."

He took a new breath and listened again for the rhythmic pounding, and he whispered, "When it gets here, the land will be dead, and the stream will stop." The sound came steadily up the hill, and Joseph, trapped with the rock, listened to it coming. Then his horse lifted its head and bickered, and an answering bicker came back from the hillside below the grove. Joseph started up and stood by his little fire, waiting with his shoulders set and his head forward to resist the blow. In the dim night light he saw a horseman ride into the glade and pull up his horse. The horseman looked taller than the pines, and a pale blue light seemed to frame his head. But then his voice called softly, "Señor Wayne."

Joseph sighed, and his muscles relaxed. "It is you, Juanito," he said tiredly. "I know your voice."

Juanito dismounted and tied his horse and then he strode to the little fire. "I came first to Nuestra Señora. They told me there that you were alone. I went to the ranch, then, and the houses were deserted."

"How did you know to look for me here?" Joseph asked.

Juanito knelt by the fire and warmed his hands, throwing on twigs to make a fresh blaze. "I remembered what you told your brother once, señor. You said, 'This place is like cool water.' I came over the dry hills, and I knew where you'd be." Now that the blaze was leaping, he looked into Joseph's face. "You are not well, señor. You are thin and sick."

"I am well, Juanito."

"You look dry and feverish. You should see a doctor tomorrow."

"No, I am well. Why did you come back, Juanito?"

Juanito smiled at a remembered pain. "The thing that made me go was gone, señor. I knew when it was gone, and I wanted to come back. I have a little son, señor. I just saw him tonight. He looks like me, with blue eyes, and he talks a little. His grandfather calls him Chango, and he says it is a little *piojo*, and he laughs. That Garcia is a happy man." His face had grown bright with all this gladness, but he grew sad again. "You, señor. They told me about you and the poor lady. There are candles burning for her."

Joseph shook his head a little against the memory. "There was this thing coming, Juanito. I felt it coming. I felt it creeping in on us. And now it is nearly through, just this little island left."

"What do you mean, señor?"

"Listen, Juanito, first there was the land, and then I came to watch over the land; and now the land is nearly dead. Only this rock and I remain. I am the land." His eyes grew sad. "Elizabeth told me once of a man who ran away from the old Fates. He clung to an altar where he was safe." Joseph smiled in recollection. "Elizabeth had stories for everything that happened, stories that ran alongside things that happened and pointed the way they'd end."

A silence fell upon them. Juanito broke up more sticks and threw them on the fire. Joseph asked. "Where did you go, Juanito, when you went away?"

"I went to Nuestra Señora. I found Willie and took him away with me." He looked hard at Joseph. "It was the dream, señor. You remember the dream. He told me often. He dreamed he was on a hard dusty land which shone. There were holes in the ground. The men who came out of the holes pulled him to pieces like a fly. It was a dream. I took him with me, that poor Willie. We went to Santa Cruz and worked on a ranch nearby, in the mountains. Willie liked the big trees on the hills. The country was so different from that place in the dreams, you see." Juanito stopped and looked up into the sky at a half moon that showed its face over the tree-tops.

"One moment," Joseph said, and he lifted the full bucket from the hole and flung the water on the rock.

Juanito watched him and made no comment. "I do not like the moon any more," Juanito continued. "We worked there on the mountain, herding cattle among the trees, and Willie was glad. Sometimes he had the dream, but I was always there to help him. And after each time he dreamed, we went to Santa Cruz and drank whiskey and saw a girl." Juanito pulled his hat down to keep the moonlight from his face. "One night Willie had his dream, and the next night we went to town. There is a beach in Santa Cruz, and amusements, tents, and little cars to ride on. Willie liked those things. We walked along in the evening by the beach, and there was a man with a telescope, to see the moon. Five cents, it cost. I looked first, and then Willie looked." Juanito turned away from Joseph. "Willie was very sick," he said. "I carried him in front of me on my saddle and led his horse. But Willie couldn't stand it, and he hanged himself from a tree limb with a riata that night. It had been all right when he thought it was a dream, but when he saw the place was really there, and not a dream, he couldn't stand it to live. Those holes, señor, and that dry dead place. It was really there, you see. He saw it in the telescope." He broke some twigs and threw them in the fire. "I found him hanging in the morning."

Joseph jerked upright. "Make up the fire, Juanito. I'll put some coffee to cook. It's cold tonight."

Juanito broke more twigs and kicked a dry limb to pieces with his boot heel. "I wanted to come back, señor. I was lonely. Is the old thing gone from you?"

"Yes, gone. It was never in me. There's nothing here for you. Only I am here."

Juanito put out a hand as though to touch Joseph's arm, but then he drew it back. "Why do you stay? They say the cattle are gone, and all your family. Come with me out of this country, señor." Juanito watched Joseph's face in the firelight and saw the eyes harden.

"There is only the rock and the stream. I know how it will be. The stream is going down. In a little while it will be gone and the moss will turn yellow, and then it will turn brown, and it will crumble in your hand. Then only I will be left. And I will stay." His eyes were feverish. "I will stay until I am dead. And when that happens, nothing will be left."

"I will stay with you," Juanito said. "The rains will come. I'll wait here with you for the rains."

But Joseph's head sank down. "I don't want you here," he said miserably. "That would make too much time to wait. Now there is only night and day and dark and light. If you should stay, there would be a thousand other intervals to stretch out the time, intervals between words, and the long time between striding steps. Is Christmas nearly here?" he demanded suddenly.

"Christmas is past," Juanito said. "It will be the New Year in two days."

"Ah." Joseph sighed and sank back against his saddle. He caressed his beard jealously. "A new year," he said softly. "Did you see any clouds as you rode up, Juanito?"

"No clouds, señor. I thought there was a little mist, but see, the moon has no fringe."

"There might be clouds in the morning," Joseph said. "It's so close to the new year, there might be clouds." He lifted his bucket again and threw the water over the rock.

They sat silently before the fire, feeding it with twigs now and then, while the moon slipped over the circle of sky. The frost settled down, and Joseph gave Juanito one of his blankets to wrap about his body, and they waited for the bucket to be slowly filled. Juanito asked no questions about the rock, but once Joseph explained, "I can't let any of the water go to waste. There isn't enough."

Juanito roused himself. "You are not well, señor."

"Of course I'm well. I do not work, and I eat little, but I am well."

"Have you thought to see Father Angelo," Juanito asked suddenly.

"The priest? No. Why should I see him?"

Juanito spread his hands, as though to deprecate the idea. "I don't know why. He is a wise man and a priest. He is close to God."

"What could he do?" Joseph demanded.

"I don't know señor, but he is a wise man and a priest. Before I rode away, after that other thing, I went to him and confessed. He is a wise man. He said you were a wise man, too. He said, 'One time that man will come knocking at my door.' That is what Father Angelo said. 'One time he will come,' he said. 'It may be in the night. In his wisdom he will need strength.' He is a strange man, señor. He hears confession and puts the penance and then sometimes he talks, and the people do not understand. He looks over their heads and doesn't care whether they understand or not. Some of the people do not like it. They are afraid."

Joseph was leaning forward with interest. "What could I want from him?" he demanded. "What could he give me that I need now?"

"I don't know," Juanito said. "He might pray for you."

"And would that be good, Juanito? Can he get what he prays for?"

"Yes," Juanito said. "His prayer is through the Virgin. He can get what he prays for."

Joseph leaned back against his saddle again, and suddenly he chuckled. "I will go," he said. "I will take every means. Look, Juanito. You know this place, and your ancestors knew this place. Why did none of your people come here when the drought started. This was the place to come."

"The old ones are dead," Juanito said soberly. "The young ones may have forgotten. I only remember because I came here with my mother. The moon is going down. Won't you sleep, señor?"

"Sleep? No, I won't sleep. I can't waste the water."

"I will watch it for you while you sleep. Not a drop will get away."

"No, I won't sleep," Joseph said. "Sometimes I sleep a little in the daytime when the bucket is filling. That's enough. I'm not working." He stood up to get the bucket, and suddenly he bent over exclaiming, "Look, Juanito!" He lighted a match and held it close to the stream. "It is so. The water is increasing. Your coming brought it. Look, it flows around the pegs. It's up half an inch." He moved excitedly to the rock and leaned into the cave, and lighted another match to look at the spring. "It's coming faster," he cried. "Build up a fire, Juanito."

"The moon is down," Juanito said. "Go to sleep, señor. I will watch the water. You will be needing sleep."

"No, build up the fire for light. I want to watch the water." And he said, "Maybe something good has happened where the water comes from. Maybe the stream will grow, and we shall move outward from here and take back the land. A ring of green grass, and then a bigger ring." His eyes glittered. "Down the hillsides and into the flat from this center—Look, Juanito, it is more than half an inch above the peg! It is an inch!"

"You must sleep," Juanito insisted. "You need the sleep. I see how the water is coming up. It will be safe with me." He patted Joseph's arm and soothed him. "Come, you must sleep."

And Joseph let himself be covered with the blankets, and in relief at the rising stream, he fell into a heavy sleep.

Juanito sat in the dark and faithfully emptied the water on the rock when the bucket was filled. This was the first unbroken rest that Joseph had taken for a long time. Juanito conserved his little flame of twigs and warmed his hands, while the frost that had been in the air all night settled a white gauze on the ground. Juanito gazed at Joseph sleeping. He saw how lean and dry he had grown and how his hair was turning grey. The terse Indian stories his mother had told him came into his mind, stories of the great misty Spirit, and the jokes he played on man and on other gods. And then, while he looked at Joseph's face, Juanito thought of the old church in Nuestra Señora, with its thick adobe walls and mud floors. There was an open space at the eaves, and the birds flew in sometimes, during the mass. Often there were bird droppings on Saint Joseph's head, and on the blue mantle of Our Lady. The reason for his thought came slowly out of the picture. He saw the crucified Christ hanging on his cross, dead and stained with blood. There was no pain in his face, now he was dead, but only disappointment and perplexity, and over these, an infinite weariness. Jesus was dead and the Life was finished. Juanito built a tall blaze to see Joseph's face clearly, and the same things were there, the disappointment and the weariness. But Joseph was not dead. Even in his sleep his jaw was resistingly set. Juanito crossed himself and walked to the bed and pulled up the covers around the sleeping man. And he stroked the hard shoulder. Juanito loved Joseph achingly. He watched on while the dawn came, and he tossed the water on the rock again and again.

The water had increased a little during the night. It washed around the peg Joseph had set and made a little swirl. The cold sun came up at least and shone through the forest. Joseph awakened and sat up. "How is the water?" he demanded.

Juanito laughed with pleasure at his message. "The stream is bigger," he said. "It grew while you slept."

Joseph kicked off the blankets and went to look. "It is," he said. "There's a change somewhere." He felt the mossy rock with his hand. "You've kept it well wet, Juanito. Thank you. Does it seem greener to you this morning?"

"I could not see the color in the night," Juanito said.

They cooked their breakfast then, and sat beside the fire drinking their coffee. Juanito said, "We will go to Father Angelo today."

Joseph shook his head slowly. "It would be too much water lost. Besides, there's no need to go. The stream is coming up."

Juanito answered without looking up, for he didn't want to see Joseph's eyes. "It will be good to see the priest," he insisted. "You come away from the priest feeling good. Even if it is only a little thing confessed, you feel good."

"I don't belong to that church, Juanito. I couldn't confess."

Juanito puzzled over that. "Anyone can see Father Angelo," he said at last. "Men who have not been to church since they were little children come back at last to Father Angelo, like wild pigeons to the water holes in the evening."

Joseph looked back at the rock. "But the water is coming up," he said. "There is no need to go now."

Because Juanito thought the church might help Joseph, he struck slyly. "I have been in this country since I was born, señor, and you have lived here only a little while. There are things you do not know."

"What things?" Joseph asked.

Juanito looked him full in the eyes then. "I have seen it many times, señor," he said in compassion. "Before a spring goes dry it grows a little."

Joseph looked quickly at the stream. "This is a sign of the end, then?"

"Yes, señor. Unless God interferes, the spring will stop."

Joseph sat in silence for several minutes, pondering. At last he stood up and lifted his saddle by the horn. "Let's go to see the priest," he said harshly.

"Maybe he can't help," Juanito said.

Joseph was carrying the saddle to the tethered horse. "I can't let any chance go by," he cried.

When the horses were saddled, Joseph threw one more bucket of water over the rock. "I'll be back before it can get dry," he said. They cut a straight path across the hills and joined the road far on their way. A dust cloud hung over their trotting horses. The air was chilly and stinging with frost. When they were half way to Nuestra Señora, the wind came up and filled the whole valley with the dust cloud, and spread the dirt in the air until it was a pale yellow mist that obscured the sun. Juanito turned in his saddle and looked to the west, from whence the wind came.

"The fog is on the coast," he said.

Joseph did not look. "It's always there. The coast has no danger as long as the ocean lasts."

Juanito said hopefully, "The wind is from the west, señor."

But Joseph laughed bitterly. "In any other year we would thatch the stacks and cover the woodpiles. The wind has often been in the west this year."

"But some time it must rain, señor."

"Why must it?" The desolate land was harping on Joseph's temper. He was angry with the bony hills and stripped trees. Only the oaks lived, and they were hiding their life under a sheet of dust.

Joseph and Juanito rode at last into the quiet street of Nuestra Señora. Half the people had gone away, had gone to visit relatives in luckier fields, leaving their houses and their burned yards and their empty chickenpens. Romas came to his door and waved without speaking, and Mrs. Gutierrez peered at them from her window. There were no customers in front of the saloon. When they rode up the street to the squat mud church, the evening of the short winter day was approaching. Two black little boys were playing in the ankle-deep dust of the road. The horsemen tied their beasts to an ancient olive tree.

"I will go into the church to burn a candle," Juanito said. "Father Angelo's house is behind. When you are ready to go back, I will be waiting at the house of my father-in-law." He turned into the church, but Joseph called him back.

"Listen, Juanito. You must not go back with me."

"I want to go, señor. I am your friend."

"No," Joseph said finally. "I do not want you there. I want to be alone."

Juanito's eyes dulled with rebellion and hurt. "Yes, my friend," he said softly, and he went into the open door of the church.

Father Angelo's little whitewashed house stood directly behind the church. Joseph climbed the steps and knocked at the door, and in a moment Father Angelo opened it. He was dressed in an old cassock over a pair of overalls. His face was paler than it had been, and his eyes were bloodshot with reading. He smiled a greeting. "Come in," he said.

Joseph stood in a tiny room decorated with a few bright holy pictures. The corners of the room were piled with thick books, bound in sheepskin, old books, from the missions. "My man, Juanito, told me to come," Joseph said. He felt a tenderness emanating from the priest, and the soft voice soothed him.

"I thought you might come some time," Father Angelo said. "Sit down. Did the tree fail you, finally?"

Joseph was puzzled. "You spoke about the tree before. What did you know about the tree?"

Father Angelo laughed. "I'm priest enough to recognize a priest. Hadn't you better call me Father? That's what all the people do."

Joseph felt the power of the man before him. "Juanito told me to come, Father."

"Of course he did, but did the tree fail you at last?"

"My brother killed the tree," Joseph said sullenly.

Father Angelo looked concerned. "That was bad. That was a stupid thing. It might have made the tree more strong."

"The tree died," Joseph said. "The tree is standing dead."

"And you've come to the Church at last?"

Joseph smiled in amusement at his mission. "No, Father," he said. "I've come to ask you to pray for rain. I am from Vermont, Father. They told us things about your church."

The priest nodded. "Yes, I know the things."

"But the land is dying," Joseph cried suddenly. "Pray for rain, Father! Have you prayed for rain?"

Father Angelo lost some of his confidence, then. "I will help you to pray for your soul, my son. The rain will come. We have held mass. The rain will come. God brings the rain and withholds it of his knowledge."

"How do you know the rain will come?" Joseph demanded. "I tell you the land's dying."

"The land does not die," the priest said sharply.

But Joseph looked angrily at him. "How do you know? The deserts were once alive. Because a man is sick often, and each time gets well, is that proof that he will never die?"

Father Angelo got out of his chair and stood over Joseph. "You are ill, my son," he said. "Your body is ill, and your soul is ill. Will you come to the church to make your soul well? Will you believe in Christ and pray help for your soul?"

Joseph leaped up and stood furiously before him. "My soul? To Hell with my soul! I tell you the land is dying. Pray for the land!"

The priest looked into his glaring eyes and felt the frantic fluid of his emotion. "The principal business of God has to do with men," he said, "and their progress toward heaven, and their punishment in Hell."

Joseph's anger left him suddenly. "I will go now, Father," he said wearily. "I should have known. I'll go back to the rock now, and wait."

He moved toward the door, and Father Angelo followed him. "I'll pray for your soul, my son. There's too much pain in you."

"Good-bye, Father, and thank you," and Joseph strode away into the dark.

When he had gone, Father Angelo went back to his chair. He was shaken by the force of the man. He looked up at one of his pictures, a descent from the cross, and he thought, "Thank God this man has no message. Thank God he has no will to be remembered, to be

believed in." And, in sudden heresy, "else there might be a new
Christ here in the West." Father Angelo got up then, and went into
the church. And he prayed for Joseph's soul before the high altar,
and he prayed forgiveness for his own heresy, and then, before he
went away, he prayed that the rain might come quickly and save the
dying land.

25

Joseph tightened his cinch and untied the hair rope from the old olive tree. And then he mounted his horse and turned him in the direction of the ranch. The night had fallen while he was in the priest's house. It was very dark before the moonrise. Along the street of Our Lady a few lights shone from the windows, blurred by the moisture on the insides of the glass. Before Joseph had gone a hundred feet into the cold night, Juanito rode up beside him.

"I want to go with you, señor," he said firmly.

Joseph sighed. "No, Juanito. I told you before."

"You've had nothing to eat. Alice has supper for you, waiting and hot."

"No, thank you," Joseph said. "I'll be riding on."

"But the night is cold," insisted Juanito. "Come in and have a drink, anyway."

Joseph looked at the dull light shining through the windows of the saloon. "I will have a drink," he said. They tied their horses to the hitching post and went through the swinging doors. No one was there but the bartender sitting on a high stool behind the bar. He looked up as the two entered, and climbed from his stool and polished a spot on the bar.

"Mr. Wayne," he said in greeting. "I haven't seen you for a long time."

"I don't get in to town often. Whiskey."

"And whiskey for me," Juanito said.

"I heard you saved some of your cows, Mr. Wayne."

"Yes, a few."

"You're better off than some. My brother-in-law lost every single head." And he told how the ranches were deserted and the cattle all dead, and he told how the people had gone away from the town of Our Lady. "No business now," he said. "I don't sell a dozen drinks a day. Sometimes a man comes in for a bottle. People don't like to drink together now," he said. "They take a bottle home, and drink alone."

Joseph tasted his empty glass and set it down. "Fill it," he said.

"I guess we'll be having a desert from now on. Have one yourself."

The bartender filled his glass. "When the rain comes, they'll all be back. I'd set a barrel of whiskey in the road, free, if the rain would come tomorrow."

Joseph drank his whiskey and stared at the bartender questioningly. "If the rain doesn't come at all, what then?" he demanded.

"I don't know, Mr. Wayne, and I won't know. If it doesn't come pretty soon, I'll have to go too. I'd put a whole barrel of whiskey out on the porch, free for everyone, if the storms would come."

Joseph put down his glass. "Good-night," he said. "I hope you get your wish."

Juanito followed him closely. "Alice has the dinner hot for you," he said.

Joseph stopped in the road and lifted his head to look at the misty stars. "The drink has made me hungry. I'll go."

Alice met them at the door of her father's house. "I'm glad you came," she said. "The dinner is nothing but it will be a change. My father and mother have gone visiting to San Luis Obispo since Juanito is back." She was excited at the importance of her guest. In the kitchen she seated the two men at a snow-white table and served them with red beans and red wine, and thin tortillas and fluffy rice. "You haven't eaten my beans, Mr. Wayne, since—oh, for a long time."

Joseph smiled. "They are good. Elizabeth said they were the best in the world."

Alice caught her breath. "I am glad you speak of her." Her eyes filled with tears.

"Why should I not speak of her?"

"I thought it might give you too much pain."

"Be silent, Alice," Juanito said gently. "Our guest is here to eat."

Joseph ate his plate of beans and wiped up the juice with a tortilla, and accepted another helping.

"He will see the baby?" Alice asked timidly. "His grandfather calls him Chango, but that is not his name."

"He is asleep," Juanito said. "Wake him and bring him here."

She carried out the sleepy child and stood him in front of Joseph. "See," she said. "His eyes will be grey. That's blue for Juanito and black for me."

Joseph looked at the child searchingly. "He is strong and handsome. I am glad of that."

"He knows the names of ten trees, and Juanito is going to get him a pony when the good years come."

Juanito nodded with pleasure. "He is a Chango," he said self-consciously.

Joseph stood up from the table. "What is his name?"

Alice blushed, and then she took up the sleepy baby. "He is your namesake," she said. "His name is Joseph. Will you give him a blessing?"

Joseph looked at her incredulously. "A blessing? From me? Yes," he said quickly. "I will." He took the little boy in his arms and brushed back the black hair from the forehead. And he kissed the forehead. "Grow strong," he said. "Grow big and strong."

Alice took the baby back as though he were not quite her own any more. "I'll put him to bed, and then we will go to the sitting-room."

But Joseph strode quickly to the door. "I must go now," he said. "Thank you for dinner. Thank you for my namesake."

And when Alice started to protest, Juanito silenced her. He followed Joseph to the yard and felt the cinch for him and put the bit in the horse's mouth. "I am afraid to have you go, señor," Juanito protested.

"Why should you be afraid? See, the moon is coming up."

Juanito looked and cried excitedly, "Look, there's a ring around the moon!"

Joseph laughed harshly and climbed into the saddle. "There is a saying in this country, I learned it long ago: 'In a dry year all signs fail.' Good-night, Juanito."

Juanito walked a moment beside the horse. "Good-bye, señor. See you take care." He patted the horse and stepped back. And he looked after Joseph until he had disappeared into the dim moonlit night.

Joseph turned his back on the moon and rode away from it, into the west. The land was unsubstantial under the misty, strained light; the dry trees seemed shapes of thicker mist. He left the town and took the river road, and his contact with the town dropped behind him. He smelled the peppery dust that arose under the horse's hoofs, but he couldn't see it. Away in the dark north there was a faint flicker of aurora borealis, rarely seen so far south. The cold stony moon rose high and followed him. The mountains seemed edged with phosphorus, and a pale cold light like a glow-worm's light seemed to shine through the skin of the land. The night had a quality of memory. Joseph remembered how his father had given him the blessing. Now he thought of it, he wished he had given the same blessing to his namesake. And he remembered that there had been a time when the land was drenched with his father's spirit so that every rock and bush was close and dear. He remembered how damp earth felt and smelled, and how the grass roots wove a fabric just under the surface. The horse plodded steadily on, head down, resting some of his head's weight on the bridle. Joseph's mind went wearily among the days of the past, and every event was colored like the night. He was aloof from the land now. He thought, "Some change is beginning. It will not be long before some new thing is on the way." And as he thought it, the wind began to blow. He heard it coming out of the west, heard it whisking a long time before it struck him, a sharp steady wind, carrying the refuse of dead trees and bushes along the ground. It was acrid with dust. The tiny rocks it carried stung Joseph's eyes. As he rode, the wind increased and long veils of dust swept down the moonlit hills. Ahead, a coyote barked a staccato question, and another answered from the other side of the road. Then the two voices drew together into a high shrieking giggle that rode down the wind. A third sharp question, from a third direction, and all three giggled. Joseph shivered a little. "They're hungry," he thought, "there's so little carrion left to eat." Then he heard a calf moan in the high brush beside the road, and he turned his horse and spurred it up and broke through the brittle bushes. In a moment he came to a little clearing in the brush. A dead cow lay on its side and a skinny calf butted frantically to find a teat. The coyotes laughed again, and went away to wait. Joseph dismounted and walked to the dead cow. Its hip was a mountain peak, and its ribs were like the long water-scars on the hillsides. It had died, finally, when bits of dry brush would not support it any more. The calf tried to get away, but it was too weak with hunger. It stumbled and fell heavily and floundered on the ground, trying to get up again. Joseph untied his riata and roped the skinny legs together. Then he lifted the calf in front of the saddle and mounted behind it. "Now come for your dinner," he called to the coyotes. "Eat the cow. Pretty soon there will be no more to eat." He glanced over his shoulder at the bone-white moon, sailing and hovering in the blown dust. "In a little while," he said, "It will fly down and eat the world." As he rode on, his hand explored the lean calf, his fingers followed the sharp ribs and felt the bony legs. The calf tried to rest its head against the horse's shoulder, and its head bobbed weakly with the movement. At last they topped the rise and Joseph saw the houses of the ranch, bleached and huddled. The blades of the windmill shone faintly in the moonlight. It was a view half obscured, for the white dust filled the air, and the wind drove fiercely down the valley. Joseph turned up the hill to avoid the houses, and as he went up toward the black grove, the moon sank over the western hills and the land was blotted out of sight. The wind howled down from the slopes and cried in the dry branches of the trees. The horse lowered its head against the wind. Joseph could make out the pine grove darkly as he approached it, for a streak of dawn was coming over the hills. He could hear the tossing branches and the swish of the needles combing the wind, and the moan of limbs rubbing together. The black branches tossed against the dawn. The horse walked wearily in among the trees and the wind stayed outside. It seemed quiet in the grey place; more so because of the noise around it. Joseph climbed down and lifted the calf to the ground. And he unsaddled the horse and put a double measure of rolled barley in the feed-box. At last he turned reluctantly to the rock.

The light had come secretly in, and the sky and the trees and the rock were grey. Joseph walked slowly across the glade and knelt by the little stream.

And the stream was gone. He sat quietly down and put his hand in the bed. The gravel was still damp, but no water moved out of the little cave any more.

Joseph was very tired. The wind howling around the grove and the stealthy drought were too much to fight. He thought, "Now it is over. I think I knew it would be."

The dawn brightened. Pale streaks of sunlight shone on the dust-clouds that filled the air. Joseph stood up and went to the rock and stroked it. The moss was growing brittle already, and the green had begun to fade out of it. "I might climb up on top and sleep a little," he thought, and then the sun shone over the hills, and the shaft of its light cut through the pine trunks and threw a blinding spot on the ground. Joseph heard a little struggle behind him where the calf tried to loosen its legs from the riata loops. Suddenly Joseph thought of the old man on the cliff-top. His eyes shone with excitement. "This might be the way," he cried. He carried the calf to the stream-side, held its head out over the dry bed and cut its throat with his pocketknife, and its blood ran down the stream bed and reddened the gravel and fell into the bucket. It was over too soon. "So little," Joseph thought sadly. "Poor, starved creature, it had so little blood." He watched the red stream stop running and sink into the gravel. And while he watched, it lost its brightness and turned dark. He sat beside the dead calf and thought again of the old man. "His secret was for him," he said. "It won't work for me."

The sun lost its brilliance and sheathed itself in thin clouds. Joseph regarded the dying moss and the circle of trees. "This is gone now. I am all alone." And then a panic fell upon him. "Why should I stay in this dead place?" He thought of the green canyon over the Puerto Suelo. Now that he was no longer supported by the rock and the stream, he was horribly afraid of the creeping drought. "I'll go!" he cried suddenly. He picked up his saddle and ran across the glade with it. The horse raised its head and snorted with fear. Joseph lifted the heavy saddle, and as the tapadero struck the horse's side, it reared, plunged away and broke its tether. The saddle was flung back on Joseph's chest. He stood smiling a little while he watched the horse run out of the glade and away. And now the calm redescended upon him, and his fear was gone. "I'll climb up on the rock and sleep a while," he said. He felt a little pain on his wrist and lifted his arm to look. A saddle buckle had cut him; his wrist and palm were bloody. As he looked at the little wound, the calm grew more secure about him, and the aloofness cut him off from the grove and from all the world. "Of course," he said, "I'll climb up on the rock." He worked his way carefully up its steep sides until at last he lay in the deep soft moss on the rock's top. When he had rested a few minutes, he took out his knife again and carefully, gently opened the vessels of his wrist. The pain was sharp at first, but in a moment its sharpness dulled. He watched the bright blood cascading over the moss, and he heard the shouting of the wind around the grove. The sky was growing grey. And time passed and Joseph grew grey too. He lay on his side with his wrist outstretched and looked down the long black mountain range of his body. Then his body grew huge and light. It arose into the sky, and out of it came the streaking rain. "I should have known," he whispered. "I am the rain." And yet he looked dully down the mountains of his body where the hills fell to an abyss. He felt the driving rain, and heard it whipping down, pattering on the ground. He saw his hills grow dark with moisture. Then a lancing pain shot through the heart of the world. "I am the land," he said, "and I am the rain. The grass will grow out of me in a little while."

And the storm thickened, and covered the world with darkness, and with the rush of waters.

26

The rain swept through the valley. In a few hours the little streams were boiling down from the hillsides and falling into the river of Our Lady. The earth turned black and drank the water until it could hold no more. The river itself churned among the boulders and raced for the pass in the hills.

Father Angelo was in his little house, sitting among the parchment books and the holy pictures, when the rain started. He was reading *La Vida del San Bartolomeo*. But when the pattering on the roof began, he laid the book down. Through the hours he heard the roaring of the water over the valley and the shouting of the river. Now and then he went to his door and looked out. All the first night he stayed awake and listened happily to the commotion of the rain. And he was glad when he remembered how he had prayed for it.

At dusk of the second night, the storm was unabated. Father Angelo went into his church and replaced the candles before the Virgin, and did his duties to her. And then he stood in the dark doorway of the church and looked out on the sodden land. He saw Manuel Gomez hurry past carrying a wet coyote pelt. And soon afterward, Jose Alvarez trotted by with a deer's horns in his hands. Father Angelo covered himself with the shadow of the doorway. Mrs. Gutierrez splashed through the puddles holding an old moth-eaten bear skin in her arms. The priest knew what would take place in this rainy night. A hot anger flared up in him. "Only let them start it, and I'll stop them," he said.

He went back into the church and took a heavy crucifix from a cupboard and retired with it to his house. Once in his sitting-room he coated the crucifix with phosphorus so that it might be better seen in the dark, and then he sat down and listened for the expected sounds. It was difficult to hear them over the splash and the battering of the rain, but at last he made them out—the throb of the bass strings of the guitars, pounding and pounding. Still Father Angelo sat and listened, and a strange reluctance to interfere came over him. A low chanting of many voices joined the rhythm of the strings, rising and falling. The priest could see in his mind how the people were dancing, beating the soft earth to slush with their bare feet. He knew how they would be wearing the skins of animals, although they didn't know why they wore them. The pounding rhythm grew louder and more insistent, and the chanting voices shrill and hysterical. "They'll be taking off their clothes," the priest whispered, "and they'll roll in the mud. They'll be rutting like pigs in the mud."

He put on a heavy cloak and took up his crucifix and opened the door. The rain was roaring on the ground, and in the distance, the river crashed on its stones. The guitars throbbed feverishly and the chant had become a bestial snarling. Father Angelo thought he could hear the bodies splashing in the mud.

Slowly he closed the door again, and took off his cloak and laid down his phosphorescent cross. "I couldn't see them in the dark," he said. "They'd all get away in the dark." And then he confessed to himself: "They wanted the rain so, poor children. I'll preach against them on Sunday. I'll give everybody a little penance."

He went back to his chair and sat listening to the rush of the waters. He thought of Joseph Wayne, and he saw the pale eyes suffering because of the land's want. "That man must be very happy now," Father Angelo said to himself.

EXPLANATORY NOTES

Additional notes are available in John Steinbeck, *Novels and Stories, 1932–1937*, ed. Robert DeMott and Elaine Steinbeck (New York: Library of America, 1994), p. 906.

page xlv [Epigraph] Steinbeck compressed ten stanzas of the original hymn (from Book X of the *Rigveda*) into six. He told his publisher Robert O. Ballou on January 3, 1933, that he had adapted it by himself. "This is not Max Muller's translation, but one I made from literal transcriptions. I do not read Sanscrit. It was necessary to have the words translated. In one or two places where his phraseology has been lacking (not often with Muller) I have used his line." Steinbeck's source was a book his wife owned: Epiphanius Wilson's *Sacred Books of the East* (New York: P.F. Collier, c. 1900). Müller's refrain reads, "Who is the God to whom we shall offer sacrifice?" On February 11, 1933, Steinbeck told Ballou that he thought the publisher's request to set "Sanskrit characters in the end papers" would not work because ". . . it would give an Eastern look to the book."

4 [the long valley called Nuestra Señora] The setting of Joseph Wayne's homestead is Jolon (about halfway between Salinas and San Luis Obispo), south and west of the Salinas Valley proper, Steinbeck's characteristic landscape. The vacant church is Mission San Antonio de Padua (founded in 1771 by Father Junipero Serra), a few miles northwest of Jolon ("the Valley of the Oaks"). Jolon is an aboriginal site of Salinan Indians. The San Antonio River is fictionalized as "river San Francisquito."

10 [Castillian] Of pure Spanish blood, descendant of Castille, historic kingdom of Spain; after the sixteenth century, it became the core of Spanish aristocracy, its monarchy centered in Madrid.

23 [Abraham] The Lord's promises to Abraham (in Hebrew, "father of a multitude") are in Genesis 17:1–8; 22:15–19.

27 [Methuselah] A patriarch said to have lived 969 years (Genesis 5:27).

36 [*Maxwellton's braes are bonnie*] Popular nineteenth-century Scottish song, sometimes called *Annie Laurie*, which concludes: "She's a' the world to me, And for bonnie Annie Laurie, I'd lay me doun an' dee."

38 [Pacific Grove] Town on Monterey Peninsula founded originally as a summer tent city and a religionist retreat by the Methodist Church in 1874. Its permanent site was laid out by the Pacific Improvement Company in

1883, and it was incorporated in 1889. It became known as a strict "blue law" town because of a deed restriction banning sale of alcohol within its boundaries.

41 [Caesar . . . Nicene] Julius Caesar entered Britain in 55 B.C. and again in 54 B.C. when he defeated the Britons, led by Cassivellaunus. The Nicene Council refers to one or both of two ecumenical councils held at Nicea: the first in A.D. 325 discussed the Arian heresy (whether God the Father and Jesus Christ were one god or two; resolved that Christ was "of the same substance as the Father"); the second in 787 to refute Iconoclasm, by establishing the value of veneration (but not worship) of images, and by restoring icons to churches.

41 [Pippa Passes] Dramatic poem published in 1841 by British poet Robert Browning (1812–1889).

78 [All Souls' Eve] The evening of November 1, the night before All Souls' Day, which is the traditional day to honor the dead, who are believed to return to visit the living.

88 [hamadryad] In classical mythology, a dryad or nymph who is the spirit of a particular tree.

105 [Persians invaded . . . how Orestes came] The story of the Persian Wars, waged in the sixth and fifth centuries B.C., was told by Greek historian Herodotus in his History, one of Steinbeck's favorite classical works. Aeschylus's play The Eumenides, the third in his Oresteian trilogy (produced in 458 B.C.), contains the standoff between Orestes and the Furies around the Navel-Stone at the temple of Apollo.

165 [man who ran away from the old Fates] Orestes.

166 [big trees] The mountains around the coastal town of Santa Cruz are known for their ancient stands of giant redwoods (Sequoia sempervirens).

182 [La Vida del San Bartolomeo] Steinbeck is not referring to St. Bartholemew, one of Christ's twelve apostles, but to the Portuguese holy man and venerated Dominican bishop Bartholomew of the Martyrs (sometimes called Bartholomew of Braga), who lived from 1514 to 1590. His source may have been an English translation by Lady Herbert, Life of Dom Bartholomew of the Martyrs, published in 1890 in London. Herbert's book was a compilation of five early Portuguese biographies.

ALSO BY JOHN STEINBECK

Nonfiction:

America and Americans
ISBN 978-0-670-11602-7

America and Americans and Selected Nonfiction
Edited by Susan Shillinglaw and Jackson J. Benson
ISBN 978-0-14-243741-4

Bombs Away
Introduction by James H. Meredith
ISBN 978-0-14-310591-6

Journal of a Novel: The East of Eden Letters
ISBN 978-0-14-014418-5

The Log from the Sea of Cortez
Introduction by Richard Astro
ISBN 978-0-14-018744-1

Once There Was a War
Edited by Mark Bowden
ISBN 978-0-14-310479-7

A Russian Journal
Introduction by Susan Shillinglaw with Photographs by Robert Capa
ISBN 978-0-14-118019-9

Sea of Cortez
A Leisurely Journal of Travel and Research
By John Steinbeck and Edward F. Ricketts
ISBN 978-0-14-311721-6

Travels with Charley in Search of America
Introduction by Jay Parini
ISBN 978-0-14-018741-0

Working Days
The Journals of The Grapes of Wrath
Edited by Robert DeMott
ISBN 978-0-14-014457-4

Plays:

Of Mice and Men and The Moon Is Down
Foreword by James Earl Jones
ISBN 978-0-14-310613-5

Collections:

The Portable Steinbeck
Edited by Pascal Covici, Jr.
Introduction by Susan Shillinglaw
ISBN 978-0-14-310697-5

The Short Novels of John Steinbeck
ISBN 978-0-14-310577-0

Steinbeck
A Life in Letters
Edited by Elaine Steinbeck and Robert Wallsten
ISBN 978-0-14-004288-7

Other works:

The Forgotten Village
Photographs by Rosa Harvan Kline and Alexander Hackensmid
ISBN 978-0-14-311718-6

Viva Zapata!
The Original Screenplay
ISBN 978-0-670-00579-6

Zapata
Edited with Commentaries by Robert E. Morsberger
ISBN 978-0-14-017322-2

Critical Library edition:

The Grapes of Wrath
Text and Criticism
Edited by Peter Lisca and Kevin Hearle
ISBN 978-0-14-024775-6